THE AMSTERDAM ENIGMA

THE CONTINENTAL CAPERS OF MELODY CHESTERTON
BOOK THREE

SARAH F. NOEL

Also By Sarah F. Noel

Acknowledgements

I want to thank my wonderful editor, Kieran Devaney and the eagle-eyed Patricia Goulden and the members of my amazing ARC team for doing a final check of the manuscript.

To my mother, Pamela, whose father's family were Dutch Jews who emigrated to London

FOREWORD

This book is written using British English spelling. e.g. dishonour instead of dishonor, realise instead of realize.

British spelling aside, while every effort has been made to proofread this thoroughly, typos do creep in. If you find any, I'd greatly appreciate a quick email to report them at sarahfnoelauthor@gmail.com

CHAPTER 1

August 1, 1911, Amsterdam

"I don't know how much more of this heat I can take. Amsterdam was supposed to be a relief after Morocco, not worse." As she said this, Mary slumped down on a chair and mopped her brow with a handkerchief.

"It really is less hot here, Mary. I think the problem is that the Moroccans are prepared for heat and have their homes and lives set up to manage its effects, whereas the Dutch seem only prepared for long periods of damp cloudiness with intermittent drizzles. Much like the British, in fact."

Even as she said these words, Melody wondered why she bothered; Mary was right. The heat was stifling. It seemed to hang over the canals like a physical mass. When they arrived days before, there had at least been a breeze from the IJ, the body of water that separated Amsterdam proper from Amsterdam-Noord. Now, even that slight relief was at an end.

It seemed that everyone was suffering as they were. Locals sought the shade of the trees in the nearby Wertheimpark, but in truth, there was no escape; the air was dry, the grass parched, and tempers short after weeks without rain.

Just that morning at breakfast, Rat was uncharacteristically snappish when Melody casually inquired about his plans for the day. He apologised immediately, and Melody hadn't been upset. Instead, she realised that the unpleasant weather was merely exacerbating his underlying frustration at his lack of progress in his current mission.

As much as Melody empathised with her brother's frustrations, she had quite a few of her own. Rat was a newly fledged operative for the Foreign Section of the British Secret Service Bureau. Despite acknowledging Melody's indispensable help during his last two missions, he seemed unwilling to involve her in his latest investigation in Amsterdam.

Melody understood that this hesitancy stemmed from both her older brother's over-protectiveness and the insecurities that continued to plague him. Despite Rat's intelligence and indisputable cryptology skills, the young man struggled with self-doubt, questioning if he was ready for such assignments and worrying about failing his mentor, Lord Langley, or worse, his country. His confidence had been sorely shaken by the events in Venice and the revelation that Alessandro was monitoring him. His capture in Marrakesh, which necessitated his rescue by Melody and Captain Somerset, hadn't helped diminish those doubts.

Thinking about Captain William Somerset made Melody sigh aloud.

"It is brutally hot outside, but I do think it would do you some good to get out of this hotel and stop moping about." Mary tried to say this in a light tone, but it was immediately obvious she'd failed and that her charge was irritated.

"I am not moping about," Melody replied petulantly.

Mary knew she ought to let the subject drop, but she loved the young woman too much to take the easy way out of the conversation. "I haven't even seen you write in your diary since we arrived back in Europe."

It was true; Melody hadn't written in her diary for days, perhaps weeks. In fact, the last time she remembered taking it out was on the boat to Marseilles. She wasn't sure she was able or willing to express in words the reasons why.

Of course, Mary did have some sense of how the handsome and suave Conte Alessandro Foscari hurt Melody when the truth about his apparent courtship in Venice came to light. The observant older woman even had some understanding of the confusion and disappointment Melody experienced when the charming and attentive Captain Somerset suddenly walked out of her life. However, despite the closeness between Melody and Mary, who'd been her nursery maid, then lady's maid, and now companion for fourteen years, Melody wasn't sure she was ready to discuss what was troubling her.

Melody recalled William's last words to her, "I saw your face when Conte Foscari arrived, and I knew that my cause was a lost one." Then, he'd admitted, "I have been down this path before and know better than to attempt it again. Loving a woman who is in love with another man only leads to heartache."

Could she have stopped him at that moment, while his hand remained on the door handle? Could she have convinced him that her reaction to Alessandro was nothing more than relief over a friend's safety? Melody went over this question repeatedly in her mind. Previously, this was the sort of internal turmoil she would have documented in the pages of her diary. Mary's question was a valid one: why wasn't she writing in it anymore?

Finally, she responded to Mary with an abbreviated yet honest answer. "Writing in a diary seems childish. It has only been three months since we left London, yet I am a totally different person. And that person does not scribble down her every thought."

Mary stood and crossed to where Melody was seated. Bending over the young woman, she kissed her forehead and stroked her beautiful, thick, wavy auburn hair. "Do not be so hard on yourself, Miss Melody. You have been through a lot since we left home." Mary said nothing else; she didn't have to. Melody knew she was right, yet it didn't change her lingering discomfort. Perhaps sensing this, Mary left her young charge to her thoughts and withdrew to her bedroom in the luxurious suite.

Melody guessed why Mary left, but perhaps she didn't want to be alone with her thoughts. Perhaps she didn't wish to ponder where Rat went off to that morning or why she'd not heard from or seen Alessandro since their arrival in Amsterdam.

While she and Rat were staying in the opulent Hotel Victoria, Alessandro and Fatima were staying elsewhere. Fatima! Why had that woman accompanied them to Amsterdam? The beautiful, sophisticated, half-Moroccan, half-French Fatima had become Melody's nemesis in

3

Morocco. Quick to condescend to Melody regarding everything from her lack of foreign language fluency to her clothing, Fatima was even quicker to flirt with every man she encountered and clearly relished being the centre of male attention.

While Alessandro was imprisoned by the Sultan, Melody and Fatima had set aside their mutual dislike to work together for his release. It was indisputable that without Fatima's help, Alessandro would likely still be imprisoned, or worse. Nevertheless, whatever respite from Fatima's petty insults and preening Melody had enjoyed while their common goal was clear, once Alessandro was released, the infuriating woman reverted to form.

Perhaps even more than Fatima's almost constant flirtation with Alessandro, Melody couldn't bear the woman's toying with Rat. It was obvious that the impressionable young man was smitten with the graceful, worldly beauty. Unlike the worldly Conte Foscari, Rat was quite the innocent when it came to women, and his infatuation with Fatima was both irritating in its naivety and troubling for the inevitable heartbreak it would bring.

Determined not to dwell on Alessandro or Fatima, Melody reached for the newspaper. The hotel provided day-old British newspapers, and Melody longed for news from home. Given her eagerness to leave Britain, it surprised her to experience these pangs of homesickness. Melody rationalised these feelings as nothing more than missing Tabby Cat, Wolfie, Granny, and Uncle Maxi. Even so, she found she devoured the news from home each day.

Usually, she read the newspaper while having breakfast, but she'd been distracted that morning by her tiff with Rat. Now, as soon as she picked up the newspaper, her eyes were drawn to the headline. Ever since Germany sent a gunboat to moor off the coast of Agadir in early July – a direct provocation to the British and French governments – British public opinion had turned firmly against its Teutonic neighbours.

Previously, although there'd been an acknowledged tension between the two countries, with Germany seen as a rapidly growing industrial power eager to expand its influence beyond its borders, the British public and press had drifted towards a far more conciliatory, pro-German mood. The crisis in Morocco, which Rat and Melody tried so hard to avert, ensured that any softening of opinion towards Germany was now at an end. This sea change in sentiment was reflected in the newspaper's headline: Germany – belligerent, imperialistic, and dangerously ambitious.

Melody assumed that this change in attitude towards Germany was at least part of the reason they were sent to Amsterdam. She'd posed that very question to Rat during dinner the previous evening. He'd been evasive in his response, while acknowledging that the prevailing sentiment in the British Government now aligned more closely with the anti-German stance of the Foreign Secretary, Sir Edward Grey, than prior to the crisis. However, that did not provide her with any insight she couldn't have already deduced.

Inevitably, this line of thinking brought her back to Captain William Somerset, whose brother, Adam, was Grey's private secretary and was heavily implicated in the disappearance of a British operative in Morocco, as well as Rat's kidnapping.

What was William doing now? There'd been an attempt by elements in the British Government to blame him for the Moroccan shenanigans instigated by his brother. Given that both brothers worked for the Foreign Office, William's role in exposing his brother – and by extension, Sir Edward – was unlikely to have benefited his career.

Melody threw down the newspaper. It was no good moping around the hotel. She realised she needed to get out, despite the unpleasant weather. It was well past three o'clock in the afternoon, and the worst of the midday heat should be subsiding. And even if it wasn't, she simply couldn't sit in this hotel suite for another minute obsessing over Alessandro, William, and Fatima.

She wondered whether to knock on Mary's door and tell her she was leaving. But if she did that, there was little doubt that Mary would consider herself obliged to join her charge. Melody neither wanted to impose the heat on Mary, nor did she feel like company. Finally, Melody wrote a note explaining that she wouldn't be long and left it where she was sure Mary would find it, grabbed her hat and a reticule, and escaped before her companion could return.

CHAPTER 2

Melody made her way down to the lobby in the lift, which was operated by a very tall young man. In fact, Melody wasn't sure if she'd met anyone in Amsterdam who wasn't tall. The young man nodded and said, "Good afternoon," in English. That was another thing she'd noticed: everyone seemed to speak excellent English, which was fortunate, given that she hadn't mastered more than a couple of words in Dutch.

The lift reached the ground floor, and the doors opened onto the sumptuous lobby adorned with crystal chandeliers, velvet curtains, and marble columns. While they made their way to Amsterdam by train from Marseille, Rat informed her they were resuming the charade of her being an upper-class young woman travelling around Europe, chaperoned by her brother. At the time, Melody didn't realise that, for at least one of them, this wouldn't be much of a charade.

Given this story, it was entirely plausible that they were staying in one of Amsterdam's grandest hotels. In addition to its palatial furnishings, the hotel was one of the first buildings in the Netherlands to feature electric lighting, hot running water, and a telephone exchange. The first two were great luxuries after the deprivations experienced during much of their trip to Morocco, the last, a significant advantage considering the true nature of their stay.

As Melody crossed the highly polished marble floor, periodically punctuated by plush Persian rugs, she noticed the mingling scents of polished wood, beeswax, cigars, and roses. The latter emanated from the glorious flowers that seemed to adorn almost every flat surface.

Melody planned to make her way directly to the revolving oak-and-glass doors, bypassing the rich mahogany front desk manned by an eager young man in a smart black suit. The young fellow, whose name she thought was Robert, was busy talking to a man. As she got closer, Melody started; the man was Alessandro. She was so flustered at the sight of him that she instinctively hid behind the nearest marble column.

Almost immediately, Melody realised the absurdity of her behaviour. What on earth would she say if Alessandro caught sight of her hiding?

She was just about to reveal herself when she heard him say to Robert, "I need to speak with Mr Sandworth as soon as possible. Do you know when he will return?" Robert was quite soft-spoken, and she couldn't hear his response, but the shake of his head was a good clue. Alessandro asked for a pen and paper, wrote a note, and handed it to Robert. "Please make sure he receives this as soon as possible." With that, Alessandro thanked the man and turned to leave.

Without a moment's thought, Melody allowed him to leave the hotel before slipping out of her hiding spot to follow him. If she'd taken a moment to reflect on her actions, Melody might have considered how it would appear if Alessandro realised she was trailing him.

Despite Alessandro's professed gratitude for all that Melody had done to secure his release, most of their interactions since had been marked by awkwardness and stiff formality. Of course, things were uncomfortable between them even before Alessandro was arrested. She'd been unable to forgive or forget ever since Venice, when it became painfully obvious to Melody that Alessandro's supposed courtship was nothing more than an attempt to stay close to her brother in order to monitor his activities.

Perhaps the most irritating aspect was that, most of the time, Alessandro appeared oblivious to her coldness towards him. Or when he did notice it, he seemed to find it almost amusing, as if he were dealing with a precocious yet truculent child. Melody assumed – well, she'd hoped – that she'd proven herself capable and worthy of his professional respect by the end of their Moroccan adventures, but this seemed not to be the case.

Now, it occurred to her that if she wanted to be taken seriously as someone mature and competent enough to aid Alessandro and Rat on whatever mission they were undertaking in Amsterdam, her case wouldn't be helped by stalking him like a jealous lover. This thought flickered through her mind as she made her way out of the hotel, but by the time she stopped to see which way Alessandro was going, it had vanished.

Luckily, the streets were busy enough that she could keep her distance and remain unnoticed, yet not so busy that she lost sight of her prey. Amsterdam's carriages jostled for space with rumbling carts and the occasional clanging tram. Alessandro navigated the bustle easily, crisscrossing streets and navigating canals and bridges with the familiarity of a local. Once again, Melody wondered what else she didn't know about Alessandro; did he once reside in Amsterdam?

Melody followed at a distance, constantly attempting to judge if she was too close. As Alessandro passed the grand front of St. Nicolaaskerk, its bell tower casting long shadows across the street, he paused for a moment. Quickly, Melody turned and feigned interest in a florist's pushcart.

After a brief pause, Alessandro turned west, walking briskly along Prins Hendrikkade, past a procession of freight offices and tobacco merchants. Melody kept pace behind a pair of women strolling with a gaggle of children, thankful for their cover.

At the corner of Brouwersgracht, he turned left, and the bustle of the previous streets began to fade. It occurred to Melody to wonder what on earth she was doing; Alessandro might be engaged in something as mundane as visiting a tailor or strolling without a particular destination in mind. Why on earth did she assume she would learn anything by following him?

As she thought this, Melody slowed, trailing behind a coal delivery cart, almost ready to stop her foolishness and return to the hotel. Then, she watched as Alessandro crossed the Papiermolensluis bridge before turning onto Herengracht. The street boasted rows of stately houses, complete with brass nameplates, lace-curtained windows, and well-maintained facades.

Alessandro stopped at Herengracht 76, a tall, narrow house with a blond brick façade, large windows, and dark green shutters. She watched him run up the steps and unlock the front door with a key. Was this where Alessandro was living?

While Melody sensed she'd learned something interesting, she wasn't sure how useful the information was; after all, she already knew Alessandro wasn't staying at the Hotel Victoria, and he must be lodging somewhere. Discovering that he'd rented a house was not altogether surprising. Or perhaps he owned this house. Just as she was about to leave to try to find her way back to the hotel, she caught sight of a woman approaching number 76.

Something about the way the woman sashayed down the street seemed familiar, and quickly Melody realised it was Fatima. It seemed that, unlike Melody, Fatima knew where to find Alessandro. Despite herself, the realisation caused Melody a stab of jealousy. However hurtful this knowledge was, it paled compared to the sharpness of the pain she experienced when Fatima climbed the elegant stone steps and used a key to let herself into the house. Alessandro and Fatima were living there together!

Melody always suspected that Alessandro and Fatima shared a romantic history. Certainly, this was what Fatima hinted at multiple times in Morocco. Now it seemed indisputable.

Melody understood that Alessandro was an older, more experienced man. In fact, this was one reason he'd given her for not continuing their putative courtship, telling her on their romantic moonlit gondola ride that she was a maiden, not a woman of the world, and that to continue kissing her would not be right. That he and the beautiful Fatima shared a past should not be surprising. More to the point, given that Melody was sure she'd put any romantic thoughts about Alessandro aside, it shouldn't matter to her. Yet it did matter. And realising that the romance with Fatima had reignited, or perhaps had never paused, mattered even more.

Tears were already welling up as Melody turned away and began to walk back to the hotel. Even as the pain of her discovery caused those tears to fall down her cheeks, a voice in her head tried to rationalise that now she could set aside her feelings for Alessandro for good. He'd never been and would never be hers. Whatever small part of her heart remained open to the hope that he would finally declare his love for her needed to be locked away, with the key thrown away permanently.

Melody wiped the tears from her cheeks and muttered under her breath, "Did you really think he would be so grateful that you saved him that he'd throw himself at your feet?" Even as she uttered these words to herself, it occurred to her that perhaps Alessandro had been so grateful to be released from the Sultan's prison that he'd thrown himself at one of his saviour's feet: Fatima's.

She did not doubt that the other, cunning woman would be all too eager to take the lion's share of the credit for herself, especially if Alessandro's love was the prize. Melody reflected on all she'd endured to secure Alessandro's release: the long and arduous trek through the Atlas Mountains, her secret visit to the Sultan's harem to meet with one of his wives, and the danger that Rat faced when he was held captive by the deceitful Alistair Blackadder.

Of course, Melody acknowledged Rat would have gone to Alessandro's aid and travelled to Fes regardless of whether she'd accompanied him; her brother was totally in the other man's thrall at this point. Nevertheless, Melody believed her point was valid: she'd endured a myriad of challenges and trials in order to save Alessandro, yet it seemed that all the credit and reward fell on Fatima's dainty shoulders. Melody felt foolish and naive.

By the time she found her way back to the hotel after several wrong turns, Melody had worked herself into a state of righteous indignation. She might not confront Alessandro for his ingratitude or Fatima for her duplicity, but she could compel Rat to tell her what was happening and recognise how much he needed her help.

As she entered the hotel, Melody endeavoured to maintain a calm and casual demeanour while approaching Robert at the front desk.

"Good afternoon, Miss Chesterton. How can I help you?" the young man asked politely.

"Has my brother returned yet?" Melody asked as nonchalantly as possible. When Robert shook his head, she continued, "Are there any messages for either of us?"

Robert turned to the wall of small cubbies where messages for each room were kept, before returning with Alessandro's note. "A gentleman left this for Mr Sandworth."

"Thank you. I'll see that he gets it." Melody took the note before Robert reconsidered handing it over to anyone other than Rat. Then she hurried to the lift, eager to read it in privacy.

CHAPTER 3

R at tried to contain his frustration. This was the third time he'd sat in Café Suisse in as many days. As he'd done previously, he displayed a copy of Tolstoy's Anna Karenina prominently on the table. He was sipping yet another overly creamy Koffie verkeerd, a milky Dutch coffee, while picking at an apple strudel. Given that the pastry, as well as the coffee, was part of the agreed-upon signal with the man he was meant to meet, Rat was careful not to do more than occasionally nibble at it.

Two days prior, he occupied this table for two hours. Yesterday, he'd been there for nearly as long. It was only when he began receiving dirty looks from the waitress that he packed up his book and left.

The message had been clear about the date and time: two o'clock. When the man hadn't turned up, Rat assumed there was some problem and returned the following day. After another wait, Rat resolved to be in the cafe every day at two until contact was made.

Alessandro offered to accompany him that first day, but Rat declined. This was his mission to accomplish. As much as he admired and respected Alessandro, Rat thought he still had something to prove, particularly to himself.

While he could accept credit for uncovering Alister Blackadder's duplicity and his involvement in Brett Rothnie's disappearance, and likely

Timothy Shandling's death, Rat couldn't forget that he had allowed himself to be kidnapped by Blackadder. Even worse, it took Melody, with Captain Somerset's assistance, to rescue him.

That what Rat had uncovered was a plan by the British Foreign Office, or at least some elements within it, to influence world events, suggested that its revelation might not reflect well on Rat's abilities as an operative.

Given the fiasco the missions in Venice and then Morocco had devolved into, Rat believed that, more than ever, Amsterdam might be his last opportunity to prove he was a capable field agent, or risk being sent back to his desk in Whitehall in disgrace.

He had penned a lengthy letter to Lord Langley, expressing his concerns, and received an equally lengthy reply, assuring Rat he bore him no blame for what transpired in Morocco. Yet, Rat couldn't ignore the fact that Langley hadn't said that no one blamed him.

On its face, this mission was quite clear-cut: Britain had received intelligence that a German-backed network was attempting to interfere with the Netherlands' stated neutrality in the event of a continental war and to, at the very least, make the country dependent on and more aligned with Germany's interests. Given that the two countries shared a border and that at least some elements of Dutch society might be considered more culturally aligned with conservative Germany than with liberal Britain, there was a genuine concern that if the Dutch were dissuaded from neutrality, then there would be little question where their allegiances would lie.

There had already been what Britain believed were false flag disruptions to Dutch shipping and other events. These had been blamed on anarchists and Jewish Zionists. Yet, the Foreign Office was certain they originated in Germany.

Britain was viewed as being tolerant of both anarchists and Jews, which included providing safe haven for refugees from other European countries fleeing what they saw as political persecution for such beliefs. It would be quite easy to point the finger of blame. Even if a link couldn't be proven to British-based groups, it could be enough to imply that British influence invited instability and thus to rile up Dutch public opinion, causing them to look to their nearest neighbour for protection.

With Alessandro's assistance, Rat was to do everything possible to preserve Dutch neutrality and ensure the ongoing protection of British shipping and trade routes. This might involve uncovering, disrupting, and securing evidence of German covert operations. It would certainly entail doing whatever he could to prevent Germany from framing anarchists, Jews, or Zionists in ways that would justify severe crackdowns and sway Dutch opinion.

As he took a tiny bite of his strudel, Rat considered the task ahead of him. While he wasn't the only operative in the Netherlands with this mission – he knew for a fact that someone was stationed in Rotterdam and another in the town of Arnhem, which was on the German border – Rat felt the enormous weight of it all. Despite their efforts, Germany's sending of the gunboat to Agadir heightened tensions in Europe. The very last thing Britain wanted now was to jeopardise Dutch neutrality. This was an opportunity to redeem himself. Of course, it was also an opportunity to add the final nail to the coffin of his career.

Finally, Rat could no longer ignore the dirty looks being sent his way by the waiter. The cafe was filling up, and there was only so long he could sit at a table with a partially eaten strudel and a cold cup of coffee. Rat admitted that his contact wasn't coming, scooped up his book, and left.

By the time he returned to the hotel, Rat was in a foul mood that was only worsened by the weather. Initially, he considered going to Alessandro's townhouse, but quickly dismissed the idea. What was the point? Alessandro couldn't magically conjure the informant. Moreover, Rat had little desire to run into Fatima or confront the undeniable truth that she and Alessandro were sharing the house.

When they first arrived in Amsterdam, Alessandro nonchalantly mentioned to Rat that he and Fatima would be staying together. His sole explanation was the greater simplicity of the arrangement compared to splitting their group across three different locations. Under normal circumstances, Rat would have agreed. However, he couldn't shake off the insidious grip of jealousy. He had always suspected that Alessandro and Fatima shared a romantic past, and their cohabitation implied that it might also be a present.

Thoughts of Alessandro and Fatima so consumed Rat that he hardly knew how he got back to the hotel. He walked into the lobby, paying no attention to where he was going.

"Excuse me!" a voice exclaimed.

Shaking himself free from his preoccupied state, he realised he'd collided with a young woman. Not only had he collided with her, but he'd also knocked a pile of books from her arms.

"I am so sorry. I wasn't paying any attention to where I was going," Rat apologised.

"No! You were not," the young woman replied irritably. She was already stooping to retrieve her books.

"Please, let me carry them for you. It's the very least I can do," Rat stammered as she collected them.

"Well, that's true enough. But you don't know where I'm going with them. If I'm about to walk across Amsterdam, are you going to accompany me?" While this was said tartly, Rat sensed an underlying teasing tone.

For the first time, he took notice of the woman he'd jostled. She was perhaps Melody's age and very pretty. Unlike Melody, who was almost as tall as Rat, given his short height of five feet seven, this young woman was petite in stature. She had red-gold hair, with a few ringlets framing her face, and deep brown eyes. Rat's first thought was that it was unusual to see someone so fair with such dark eyes. His second thought was how soulful yet intelligent those eyes appeared.

"Are you about to walk across Amsterdam?" he asked.

"No. In fact, I have just come from the Anglo-Continental Lending Library and am taking these books up to my room." Then, in an unmistakably teasing tone, she asked, "Do you not think it would be quite scandalous for a young man I have just met, and whose name I have not been given, to come up to my room?"

Rat blushed and stammered, "I didn't mean... Of course I wouldn't... Please excuse me." He lifted his hat off his head as if this were some kind of gentlemanly apologetic act, then promptly dropped it onto the marble floor.

"Perhaps a better answer would be to introduce yourself so that we might at least deal pre-emptively with one aspect of the likely scandal"

After picking up his hat and then fidgeting with it nervously, Rat extended a hand and said, "I am Matthew Sandworth, of Mayfair, London."

The young woman's eyebrows raised slightly. "Mayfair? That is a very nice address, Mr Sandworth. And what are you doing in Amsterdam? Your grand tour?"

Rat was very conscious of being judged both as an interloper in the upper classes and as a man of means who didn't need to work for a living. Although he couldn't admit what his actual employment was, he'd honed his answer ever since Venice.

Now, he gave the explanation he was most comfortable with, both for its proximity to the truth and its modesty. "I am accompanying my sister, Melody, on her tour of Europe, while also doing some research for my guardian and mentor who is a member of the House of Lords."

Rat was uncomfortable disclosing that his guardian was a peer of the realm, but as it was indeed the truth, he was compelled to acknowledge it.

"Well, it is nice to meet you, Mr Matthew Sandworth of Mayfair. I am Jemima Edwards of Hampshire." She shook his outstretched hand and gave Rat a smile of such sweetness that he almost dropped his hat again.

Jemima continued, "I am a modern young woman and will allow you to escort me to my room while carrying my books. And if the fussy old biddies who sit in the lobby ready to judge anyone who passes by see fit to gossip about me, I shall rise above it."

Were there old biddies sitting in the lobby? Rat hadn't noticed. Now he glanced around him, only to find Jemima laughing at him.

"Well, perhaps they are all taking naps at this moment. But mark my words, there will be gossip, and I will rise above it." With these words, Jemima thrust her books into his arms, turned, and led the way towards the lift. Rat hurried to catch up with her, unsure what was happening.

Most of Rat's experiences with young women, other than his sister, were with the snooty young women in society who looked down on him with disdain because he worked. Of course, there was also Fatima, though Rat wasn't sure how he would characterise his experience with her. Rat sensed that Jemima Edwards was unlike any young woman he'd ever met. Perhaps that wasn't entirely true; there was something of Melody's liveliness and pertness about the young woman. However, there was also a directness and confidence that were uniquely Jemima's.

Rat was sure the lift operator raised his eyebrows slightly at the sight of the young man following the pretty girl. Rat smiled a little self-consciously and averted his eyes from any judgement he might see in the other man's face. He only hoped Jemima's room was on a low floor and that the ride would be quick.

When the lift stopped at the third floor, it occurred to Rat that this was also the floor that Melody's room was on. However, he didn't think much of that, at least until the moment her door opened, and he found himself face-to-face with his sister.

Melody had sat in her living room, stewing for some time. Finally, when her initial righteous indignation had simmered long enough to morph into fury, she stood and made her way to the door. She would not simply sit there waiting for some man to toss her a titbit and pat her on the head. No! She would go and find her brother and demand to be included in whatever mission he was undertaking with Alessandro.

As determined as Melody was to find her brother, she didn't expect to open her door and find him standing before her. She certainly hadn't anticipated seeing him in the company of a young woman. And what was he doing with all those books?

From the look on Rat's face, he was as surprised to come face-to-face with Melody as she was with him.

"Melody. I didn't realise you were here," Rat stammered, immediately recognising how inane the observation was.

"Well, where else would I be?" Melody retorted bitterly. "It isn't as if I have anything better to do, is it now?"

Rat's eyes widened, hoping to alert his sister that they were not alone. Whatever grievance she was about to air, he didn't want her to let slip anything about their real reason for being in Amsterdam. If she'd known his thoughts, Melody might have pointed out acidly that she didn't know what that reason was. Jemima had walked slightly past Melody's door when it opened. Now, she turned and returned.

Extending her hand, she said, "You must be Miss Sandworth, Mr Sandworth's sister. I am Miss Jemima Edwards."

Melody regarded the young woman. Then, in an icy tone worthy of Granny, she said, "Then you have the advantage of me, I am afraid. And, it is Miss Chesterton, not Miss Sandworth."

If the other woman wondered why siblings didn't share the same surname, she did not comment. However, she did ask, "But I am correct in assuming you are Mr Sandworth's sister?"

Melody would have preferred not to answer. Nevertheless, Tabby Cat had raised her to be a well-bred young woman, and the habit of good manners was too strong to ignore.

"Yes. I am Matthew's sister, Miss Melody Chesterton."

"It is so lovely to meet you," Jemima said breezily. "Mr Sandworth was just helping me take these books to my room."

Rat understood this statement needed further clarification. "I bumped into Miss Edwards in the lobby and sent her books flying everywhere. The least I could do was offer to carry them up for her."

There was something about this situation that irritated Melody, though she couldn't quite articulate what it was. Under normal circumstances, she might have found it mildly amusing, perhaps even charming.

That her socially awkward older brother had somehow connected with a very pretty young woman should have provided fodder for many days of sisterly teasing. Furthermore, considering how she felt about Rat's infatuation with Fatima, Melody should have been thrilled at the prospect that his attention might have been diverted, however briefly, to someone else.

Yet Melody didn't find it amusing, charming, or even a relief. Instead, she found it irritating. She'd intended to barge into Rat's room and unleash the full power of her fury on him, hopefully cowing him with her steely gaze and forcing a confession of his mission. Her crowning glory would be if Rat then admitted he needed Melody's help. Now, she was forced to smother her anger as best she could or at least feign an insincere smile while engaging in meaningless small talk with this stranger who seemed to have attached herself to Rat.

While Rat did not know what Melody's particular annoyance was, there was no doubt she was stewing about something. He was caught; he'd promised to escort Miss Edwards to her room, but turning his back on Melody's undeniable anger would be unacceptable to his sibling.

Fortunately, his dilemma was resolved by Melody herself. "Matthew, when you have finished escorting Miss Edwards to her room, please return so that we might speak." Rat nodded his assent, and Melody retreated into her room, closing the door behind her, coming very close to slamming it.

It appeared that Miss Edwards' room was only three doors down from Melody's own. Upon arrival, Jemima turned and reached for her books. "It seems wise not to keep your sister waiting, Mr Sandworth."

Rat wasn't certain how to respond. That Melody was angry with him was undeniable. However, he knew better than to air his family's linen in public.

Instead, Rat found himself saying the last thing he would have imagined would come out of his mouth, "Might I see you again, Miss Edwards? Perhaps we could take a walk tomorrow or even visit a museum."

Almost as soon as he'd said it, Rat regretted speaking. What on earth was he thinking? Aside from anything else, he was on a mission for the British Government of great importance and sensitivity. He didn't have time for a romantic dalliance. And was that what he'd just suggested starting? Rat had never asked a girl if he might call on her before. He wasn't even sure if he had done it right.

It appeared his execution of such a request was correct, as Jemima replied, "That would be lovely, Mr Sandworth. Might I suggest afternoon tea at the Café Riche? You may call for me at four o'clock."

Rat was so unsure of the etiquette of such matters that he'd no idea whether she would be chaperoned. However, it appeared that for all his innocence, Miss Edwards was in complete control of the situation; thus, he assumed she would do whatever was appropriate and that he needn't worry. He gave a slight bow and agreed to present himself at the allotted time. He would have more than enough time to return to wait for his informant before that.

CHAPTER 4

There was only so long Rat could delay the walk back to Melody's room. He was tempted to continue to his room and ignore his sister's demand, but that would not only postpone the inevitable; it would also provoke her temper even further. Rat wasn't certain what precisely to make of Melody's anger, but he sensed she was unhappy about being left in the dark regarding their purpose in Amsterdam.

Rat's initial inclination was to share the details of his mission with his sister. However, Alessandro indicated he shouldn't disclose anything for the time being. Of course, he hadn't witnessed all that Melody was capable of in Morocco. All that Alessandro knew was that she was involved in helping to free him. Though, perhaps he did realise more than that. After all, he'd been informed how Melody and Captain Somerset tracked and rescued Rat from Alister Blackadder. Still, Rat knew Alessandro regarded Melody's role in this story as somewhat exaggerated and was inclined to believe that Somerset had been the true hero, with Melody merely insisting on tagging along. Rat knew that wasn't true and had attempted to stand up for his sister, though he wasn't convinced he had been believed.

Melody might have been surprised to learn that Rat didn't understand Fatima's true role any more than she did. It was clear that Alessandro not only had a romantic history with the woman, but also some sort of professional connection through his work with the British Secret Service Bureau. However, what that history entailed, and more importantly, what exactly Fatima's current role was, were matters Rat had been reluctant to discuss with either Alessandro or the woman herself.

What Rat did know was that, whatever Fatima's role, it rubbed salt into the wound that she was trusted where Melody wasn't. He didn't blame his sister for being upset by this; Rat just wished she wouldn't take it out on him.

Taking a deep breath and preparing himself for a difficult conversation, Rat knocked on Melody's door. She answered, said nothing, but stepped aside to let him enter. Rat glanced around the luxurious suite, hoping to see Mary. Melody's companion was usually a voice of reason and very adept at managing her charge's temper. Unfortunately, Mary was nowhere to be found, and it seemed Rat would not be saved.

Rat accepted his fate and took a seat facing his sister, who was in a state of high dudgeon that Granny, the Dowager Countess of Pembroke, would have been proud of. As resigned as Rat was to the conversation, he would not throw himself into the lion's den voluntarily. Instead, he sat silently, waiting to hear what he was to be accused of.

Now that her brother was in her sights, Melody paused before berating him. What did she want to focus on? There was so much fuelling her anger, even the overly perky Miss Edwards. However, Melody realised the irrationality of this irritation, or at least that mentioning Rat's companion would dilute the power of her indignation. Admitting that she had followed Alessandro and now realised that no one had bothered to inform her he was sharing accommodations with Fatima was also not the strongest card she had to play.

Instead, Melody chose to focus on the issue where she believed there was both the strongest reason for her ire and, perhaps more importantly, the best argument against what was currently happening.

"Why am I being kept in the dark about the mission you and Alessandro are involved with in Amsterdam?"

While Rat anticipated some version of that question, he wasn't expecting such directness. Of course, if he'd known all the other things that were fuelling Melody's anger, he might have better understood.

Now it was Rat's turn to pause as he considered the most effective way to put his sister off. Unfortunately for him, this pause inflamed Melody, as she correctly deduced that what he was looking for was a way to evade her question.

"Rat! I deserve better than to be kept in the dark. You know I do. I proved myself in Venice and Morocco; you cannot deny that. I did not wish to press this point, but without my help, what would have become of you and Mr Rothnie?" Melody felt awful, reminding Rat of such a humiliating memory for him, yet he left her no choice.

Now that she'd started down this path, Melody realised she needed to press on with even more determination. "I have earned the right to be informed, to be involved. Can you say otherwise?"

Rat sighed. Given that this conversation had been as certain as night followed day, he really should have given his answer more consideration.

Because he hadn't considered it until that point, Rat said the first thing that came to mind. "We don't have sufficient intelligence at this point for involving you to make sense, Melody."

Hearing this, Melody wished she were standing, as the perfect gesture to respond to her brother's absurdity would have been to place her hands on her hips in an indignant pose. However, since she was sitting, she resigned herself to employing a smaller range of gestures to convey the outrageousness of his reply, simply raising her eyebrows as high as they would go.

"You cannot possibly believe that is an acceptable answer?" she stated in a tone that made clear just how unacceptable it was. Not waiting for a response, Melody continued, "Did Alessandro wait to have more intelligence before briefing you?"

"Don't be absurd, Melly. Of course he didn't. He and I are equals in our investigative activities."

As soon as he spoke these words, Rat realised what a terrible mistake he'd made. At this point, Melody stood and glared at him. Rat's first thought was how proud the dowager would be of what her years of training had produced; Melody, in full righteous wrath, was a sight to behold.

Then, in a tone so cold Rat almost shuddered in response, she said, "Matthew, did you ever witness Wolfie treating Tabby Cat as anything but his equal? Yet, here we are in a new century, and still, you and Alessandro continue to behave as if this investigation is a men-only club."

Rat wasn't sure that Melody had ever used his given name before, and hearing it was perhaps the most shocking part of this conversation. So shocking, in fact, that he was compelled to consider her question seriously: did he treat her as anything less than his equal? Maybe. However, if he did, it was based purely on the indisputable facts of their situation; he and Alessandro were employees of Britain's Secret Service Bureau, while Melody was not. Perhaps that would have been the safest answer to give.

While Rat had given Lord Langley a fairly accurate representation of the missions in Venice and Morocco, he'd been circumspect about Melody's role. More than anything, this was because of Langley's original insistence that the young woman not be involved in Rat's work. Initially, when Rat's trip to Europe was being arranged as a cover for his intelligence work, Lord Langley was reluctant to put Melody in any potential danger. He had needed to be persuaded by the dowager of the merits of the trip for the young woman. Even then, Rat recognised his guardian was concerned about Melody's safety.

Since then, Rat believed he couldn't completely neglect to mention his sister's role in his missions. However, while Lord Langley now knew that Melody had been involved, the extent of her role was something Rat had been vague about. Of course, it had turned out that Langley hadn't even known that Alessandro had been assigned as a secret handler to monitor Rat's activities, and Rat did not believe he possessed the authorisation to disclose this information. Given this, there was always only so much Rat could discuss, even in his highly encrypted letters and telegrams back to his mentor.

If Lord Langley couldn't be informed about Melody's involvement, Rat wasn't certain who else could be. If Alessandro believed he was compelled to report it to his superiors, he mentioned nothing about it.

As these thoughts raced through Rat's mind, he realised that using this as an excuse was disingenuous; while it was part of what he meant, it wasn't everything, and Melody was too astute to believe otherwise.

Finally, Rat decided to navigate a challenging course between fact and feeling. "Melody, there is no doubt of your contribution to the work

Alessandro and I have undertaken in Venice and Morocco. I have nothing but admiration for your intelligence, observational skills, and bravery."

It was evident that Melody was about to interject, but Rat raised his hand. "Let me continue. However, it is an indisputable fact that Alessandro and I have been trained for this work." In truth, while Rat had been preparing for the work, or at least aspects of it, since childhood, he possessed no knowledge of what training Alessandro had received. He also suspected that Melody possessed no clearer idea either, and so he took a chance by stating this.

"This isn't a game, Melody. As much as I realise you crave involvement, the work we are doing may be a key factor in determining if Britain ends up at war with Germany and, if it does, who wins. You must see that there are larger forces at work than your hurt pride at being excluded."

Whatever excuse Melody expected her brother to give, this was the one that had been creeping around the edges of her conscience even as her indignation grew; was she being immature and unreasonable in failing to realise that these missions were far more than opportunities for adventure and daring? She had tried to push such thoughts aside in favour of her certainty that she was being unfairly ignored.

Now, Rat's words took the wind out of Melody's sails. She sat back down and replied in a far calmer voice, "I do realise that, Rat. I really do. But don't you see that I could help you, have helped you, and should be given the opportunity to do so again?"

Rat acknowledged the truth of her words. "Melody, we don't even know what we are dealing with." Then, deciding there was nothing to be lost by the admission, he added, "I have been waiting in a cafe for three days for an informant to make contact. We have been communicating via classified advertisements in the newspaper. Until he turns up, I am not even sure what I am supposed to do. I've sat there at two o'clock each day as requested, yet no one appeared."

At these words, Melody remembered the note left by Alessandro. She stood up to retrieve it from where she had angrily thrown it upon entering the room earlier. "The desk clerk gave me this message that was left for you." She omitted to mention that she was aware Alessandro had left it.

Rat took the note and opened it. As his words appeared to be innocuous, Alessandro hadn't bothered to seal the envelope. The note read, "Our favourite artist has died. I will be holding a memorial for him tonight at 7 p.m. I am sure it would mean a lot to him if you were to attend."

"Did you read this?" Rat asked. Melody didn't deny it and nodded.

"What does it mean? Who is your favourite artist?"

"It is a note from Alessandro. It appears that the man I have been waiting for at the cafe for three days has turned up dead."

"And the memorial?" Melody asked.

"I am to meet Alessandro where he is staying," Rat admitted.

"Will you take me with you?" Melody almost demanded this, but at the last moment, chose to soften her tone. It worked.

"It is about a twenty-minute walk, so be ready to leave just after half-past six," Rat said as he rose to leave.

As Melody watched Rat leave, she experienced a disconcerting jumble of emotions. She was glad he was willing to open up about the mission and to take her to meet Alessandro. However, Melody also experienced some guilt; there was no denying that she had manipulated the situation to leave Rat little choice. Her brother's words rang in her ears: "You must see that there are larger forces at work than your hurt pride at being excluded."

Well, she would simply have to ensure that her contributions were meaningful and served that larger cause. Of course, it was easy enough to tell herself this with a measure of bravado. However, Melody still couldn't shake the feeling that she had been petulant and childish, putting her beloved brother in an impossible situation.

CHAPTER 5

As they walked the route to the house Alessandro was sharing with Fatima, Melody kept reminding herself that she was not supposed to know where they were going. Even when, on one occasion, she was certain they'd taken a wrong turn, Melody held back from suggesting they should have gone down another street. Instead, she bit her tongue and endured the unnecessary addition of an extra ten minutes to their journey as Rat finally realised his mistake and they doubled back.

Eventually, they arrived at the elegant, if low-key, street Melody recalled from earlier that day. At this point, Melody commented on the obvious: "Why is Alessandro not staying in a hotel?"

"He owns a house in Amsterdam," Rat answered, confirming Melody's earlier suspicion.

Melody then forced herself to pose the question she already knew the answer to. "Where is Fatima staying, given that she is not in our hotel?"

As they walked side by side, Melody had only a partial view of her brother's face. What she saw convinced her he felt no happier about Fatima's living situation than she was.

He paused for a moment before responding, and then Rat said in a stiff tone, "Lalla Fatima is residing with Alessandro for the moment."

There was so much that Melody could have said in response to that statement, and she believed Rat wanted to say much more in addition. However, they both suppressed their emotions regarding the matter, and nothing further was said on the subject.

Upon arriving at Herengracht 76, Rat knocked on the door. Beside him, Melody was anxious yet curious. Would Fatima be openly presenting herself as the lady of the house, or would there be an attempt to uphold the charade that she was merely a guest? For a moment, Melody considered the possibility that Fatima was, in fact, only a guest. Then, the door was opened by the woman herself, looking more beautiful and radiant than ever.

Melody didn't think it was only her dislike of Fatima that made her imagine the other woman smirking with self-satisfaction as she welcomed them into the house.

"Melody, what a surprise. Sandro didn't mention that you would be accompanying Matthew." Once again, this was said with such an obvious smirk that Melody was certain Fatima realised how upset she was at being excluded from the details of the mission and at discovering the truth about Alessandro's living situation.

Determined not to play into the woman's hands, Melody summoned all the dignity she could muster and answered, "Given my pivotal role in discovering Brett Rothnie and therefore ensuring Alessandro's release from prison, Matthew agreed that my assistance was necessary again." Of course, Rat had agreed to nothing of the sort, and Melody made sure not to glance over at her brother for fear her lie would be evident from his face.

After her distortion of the earlier conversation with Rat, Melody was shocked to hear him agree with her. "When I read Alessandro's note, I realised that we were negligent in excluding Melody and took pains to rectify the situation immediately."

As they spoke, Fatima led the siblings into a bright, well-appointed drawing room at the front of the house, where Alessandro was seated, reading a book. Upon their entrance, he stood, displeasure writ large on his face.

Upon hearing Rat's words, Alessandro raised his eyebrows. "I can see that, Matthew. I wish we'd discussed involving Miss Chesterton before you acted."

And with that, Melody snapped. "Do you, Conte Foscari? Do you wish you'd discussed it first? Perhaps you and Matthew should have discussed my involvement in Morocco before I risked my life to save you both."

"Melody, dear. While no one is withholding credit from you for your well-meaning actions, let us not pretend that it wasn't I who was the key player in securing darling Sandro's release." Melody was so outraged by what Fatima had said it took her a moment to react.

Fatima took advantage of that pause to continue. "It was my men who saw to our safe passage across the Atlas Mountains. I was the one who obtained an audience with the Sultan which enabled a private audience with Sandro, where I was the one who learned key information from him. To say nothing of the invaluable help I gave around local culture and language to you and your brother. I cannot imagine how either one of you would have fared without my assistance."

Finally, Melody composed herself sufficiently to respond. Simultaneously, Rat placed his hand on her arm, whether as a gesture of support or a caution against losing her temper, Melody did not know or care.

Shaking off her brother's hand, Melody uttered in yet another excellent impersonation of the dowager, "Miss Amrani, it is indeed true that when one needs assistance with staffing, catering, or indeed advice on where to shop, your help is second to none. However, I do not recall you being present when Captain Somerset and I tracked down Alister Blackadder and risked our lives to free Matthew and Mr Rothnie. And without Mr Rothnie's assistance, Conte Foscari's release would never have been secured."

Alessandro and Rat exchanged glances; someone needed to intervene before the situation escalated further. Rat signalled silently that this responsibility rested with Alessandro.

Whether his message had been received or Alessandro had reached a similar conclusion, the result was the same: Alessandro addressed Fatima in a firm voice, "Please go and see about some refreshments for our guests."

The furious look Fatima gave him spoke volumes, but she didn't argue. Instead, she turned and stomped out of the room.

Alessandro indicated that Rat and Melody should take a seat before saying in a placatory tone, "You are correct, of course, Miss Chesterton.

Your help was invaluable. However, this is a very different situation, and I am not sure why you believe it is either necessary or appropriate for you to be involved."

Rat realised this was the point when he either defended his sister or caused a rift in their relationship that might never be healed. He knew what he had to do.

In a polite yet firm tone, he supported Melody. "My sister is intelligent, resourceful and her bravery has been demonstrated beyond doubt. Not only does she deserve to be included, but our mission will also be more effective for her involvement. If necessary, I am prepared to telegram Whitehall and make this request formally."

At his words, Melody had to exert all the self-control she could not to cry with gratitude. As irritating as Fatima's attempts to minimise her role in Morocco, and devastating as Alessandro's dismissiveness had been, what had upset Melody the most since their arrival in Amsterdam was what she perceived as Rat's disloyalty. To hear her brother give such a resounding defence of her and endorsement of her abilities was almost all Melody needed.

Even if Alessandro somehow overruled Rat and prevented her involvement, she would never forget what Rat had said.

As true as this was, still, Melody was relieved when Alessandro sighed, raised his hands in a gesture of surrender, and replied, "That will not be necessary. By all means, let us include Miss Chesterton. Shall we get down to business?"

CHAPTER 6

T he door opened, and a young maid entered with a tray of light
refreshments. The tray held small silver bowls filled with what
appeared to be olives, gherkins, cubes of aged Dutch cheeses, and salted
almonds.

"I dine quite late when in Amsterdam, so hopefully this will tide us all
over while we chat. Can I get anyone a drink? Perhaps sherry or madeira?"

Melody and Rat both demurred, but Alessandro rose and poured
himself a glass of sherry. Everyone helped themselves to some snacks.
Melody wondered if Fatima would return to join them, but it seemed she
was either too much in a pet or didn't think Alessandro would welcome
her. Either way, Melody relaxed, realising the infuriating woman wouldn't
be returning, at least for now.

"I assume you received my message," Alessandro asked Rat, who
nodded in response.

Melody realised that it was one thing to be reluctantly included in the
conversation and another to be treated as a full member of the operation.
If she didn't assert her right to be more than involved in name only from
the outset, then it had all been for nothing.

After clearing her throat slightly, Melody said firmly, "Please explain
your message. Who is the artist and what has happened to him? Your note

was obviously in code, given that there is no memorial service taking place now."

Rat realised Melody needed to be told everything. If he was going to honour his own words from earlier and involve her, it couldn't be by cherry picking what information to share. He also suspected that, if given a choice, Alessandro would not be forthcoming.

Putting down his plate, Rat explained, "I have been waiting in a cafe for the past three days for a German defector who has become a British informant. His code name is Vermeer. He claims to have identified a new cypher used by Germany as they attempt to sway Dutch public and political opinion against Britain. As you know, he never showed up. What Alessandro's note told me was that he is dead. Now, you know as much as I do."

Melody doubted that was true, but she let the statement stand for now. While she wanted to ask why a German might choose to help Britain, Melody didn't want to interrupt the story. She could also press Rat for more details on their walk back to the hotel.

"How did you learn of the dead body?" Rat asked Alessandro.

"Through the newspaper I own here in Amsterdam which found out today that a body was found floating in the Prinsengracht canal. Though his body was already waterlogged, Vermeer's right fist remained firmly clenched. Perhaps it was rigour mortis that kept it tight. When the police pried it open, they found a torn scrap of thin paper, smeared, but still legible. Based on what one of my journalists heard, I am hopeful it might be a torn fragment of a cypher that Matthew can unravel."

"How can we be sure the body is Vermeer?" Rat asked.

Alessandro explained, "In his pocket, the dead man had a copy of Anna Karenina." Melody wondered what the significance of this was, but it seemed it was answer enough for Rat, who nodded his head. "According to my man, the coroner said the body couldn't have been in the water for long, given that the paper hadn't disintegrated."

"Is there any way to find out what is written on the paper? Or did your journalist manage to discover that already?"

"Unfortunately not," Alessandro admitted. "His body was found drifting near the Westerkerk bell tower, not far from the Bloemgracht bridge, just past dawn on Tuesday. It is being dealt with by the local police force, Bureau Elandsgracht. My journalist, Hans, has a contact over there. He thinks he can find out."

"Let us hope so. And let us hope that the paper turns out to be decipherable." His cryptography skills were the aspect of his job in which Rat was the most confident. However, decoding a fragment of something that might or might not be a cypher on a piece of paper that had been in a canal for days did not seem like a simple proposition, and he was hesitant to raise anyone's hopes.

When Alessandro returned to nibbling on the cheese on his plate, Melody thought there was nothing to be lost by trying to glean more information. "While I will admit to not knowing as much about European politics as either of you, I thought that the Netherlands maintained a long-held policy of neutrality. Certainly, I have never heard either of you speak of it in the context of fears of German influence."

Rat acknowledged the truth of her statement. "The Netherlands has been famously neutral for many decades. While, of course, Britain would like to think that it would take her side in the event of war with Germany, at the very least it would like to ensure this neutrality remains. Although it is not far across the British Channel to Dutch shores, the country's shared border with Germany makes it more susceptible to German influence."

Alessandro seemed to realise that this conversation was going to take place whether or not he was involved, and he picked up the narrative. "Apart from how precariously it is located geographically, there are other reasons for the Netherlands to maintain this neutrality: it helps protect its overseas holdings, specifically, in the Dutch East Indies, and trade with both Germany and Britain is important to the local economy."

While this was all quite interesting, Melody wanted specifics about the mission that Rat and Alessandro were involved in. She feared she would receive nothing more than a history lesson.

"And so, what are you both here to do?" she pressed.

Rat and Alessandro exchanged glances. Then, Rat answered, "There is a fear that Germany is trying to manipulate public or diplomatic opinion to keep the Netherlands out of Britain's sphere of influence. If it can sway it over to the side of Germany's Triple Alliance, even better."

"This is starting to sound a lot like the situation we ended up facing in Morocco," Melody observed. Then, it had turned out to be the British

Foreign Secretary who was trying to turn British public opinion against Germany.

Rat shrugged his shoulders. "It isn't exactly the same, but I understand your point. Yes, again, this is a covert war to manipulate sentiments against the other side. We believe that more false flag operations are underway; we learnt that much from Vermeer. He claimed to have evidence that would prove definitively what Germany was doing and was going to hand it over at our meeting."

"So, we believe something is happening. But the only person who could prove what it was is now dead?" Melody summarised. Alessandro and Rat both nodded their heads in a manner that Melody found depressingly defeatist.

"Yet that isn't all you know, is it?" she pointed out. Noticing the confusion on the faces of both men, Melody continued, "Who was this Vermeer communicating with before? There must be someone; after all, someone was able to tell you how to contact him. And how did Vermeer even come to the attention of the Secret Service Bureau?"

Whatever reaction Melody had anticipated to this question, it wasn't the evident discomfort that Rat and Alessandro displayed. Rat began tapping his foot, and Alessandro couldn't meet Melody's gaze. What on earth was going on?

When it appeared that neither man was willing to respond to her, Melody demanded, "What is happening here? There is clearly something you do not wish to tell me."

Alessandro shot Rat a look that was accurately interpreted as, "This one is your problem."

Rat sighed and explained. "The Foreign Office had been cultivating this informant for some time and had an established communication protocol. Until perhaps six weeks ago, Vermeer's liaison was Captain William Somerset. For reasons that I truly do not know, Somerset was sent to Morocco under some kind of cloud. From what I understand, the events we were involved with in Fes have reflected particularly badly on the captain, coming as they did after whatever occurred here."

"William? He was here?" Melody gasped.

When Captain William Somerset walked out of that door on that fateful day in July, Melody resigned herself to the fact that it was the end of their story. She wasn't even certain of her emotions regarding this. William had sensed her feelings for Alessandro, which led her to question whether she had genuinely moved on from her infatuation with the conte.

Now, hearing his name and involvement with whatever they were hoping to do in Amsterdam brought everything to the fore once more. She hadn't heard from, or about, the captain since he'd said goodbye. Of course, she still did not know where he was; she assumed he was in Morocco. Just because he had been in Amsterdam meant nothing. Even so, his connection to this city and to this mission caused her enormous discombobulation and, despite her best efforts, Melody blushed deeply.

CHAPTER 7

Hearing William Somerset's name had so thoroughly unsettled Melody that Alessandro could steer the conversation away from Vermeer without her even attempting to bring it back.

Her mind was suddenly so filled with William that she couldn't say what Alessandro and Rat were discussing. There was no doubt that she had developed genuine romantic feelings for Captain Somerset in Morocco. Although their relationship began somewhat unevenly, with her mainly flattered by his overt admiration, over the last few weeks in Morocco, Melody had grown to trust and admire William and thought that he was the kind of man with whom she would happily share her life. He neither condescended to her nor was he overly protective. He saw her for who she was, not as an idealised female on a pedestal, but as an independent, strong-willed young woman.

Yet, just as Melody allowed herself to imagine a future with him, he walked out of her life. His last words to her were, "Be well, Melody. Love well." She couldn't pretend not to understand his meaning; William had observed her reaction to Alessandro upon his release from jail, and it revealed everything, as far as he was concerned.

Fatima had rejoined them for dinner, and the group discussed such mundane topics that Melody could occasionally contribute a comment, all the while remaining preoccupied with her thoughts about the handsome captain. Despite her intention to question Rat further during their walk home, she once again found herself lost in her thoughts. If he thought anything of her absent-minded replies to his casual remarks, Rat was wise enough not to mention it.

It was only as he walked her to the door of her hotel room that Melody thought to ask, "What do we do now?"

"Well, let us see if Alessandro has any luck with the paper the deceased man was found clutching. If he does, then hopefully that will provide us with what we need to move forward." Melody couldn't see any need to argue with that line of reasoning.

Just as she was fishing for her room key in her reticule, Rat said, as casually as possible, "I am taking Miss Edwards to tea at Café Riche tomorrow afternoon, just in case you are looking for me."

Melody paused, her key halfway to the lock, and turned in astonishment. Her initial thought was one of surprise that her shy brother had found the courage to pursue a young woman. Melody's second thought was less charitable as she recalled her immediate aversion to Jemima Edwards.

In that brief moment, Melody envisioned how her future might unfold: Rat and Jemima would fall in love, and Melody would, gradually at first, but surely, be pushed out of his life. They would marry, and ultimately, she would be relegated to seeing her brother only at Christmas dinner and other significant family events. It never occurred to Melody that the possibility of such a grim future was something she could influence by not acting on her initial reactions to Jemima.

Melody turned to face her brother. "You do not even know this woman, Rat. You bumped into her in the lobby then carried her books up. That is all. She could be anyone."

Very stiffly, her brother replied, "And yet you allowed Captain Somerset to call on you after a brief introduction at a party. How is that any different?"

How was it different? Melody said the first thing that came to mind, even though it sounded absurd to her own ears. "William was, is, a captain in His Majesty's armed forces. If that doesn't suffice as a recommendation of character, I do not know what does."

Rat made a sound that could have been a snort of derision, or perhaps a sigh of exasperation. Rather than addressing Melody's clearly absurd rejoinder, he said, "Good night, Melody. I will see you at breakfast tomorrow."

Melody slept poorly, tossing and turning and never falling into a deep sleep. As she lay there in the middle of the night, she couldn't say what ran through her head more: thoughts of Captain Somerset or all the scenarios in which the cunning Jemima Edwards stole Rat away from her forever. Whenever she managed to put these two thoughts out of her mind for even a moment, memories of Fatima and Alessandro's apparent domesticity would pop in to torment her.

Finally, as it became clear she wouldn't be getting any more sleep, Melody got out of bed and donned her wrap. One advantage of the brutally warm weather Amsterdam was experiencing was that even in the middle of the night, the room remained warm. Melody didn't want to venture into the suite's living room and risk waking Mary. Instead, she curled up in the chair by the fireplace in her bedroom.

While Melody hadn't expected to sleep in the chair, she did doze off. It was only the discomfort of her position that finally roused her. Glancing at the clock on the mantelpiece, she noted it was seven o'clock. There was little point in climbing back into bed. Instead, she might as well bathe, get dressed, and prepare for the day ahead.

Melody had been one of the first guests in the hotel dining room that morning. After two strong cups of coffee, she was finally ready to function. By the time Rat joined her, Melody had ample time to reflect on why her sleep had been so disturbed.

As soon as her brother sat down, Melody said, "I am sorry, Rat. I was utterly unreasonable in my reaction to your outing with Miss Edwards. It was unfair and ungenerous."

"Thank you. That means a lot. I realise you were out of sorts after hearing that I have taken over Captain Somerset's mission."

Although that wasn't the only reason for her irritability, Melody was content to accept Rat's words. They finished the rest of their breakfast companionably enough.

As Melody was finishing the last of her second cup of coffee, she spotted what appeared to be Alessandro in the hotel lobby. From her vantage point, she noticed the desk clerk gesturing towards the dining room, presumably indicating where Rat could be found.

"I believe Alessandro is here," Melody informed Rat.

He turned his head just in time to see Alessandro enter the room. Rat waved, and Alessandro acknowledged him before making his way over to where they sat.

With no preamble of a welcome, he said in a low voice, "Can we speak in your room?"

While the question had been directed towards Rat, Melody set down the coffee cup she was holding and replied, "Let us go to my suite, it is larger and more comfortable than Matthew's room."

For a moment, Melody thought Alessandro might be about to ask to speak with Rat in private, but he seemed to reconsider and nodded his agreement.

Five minutes later, they were all seated in her spacious and luxurious suite. Mary had been in the living room when they entered, but she quickly and quietly slipped away into her bedroom.

Alessandro pulled out a piece of paper from his pocket. "I wasn't able to get the original, but my man was able to get a copy of the scrap Vermeer was holding," Alessandro explained as he handed the paper to Rat, who was sitting next to him.

Rat stared at the numbers and words that were written. Reading aloud, he said, "Nootmuskaat. 62 zakken. ZKL-3. Huis Jansen. I have no idea what any of this means."

"Well, I know what nootmuskaat is," Melody informed them. "It's nutmeg. I've seen it on the menu when I order that delicious rice pudding the hotel serves. I asked the waiter after I ordered it for the second time, and he pointed to what was clearly nutmeg sprinkled on top."

"What does zakken mean?" Rat asked, with little expectation that anyone would know.

"Sacks," Alessandro surprised him by answering. He reflected on what he'd said. "So, sixty-two sacks of nutmeg. I think this is part of a shipping manifest and ZKL-3 are part of the crate markings that help identify the ownership or destination of the shipment at a glance. This helps route the cargo quickly through the docks."

"How is that helpful?" Melody wondered. She knew Amsterdam was a major shipping hub, which was part of the reason the British and Germans were so intent on winning over Dutch support. "Is it possible there is nothing interesting about the paper Vermeer was holding and that it just happened to be in his hand when he fell into the canal?"

"That is the other thing my man found out; Vermee was already dead by the time he was thrown in the canal. He was strangled."

"So, there is no doubt he was killed." Rat paused after saying this and thought again about what was written on the paper. "What we do know is that Vermeer had uncovered a new cypher being used by the Germans. What if the shipping manifests are the means of communication?"

"What do you know, if anything, about this Vermeer?" Melody asked.

Rat shrugged and admitted, "Very little. As I said, he was Somerset's contact, and even then, I'm unsure how much was known. My understanding is that his willingness to turn against Germany was quite a recent thing."

They all sat in silence for several minutes. If Rat was correct, this was a crucial piece of the puzzle. However, with Vermeer dead, it was unclear where their investigation should proceed next.

"If this is a cypher, then do you think you can unravel it with only this scrap?" Melody asked Rat.

He considered the question. "Possibly. Though there is no doubt it would be easier if I had a more representative sample."

"Then, I think that we need to try to uncover where Vermeer might have obtained this and then attempt to look at other manifests." As Alessandro said this, another thought struck him. "I wonder if this is a real manifest or if ones containing cyphers are somehow swapped in at some point."

"There would certainly be less risk of exposure if the manifests were real. Though it would also involve a degree of additional complexity; presumably shipments would have to be coordinated in order to match the manifests." As Rat said this, he stood and started pacing.

"I believe we have an interesting working hypothesis, which at least gives us somewhere to start," Rat mused. "However, it could also be entirely wrong."

Melody laughed wryly. "I learned a lot from watching and listening to Wolfie and Tabby Cat over the years. I know that they always work from the position that one needs to start with a supposition and pivot and adjust as new information became available. No theory is perfectly correct from the beginning. What is important is that one does not become too wedded to an initial idea."

"Who are Wolfie and Tabby Cat?" Alessandro asked. Immediately, Melody regretted using the nicknames she had given her guardians when she was a small child. It felt like she had unwittingly shared a very personal detail with Alessandro.

When Melody didn't answer immediately, Rat stepped in. "Melody is referring to the Earl and Countess of Pembroke." He offered no further explanation, and Alessandro realised he was unlikely to receive more anytime soon. However, Rat added, "I believe that Melody is absolutely correct. Let us assume that our hypothesis is correct until we have additional information that proves otherwise."

Alessandro agreed, though it didn't escape Melody's notice that the conte didn't do so until Rat had essentially repeated what she had just said. She was tempted to make a sarcastic remark about this, but decided to bite her tongue and be grateful that her idea had been accepted.

CHAPTER 8

With their working hypothesis in place, the group spent some time debating their next steps. The most obvious starting point was for Rat to attempt to decipher the scrap of manifest, assuming it was a cypher.

Alessandro decided he would continue to leverage his journalist connections to uncover more about the deceased man, whose code name was Vermeer.

This left Melody. She recognised it was one thing for the two men reluctantly to accept her involvement in the investigation, but another entirely to assign her actual tasks. It would be all too easy to allow herself to be sidelined while Rat and Alessandro paid lip service to including her, only to struggle, very conveniently, to find tasks for her to assist with.

Once their impromptu meeting had concluded, Alessandro left the hotel, Rat retreated to his room to contemplate the meaning of the manifest, and Melody was left alone with her thoughts. She reflected on what they understood, or at least what they had as their working theories.

They knew Germany was involved in orchestrating false flag events, but it didn't seem there was certainty about the nature of all those activities. She resolved to go to the local circulating library to see if she could discern any patterns in recent events. There was only one issue: she couldn't speak or read Dutch. She knew that, in London, one might visit the library to peruse newspaper archives. However, what use would those be to her if she could not translate them?

Melody picked up her large satchel that was perfect for carrying her notebook and made her way down to the lobby. She was relieved to see the ever-helpful Robert on duty. In the lift on the way down, she'd considered what innocuous reason she might provide for wanting to read the archives. She'd decided to explain that she was assisting her brother with some research on an ancestor's legal case. She couldn't imagine that Robert would scrutinise her motives too closely or try to delve too deeply.

It seemed that Melody's supposition was correct, and Robert helpfully informed her about the Anglo-Continental Lending Library. He mentioned it provided weekly, and in some cases daily, English language summaries of bulletins from the major Dutch newspapers, particularly focusing on politics, crime, and labour issues.

What intrigued Melody was that Robert also noted that the library offered colonial news briefs, including shipping reports, trade figures, and even localised uprisings. He then provided her with detailed directions on how to reach the library. This was more than Melody had dared to hope for. She thanked the desk clerk and then set off in the direction Robert had indicated.

The library was just a few minutes' walk from the hotel, situated in a bustling area full of banks, travel offices, and even some consulates. The entire vicinity appeared to cater to international visitors, making it sensible that this was the library's location.

Housed in a respectable-looking narrow brick townhouse, the only indication that Melody had arrived at the correct building was a discreet brass plaque next to the door that read: "The Anglo-Continental Lending Library & Reading Lounge." To Melody's eye, it had the ambience of one of the exclusive clubs frequented by the upper class: not intended to be easily recognised by the hoi polloi.

Inside, the atmosphere of exclusivity and luxury persisted. After registering at the reception desk, which involved paying a small fee, Melody was guided through to a spacious room. Most of the wall space was occupied by bookshelves, while the rest was adorned with oak panelling. There were long tables fitted with brass reading lamps, comfortable leather chairs, and plush Persian carpets on the floor. The room smelled of musty old books, cigar smoke, and polished wood.

There was a table by the door, manned by a young man who welcomed Melody in English. He explained she could browse the shelves or make requests from the catalogues. Beside the table, she noticed a more comfortable reading room in the adjoining space.

Melody explained what she was seeking, and the young man assured her they had English language summaries and colonial briefs dating back to the previous century. Melody informed him she only wished to review the past six months. It occurred to her she did not know how long the German false flag operation had been ongoing. Nevertheless, she thought she would begin with six months and request additional reading material if it became necessary.

Twenty minutes later, she sat with a stack of bound periodicals in front of her. While she had waited, Melody considered what she was looking for. From what Rat and Alessandro had said, the German false flag operation intended to influence the Dutch press and public and make them more inclined to push for protection from their neighbour. In order for this plan to work, there had to be a degree of subtlety to the undertaking. If there were too many manipulated events or Germany's actions were too overt, there was the risk of pushing the Netherlands in the opposite direction, towards Britain.

Melody decided to start at the earliest date of newspapers she had in front of her and just skim for a few days to see if anything caught her eye. She paid particular attention to the translated opinion pieces.

It didn't take her long to grasp the social and political positions of the various newspapers represented in her pile: the socialist and liberal papers were clearly the ones more sympathetic to dock strikes and other worker agitation. The conservative papers appeared to be barely accepting of Jews in Dutch society, discouraging intermarriage and questioning their social insularity. There also seemed to be an effort to link them with values that clashed with Dutch Calvinist norms.

However, Dutch Jews viewed Zionism as a movement with far more overt hostility. After delving into many of the more conservative pieces, Melody sensed a theme: an open distrust of Zionism as a destabilising force in Europe.

As Melody took notes on how she characterised the press' views, she noted that the liberal periodicals admired British liberalism, industry, and naval power. They regarded Britain as a valuable trade partner and an imperial model. In contrast, these newspapers were generally cautious of German militarism but open to cooperation. A significant fear of being drawn into any upcoming conflict with Britain was alluded to frequently.

In contrast, the conservative papers, particularly those with a more Calvinist bent, regarded Britain as secular, arrogant, and a potential threat to Dutch Protestant identity. There was a strong undercurrent of resentment towards British dominance in global affairs. These opinion writers expressed a greater ideological alignment in their moral conservatism with Germany, admiring their neighbour's discipline and order. It was evident that these writers were quite sympathetic to German ambitions, if only because they were seen as a bulwark against both socialism and secularism.

If there was an overt German influence on these pieces, it was difficult to identify. Melody suspected that there was little in these opinion pieces that couldn't have been found in British papers of a similar ideological persuasion.

After an hour spent reading through opinion pieces and editorials, Melody backtracked and searched for articles referring to events that might be part of the false flag operations. Eventually, she noticed what she believed to be a pattern in many conservative newspapers: at least once a month, there was some kind of event that was subsequently followed by an opinion piece or editorial presenting a clear, if subtle, pro-Germany or anti-British argument.

In February, she read the headline, "Warehouse Ablaze: Zionist Literature Found at Scene." The article went on to say, "A fire late Wednesday night destroyed much of a spice warehouse along the Entrepotdok. Authorities report the discovery of pamphlets in Hebrew script urging colonial workers to 'rise against merchant tyranny.' While no suspects have been apprehended, sources indicate several Jewish labourers were seen near the site earlier that day. The fire disrupted outgoing shipments bound for Batavia and Bombay. A police spokesman declined to speculate but noted 'unusual political materials' were found in the rubble."

Some weeks later, another headline read, "Disorder at the Docks: Anarchists Incite Violence Amid Naval Visit." This article reported that a violent altercation had disrupted the Royal Navy's ceremonial arrival at the Amsterdam docks the previous day. Apparently, the police dispersed a crowd of dockworkers after discovering flyers bearing the anarchist 'black star' emblem and slogans decrying 'foreign empire and merchant tyranny.' An editorial piece published the same day claimed the incident had raised concerns about extremist infiltration within dockside labour.

The events and reporting continued in a similar vein every few weeks. While the events appeared unrelated and each presented a slightly different type of disruption, a theme emerged: something violent occurred and then fingers were pointed towards socialists, anarchists, Zionists, and, in one intriguing piece, towards the British. The opinion piece that referenced an attempted break-in at a government munitions depot implied the instigators were agitators with foreign loyalties. Although it wasn't directly attributed to Britain, little imagination was needed to grasp what the writer was suggesting.

Then, another pattern became apparent: despite the news articles being published in a variety of conservative-leaning newspapers, more often than not, the journalist credited with the piece was one of two men. Of course, this might simply reflect partisan journalists. Melody noted the men's names; she would ask Alessandro what he knew about the writers.

All in all, it had been a very productive two hours. Though, now she looked at the clock on the wall, Melody realised it had been closer to three hours. No wonder she was hungry; she'd missed lunch in the hotel altogether.

As she packed up her notes in her satchel, Melody heard a woman's voice behind her. "Good afternoon, Miss Chesterton."

She couldn't imagine who she knew in Amsterdam who would be in this library. It wasn't Fatima's voice, of that much she was sure. Melody turned around and her heart sank as she saw Miss Edwards standing there, an annoyingly friendly look on her face.

"Miss Edwards, what a surprise meeting you here." It was the first thing Melody thought to say, and immediately kicked herself; was it really a surprise meeting a fellow British traveller in the Anglo-Continental Library? Particularly as the other woman had been laden up with books when Melody had met her the day before.

"Oh, I do not know what I would do without this library," Jemima confided. "I am here almost every day, returning books and getting out new ones." Melody stood there, holding her notebook and pen, unsure what to say.

Jemima Edwards seemed not to feel the awkwardness that weighed Melody down. Glancing at the bound periodicals Melody had stacked up on the table for collection by the clerk, she asked, "Whatever are you researching, Miss Chesterton? I only take out romances and the occasional penny dreadful."

This was asked in a bright, unassuming tone, yet Melody was immediately on alert; was it merely a coincidence that they had met here, or had Jemima followed her from the hotel and watched her while she did her research?

Immediately, all sorts of suspicions ran through Melody's head. Did Rat just bump into the young woman in the library, or had the entire interaction been planned to lure him into Jemima's web? And if so, for what purpose?

Melody decided to be as nonchalant as possible about her reading material. "Whenever we arrive in a new country, I am always interested in learning what I can about its current political and social situation. I find that reading back issues of newspapers gives me some interesting context."

Even as she said this, Melody was embarrassed by the lie; not the fact of lying to Miss Edwards, but rather that this wasn't something she actually did when they arrived somewhere new. Perhaps, in the future, she should make a habit of doing the very thing she just lied about doing.

Melody felt so awkward that she wanted nothing more than to escape the conversation with Miss Edwards. She picked up her pretty bolero jacket that was lying on the table and put it on. Trying her best to sound carefree, she forced a bright smile and said, "Well, I must let you get on your way. I understand you are meeting my brother shortly. Good day, Miss Edwards." Without even waiting for a response, she turned to leave.

"So lovely to see you again, Miss Chesterton," Jemima called after her retreating back.

CHAPTER 9

R at had been staring at the partial manifest for what seemed like hours, yet he had little to show for the time spent. Could it be a code? Of course it could be. If his years of cryptology training had taught him anything, it was that anything could be a code. In fact, the more mundane a piece of writing seemed, the better a code it was.

He stared at the words on the paper as if hoping they would magically rearrange themselves and make sense. "Nootmuskaat. 62 zakken. ZKL-3. Huis Jansen," Rat said aloud. Did hearing them help? Not really.

One thing that Rat kept going over was whether this part of the manifest was important or if Vermeer had just wanted to suggest they should look at manifests in general. Or perhaps neither was true; perhaps he'd been holding it when he was strangled, and it meant nothing more than that. Rat considered the scenario: Vermeer was attacked, whether by surprise or by someone he knew, and the life seeped out of him. He must have fought back. Yet, at some point, he realised he was going to die, and his last thought was to clutch a piece of a manifest tightly in his hand.

Was that likely? Would someone have the peace of mind to think that clearly while fighting for their life? It didn't seem likely. Perhaps the paper was already in his hand when he was attacked? That seemed more plausible, but then why? Did he suspect he was about to be attacked and sought to hide the paper? That made some sense. Rat's head was pounding. He knew he ought to take a break, but his day so far was so unproductive that he didn't believe he had earned it.

He contemplated his planned outing with Jemima Edwards. Could he truly justify taking a few hours in the middle of the afternoon to sip tea with a lovely young woman? He worried he couldn't and considered knocking on Miss Edwards' door to cancel. However, Rat understood that sometimes it was only by taking a break that a revelation would emerge. It had often happened before that he'd been working on a particularly challenging code for hours, only to step away from it and almost immediately solve the cypher. And so he rationalised his outing with the charming Jemima Edwards.

To compensate for his outing later, Rat took no break for a midday meal and instead nibbled on a packet of biscuits he found in his bag. At half-past three, he realised he needed to stop fixating on the cypher and prepare to meet Miss Edwards. Rat changed his clothes three times before settling on a suit that, while it wasn't his smartest, was at least fashionable enough for even the poshest Dutch cafe. He had considered wearing his very finest suit, but thought it would seem as if he was trying too hard.

Just a few minutes before four o'clock, Rat smoothed a rogue lock of hair and straightened his tie. He was surprised by how nervous he was. Of course, he had little experience in courting. In fact, he had none.

This thought stopped him in his tracks: was that what he was doing? Courting Miss Edwards? Lord Langley had achieved so much in the education he'd provided Rat over the past fourteen years. Any trace of the cockney street urchin had long been smoothed away, both in Rat's accent and manners. Langley had taught his young charge how to read and then ensured he was educated to a level to match any aristocrat's son. However, courtship was not something that Langley, who was himself quite awkward in social situations, considered teaching his ward.

Rat had already been uncertain about the wisdom of his afternoon plans with Jemima. Now, he was sorely tempted to send a note with some excuse to back out. Rat even went so far as to sit at the desk in his room with his pen poised over a sheet of hotel letterhead.

As Rat sat there, pen in hand, he contemplated what excuse he might offer. He also considered the likelihood that he would be relinquishing his one chance to get to know the delightful Miss Edwards.

"Well, it isn't as if I'm making any progress here," Rat said to himself. "We will sit in a cafe for an hour or so, and then I'll come back refreshed."

Once he made up his mind to go, Rat realised that if he didn't hurry, he would be late. He decided he didn't have time to wait for the lift and instead dashed out of his room towards the staircase, which he took two steps at a time. The floor Melody and Miss Edwards were on was below Rat's, and he reached her door only a couple of minutes late. Rat took a moment to compose himself after sprinting down the stairs and then knocked. A few moments later, it was opened by Miss Edwards, who looked even lovelier than Rat remembered.

"I am so sorry I am a few minutes late," Rat stammered.

Jemima smiled. "Were you debating whether or not our little outing is a good idea, Mr Sandworth?" This was posed in a teasing tone, but given that it was precisely why he was late, Rat blushed.

"I am sorry, I just lost track of the time," he lied.

"No matter. Shall we go?"

With that, Miss Edwards stepped into the hallway, closed the door behind her, and took Rat's arm. Well, that at least answered one of his questions: she would not be chaperoned for their outing.

As if reading his mind, Jemima explained, "I am travelling with my Aunt Beatrice. However, she rarely leaves her room due to her delicate nerves."

Rat wondered why anyone would choose such a companion and why Aunt Beatrice would agree to such a trip if she had such a condition. However, he put such thoughts aside and concentrated on how delightful it was to have Miss Edwards holding his arm and talking away in her lovely musical voice.

If Rat had worried about what they would talk about, he needn't have; Miss Edwards was more than capable, and willing, it seemed, to take the lead on most of the conversation. As they walked through the lobby, Rat felt all eyes were on them. Whether that was all in his imagination, Miss Edwards acted like there was nothing noteworthy about the two of them walking together in public as if they had known each other for years.

Rat hadn't been to Café Riche and had no idea how long the walk there might take. As she led the way to Damrak, the bustling avenue connecting Central Station to Dam Square and the Royal Palace, Jemima informed Rat, "We should take a tram. It is much the quickest way to get to Café Riche."

Rat had had no reason to take a tram since arriving in Amsterdam and hoped Miss Edwards knew more about where to board than he did. Fortunately, she seemed to know exactly where she was going. Jemima Edwards even took the lead in boarding the electric tram, fishing two coins out of her reticule and dropping them in the box to pay their fares. Rat wasn't sure what to make of this; he couldn't imagine it was customary for a young woman to pay for anything on such an outing.

As they took their seats on the tram, Jemima continued to dominate the conversation. "Café Riche is one of Amsterdam's most elegant, fashionable, and cosmopolitan establishments. The local elite and most visiting foreign dignitaries know that this is the place to be seen. Did you know that?"

Rat did not know that. He was also uncertain about the idea of being seen in such a place. One lesson he had learned long ago from Lord Langley was the value of not drawing attention to oneself. While Langley himself didn't exactly live in the shadows, he was usually found on the fringes of a social gathering, quietly observing and listening.

Whether Rat might have protested earlier if he'd realised the nature of the place they were headed to was moot; they were almost there now, and he was far too much of a gentleman to complain at this point. Café Riche was as luxurious and refined as Jemima had promised. It did cross Rat's mind to wonder if they could even get a table. Certainly, the place seemed very busy. However, it appeared that Jemima had thought ahead and had Robert telephone to secure a table for them.

Rat was unsure whether to be impressed by the young woman's organisational skills or offended by how completely she had taken charge of their outing. Once they were settled at one of the nicer tables in the cafe by the window, but still with a wonderful view of everyone coming and going, the waiter handed them menus.

"They are known for their patisserie," Jemima explained. "I can never resist their mille-feuille."

Rat had no idea what mille-feuille was, but was happy to have Jemima order one for him. A few minutes later, they were each served a plate of delicate, flaky pastry, interspersed with sweet, creamy layers. This was accompanied by a pot of tea.

As Jemima poured a cup of tea for each of them, she said in a voice that would brook no dissent, "Now, isn't this nice. We can sit and have a lovely coze. You can start by telling me all about yourself."

Naively, Rat had hoped that his vague explanation of how and why he was accompanying his sister around Europe would have sufficed. He never expected to have to expand on the story he had told Miss Edward the day before.

Now, he froze, the cup of tea halfway to his mouth. "Um, ah. Well, my life isn't all that interesting. I would much rather hear about you, Miss Edwards."

For a moment, Rat thought Jemima might insist that he tell her more about himself. Luckily, she accepted his explanation and told him all about her life in Hampshire as the daughter of a solicitor. After describing the village she lived in and telling some charming anecdotes about its inhabitants, she paused to sip some tea. "I just adore the Rijksmuseum," she gushed. "Have you had a chance to visit yet?" Rat admitted he hadn't. "Then that must be our next meeting."

It seemed there was to be another outing, Rat thought as he allowed himself to be swept along by Jemima Edward's enthusiasm.

CHAPTER 10

As Melody left the library, she contemplated her next move. She knew Rat would be departing soon for his outing with Miss Edwards, and besides, he wasn't the right person to confide her insights to; Alessandro was.

Despite her general irritation with the man, he owned at least one newspaper in Amsterdam, if not more, for all she knew. Certainly, he was the one most familiar with and connected to the world of journalism. Yet Melody hesitated.

On the surface, her reluctance to return to Alessandro's townhouse stemmed from the real possibility of having another uncomfortable confrontation with Fatima. She could envision the woman's disdain as she insinuated Melody was fabricating false reasons to seek out "her Sandro."

Yet, there was more to her hesitation than merely the likelihood of encountering Fatima. Melody had been proud of what she had uncovered during her research in the library, and believed it warranted further exploration. But now, as she thought about it further, Melody feared Alessandro would mock her, because he had already discerned the pattern she had noted or, worse still, for her naivety in believing it to be significant.

Melody was so deep in thought that she nearly lost her way. At one point, she paused at a street corner and looked around; had she taken a wrong turn? At that moment, she felt a hand on her shoulder and was shoved to the ground. It took her a moment to realise that the person who had pushed her had also snatched her satchel.

Some bystanders gathered to assist the young woman. After she protested that she didn't require a trip to the doctor, the crowd lost interest and drifted away.

Aside from some grazes on her palms, Melody was unhurt. More than anything, she was angry. She assumed a footpad had set upon her. Other than her notepad, she had nothing of value in her bag. Whatever money she was carrying was in a small bag in the pocket of her skirt.

What was most annoying was having lost the notes she had made. However, as she reflected on them, Melody realised that, while she might not recall every detail, she remembered enough to relay it to Alessandro. She did remember the names of the two journalists she had identified as being behind many of the more partisan articles. Losing her notes was irritating, but not fatal.

Now, Melody was determined to reach Alessandro's house as swiftly as possible so that she could write down everything she recalled while it was still fresh in her mind. Ten minutes later, she stood outside his door, taking a moment before knocking. She took a deep breath and braced herself for an inevitable confrontation with Fatima.

Because of her attempts to prepare herself to come face-to-face with Fatima, Melody was caught off guard when a maid answered the door. It appeared that Alessandro was home, and the maid welcomed her into the house, guiding her to the room they had occupied the previous evening.

Melody took a seat and waited a few minutes before the door opened, and Alessandro entered. To her immense relief, Fatima was not with him.

"Miss Chesterton, Melody, I was not expecting you."

Melody considered making an acerbic comment about his attempts to exclude her from the investigation, but she thought better of it. There was nothing to be gained by further antagonising the man.

Instead, she said, "I believe I have found something out. I spent the afternoon in the Anglo-Continental Library taking notes." She paused. "Unfortunately, I was attacked on the walk over here and my satchel was stolen."

"Melody, are you alright?" Alessandro exclaimed. His concern at this news should have been gratifying, but given her overall irritation at the man, pretending to care about her welfare was annoying.

"I am fine. Nothing more than some grazing on my palms. However, my notes were in the satchel. I believe I can remember the main gist of what I wrote. Do you have some paper on which I can write names and details?"

Alessandro crossed to a charming little desk in the corner of the room and returned with some expensive-looking notepaper and a pen.

Melody then explained what she had discovered and noted key details, including the journalists' names, as far as she could remember them.

Any fear she'd had that Alessandro would tell her he already knew these facts, or that they were unimportant, dissipated as he said, "This is good work, Melody. Really good work. I should have thought of doing this, but I didn't."

Melody blushed at the praise. Alessandro continued, "I recognise one of those names, Hendrik Bosman, but not the other, Paul van Dijk. Bosman is a notorious apologist for some of the most extreme elements in Dutch society. Let me see what I can find out about van Dijk."

"Were you able to learn anything more about Vermeer?" Melody asked.

Alessandro nodded. "From what my journalist discovered, his name was Karl Brenner, or at least the name he had been living under. He had been working as recording clerk at the docks at Entrepotdok for a year now. It appears he had been cohabiting with a woman for several months, and when he didn't return home for two nights, she went to her local police station and identified the body."

"Well, a job at the docks explains how he must have got hold of the manifest fragment that was found in his hand," Melody mused.

"Indeed," Alessandro agreed.

While she was initially hesitant to mention William's name, Melody couldn't help but ask, "Do you know anything about how Vermeer origi-nally made contact with Captain Somerset?"

"Nothing. However, I do know that all potential informants are thor-oughly vetted, so Somerset must have had reason to trust the man's information."

"What kind of information had he passed on previously?"

Once again, Alessandro knew very little. All he was aware of was that the British Government's suspicions regarding German false flag operations had been confirmed, at least in part, by Vermeer's information.

Alessandro promised to inform her and Rat as soon as he had more information regarding the two journalists. "I want to talk to some of my people about the events you've highlighted. I'm sure my newspaper covered the events, and I want to understand their viewpoint on what happened."

Melody couldn't help expressing her next question, "Will your journalists think you want this information?"

It was a fair question, and Alessandro nodded in recognition of it. "I own the newspaper and so do not need to explain myself. However, I already mentioned to my staff that I am attempting to ensure consistency across my newspapers, which includes connecting events in one country to those my papers are reporting on in others."

Even if that wasn't entirely plausible, Melody could see that a lowly journalist would not imagine it was his place to delve too deeply into the explanation. Ten minutes later, Melody decided it was time to leave. She had avoided encountering Fatima and didn't want to overstay and risk changing that.

Despite the open windows, the hot temperatures had left the drawing room rather stuffy. Melody had once again removed her bolero jacket upon entering the room, placing it beside her on the couch. Now, she picked it up and began to put it on. As she did so, she heard a slight crinkling from within one pocket. Melody reached in and discovered a piece of paper she was certain hadn't been there earlier. Melody pulled the paper out. At first glance, it appeared to be two columns of meaningless letters and numbers.

Alessandro walked towards her and extended his hand. After examining it for a couple of minutes, he said, "I think this might be the key to the cypher."

"Really? In my pocket?" Melody asked sceptically.

"How do you think it got in there?"

Melody considered his question. Now, she second-guessed her initial certainty that the paper hadn't been there earlier. When was the last time she had worn this jacket? She thought back over the days since they'd arrived in Amsterdam.

Finally, Melody said, "I've only worn this jacket once or twice since we've been here. I put it on today because the temperature is a little cooler than it has been and it does go so nicely with this skirt."

"And you've had it on all day, or at least until you came here?"

"No. I took it off in the library. It was also quite stuffy in there. However, it was next to me on the table the entire time. I would have seen if anyone had approached me and slipped something in there."

"What about the person who stole your satchel? Is it possible they slipped something into your pocket as they grabbed your bag?" Alessandro asked.

She shrugged her shoulders. It was possible, but why bother? "If someone wanted to give me something, that seems a rather extreme way of going about it. Doesn't it? Why not walk up to me and give it to me while pretending to ask for directions?"

It was a good question, but Alessandro had no equally good response. Instead, he said, "This could be what Matthew needs to decipher the manifest. Someone wants this information in your hands, Melody. Maybe this is another informant who fears making direct contact because of what happened to Vermeer."

While that seemed plausible, Melody felt she had to point out what she thought would be obvious: "Or, someone is trying to throw us off the scent of the real cypher by giving us a false key."

Reluctantly, Alessandro accepted this was plausible. However, he insisted that they should consider the possibility that someone was trying to help them. As they talked, he became increasingly convinced that Vermeer had not been acting alone and that this additional informant was afraid to step out of the shadows.

"I have seen things like this happen before. Perhaps this associate of Vermeer's knew about his planned meeting with your brother and has been watching you both, waiting for the right moment to share whatever Vermeer was planning to give Matthew," Alessandro suggested.

Despite Alessandro's assurances, Melody couldn't shake her concerns about the convenience of a cypher key unexpectedly appearing in her pocket. However, she was still glowing from his unexpected praise earlier and didn't want to take a step back from their newfound cordiality by continuing to challenge him.

As she had this thought, Melody wondered again where Fatima was. When they were in Morocco, Melody harboured serious reservations about the other woman's trustworthiness. Half Moroccan and half French, there seemed little reason for Fatima to align herself with British interests, and even less reason to trust that she would.

Melody could easily believe that Fatima didn't possess any national allegiance and instead picked the side most likely to win in any given situation. However, Alessandro seemed to trust her totally, and there was little doubt that she knew far more about his work for the British Secret Service Bureau than he was willing to acknowledge to Melody.

Why had Fatima come with them? Melody couldn't help but wonder. "Where is Fatima today?" She asked, attempting a nonchalant tone.

"I have no idea. Probably out shopping," Alessandro answered. Then asked suspiciously. "Why?"

Melody shrugged. "I was just curious why she didn't open the door today."

Perhaps sensing the direction in which Melody's thoughts had been heading, Alessandro said with the weariness of someone resentful of having to repeat himself yet again, "Melody, Fatima can be trusted. Or at least, I trust her. She is not working against us, nor is she some wily operative who is playing both sides. I realise you dislike her, though I am not sure why. However, it's not helpful to throw up these accusations."

Melody wanted to argue that she had made no accusation. She had simply asked where the woman was. However, since suspicion had indeed been behind her inquiry, she saw no point in prolonging the discussion. She didn't trust Fatima and never would, but, at least for now, she was the only one who didn't. Melody realised it was pointless to poke at the matter any further.

Changing the subject entirely, Alessandro told Melody, "I am sending Mustafa to walk back with you. If the snatching of your bag wasn't a random act, then whoever took it may have realised they do not have what they were looking for and might try again. Do you know, the boy has the most extraordinary power of recall. I didn't realise it until we reached

Amsterdam. I showed him a map one day and he could remember the entire thing perfectly when we were next out."

Mustafa was a young, orphaned Arab boy whom they had befriended in Morocco. He was a skinny lad of about eight years who had proven resourceful and brave. They had brought him with them to Amsterdam, where Alessandro had insisted the boy stay with him. Now that she realised Alessandro owned a house in the city, it made sense why he had kept the boy. Indeed, Melody wasn't sure what she and Rat would have done with him at the hotel. Melody hadn't seen Mustafa since their arrival and suddenly felt guilty for not having even thought to ask about him.

Now, upon hearing Alessandro's suggestion, Melody was both pleased at the chance to see the boy and discover how he was doing and also irritated by the notion that she required protection.

"Do you really believe I am so weak and incapable of taking care of myself that I would be better off with a child than alone?" she snapped.

Alessandro raised his hands as if to defend himself against her attack. "It was only a suggestion."

"I will take Mustafa with me, not because I need to be guarded or shown the way back to the hotel, but because he can relay back to you whatever my brother has to say about the potential use of this note as the cypher key.

CHAPTER 11

M ustafa appeared just as happy to see Melody as she was to see him. When they first met Mustafa in the Medina in Casablanca, he had been wearing the traditional djellaba robe. Now, he was dressed like any middle-class Dutch boy of his age. Although his dark hair and skin made him stand out somewhat to anyone paying attention, overall, he resembled any well-fed, happy child. Given how skinny and hungry Mustafa had been when they first encountered him, it warmed Melody's heart to see the boy looking so content.

"Lalla Melody, I like Amsterdam very much. I like the canals and I very much like the Stroopwafels," Mustafa said, referring to the two thin waffle discs filled with a warm, spiced syrup sold by street vendors.

Melody smiled; at times, the streetwise Mustafa seemed much older than his eight years, but this was one of those moments when his chatter resembled that of any eager child his age. And Alessandro had been right about Mustafa's knowledge of the streets of Amsterdam. Whether it was because he did have a remarkably retentive visual memory, or just a good sense of direction, his knowledge of how to return to the hotel was more useful than Melody would ever have admitted.

Despite her irritation at Alessandro's suggestion that she needed protecting and that a child would do a better job than she could on her own, his point was valid: what if her supposed footpad tried again? This led Melody to ponder who might have been watching and following her.

While she would never acknowledge as much to Alessandro or Rat, Melody realised she had been rather oblivious to the people around her since their arrival in Amsterdam. Everything about their trip to Morocco had been so fraught, and it had been wonderful to relax a little. Perhaps she had relaxed too much.

As she and Mustafa ambled along, the child continued to chatter with little need for a response, and Melody retraced her steps from that day. She had gone down to the lobby and asked Robert where she might read newspaper archives. As she relived the conversation, Melody realised she had not tried to be discreet and hadn't even lowered her voice during their exchange; anyone could have overheard where she was going and why.

Then, she had been so preoccupied with following Robert's directions that someone might have followed right behind her without her noticing. At the library, she had only lowered her voice because it was the social norm in such places. However, she hadn't taken particular care to consider who might be around when she requested the periodicals she wished to see.

She had been sitting at the table in the library, reading and making notes, entirely oblivious to her surroundings. After all, Miss Edwards had sneaked up on her without Melody realising.

Glumly, Melody acknowledged to herself that someone could have been following and observing her all day and she wouldn't have known. Now, she glanced around; was she being followed now?

Melody leaned down and said in a low voice to Mustafa, "Let me know if you see anyone suspicious or think we might have someone following us."

The boy was much more attuned to the need for discretion than she had been all day and offered nothing more than a quick nod in reply.

Whether she was being followed or not, there were no further incidents during their walk to the hotel. Melody and Mustafa made their way through the lobby to the lift. It wasn't until the door had closed and the operator asked her which floor she wanted that it occurred to Melody that Rat might not have returned from his outing with Miss Edwards yet.

With Mustafa by her side, Melody knocked on Rat's door and was relieved when he opened it. He was clearly surprised to see Mustafa, but did not comment. Instead, he stepped aside to allow them to enter his room. Rat only had two armchairs in his room, so Mustafa perched on the bed. Melody explained everything since she had left the hotel earlier for the library.

When she reached the part of her story where she encountered Jemima Edwards, Melody's eyes flickered up to her brother's face. She wanted to know how their outing to the cafe had gone, but there were more important matters to discuss. Melody then described leaving the library and being attacked on the street.

"Melody! Are you alright? Why did you not lead with that part of the story?" Rat demanded in a panic.

"Because I'm absolutely fine." She raised her hands so Rat could see her palms. "This is the worst of it. And that I've now lost one of my favourite and most practical bags. But let me tell you the rest of it." She then explained how she had found the piece of paper in her pocket while she was with Alessandro.

Pulling the paper out of her jacket pocket, Melody handed it over. "Alessandro believes it might be the cypher key."

Rat took the paper and stared at it intently. "I think he is right. I spent so long looking at that piece of a manifest earlier, that I don't even need to get it now to know how to decrypt it. Nootmuskaat. 62 zakken. ZKL-3. Huis Jansen. That's what the piece of paper said." Rat stood and went to fetch a notebook and a pencil, then returned to the armchair.

Melody and Mustafa sat in silence while Rat scribbled away on the paper.

Eventually, Rat looked up and said, "So, as we already knew, this was only part of the manifest, so it isn't the entire message. However, there seems little doubt that the paper you found in your pocket is the key. The scrap of manifest we have has a date, and a name, Van Rhijn. It also mentions anarchists."

"What is the date?" Melody asked. When Rat told her it was the sixth of February, she said, "I know I saw something on that date. I wrote it in the notebook that was stolen. Think, think. What was it?"

Melody stood up and began pacing the room as she cast her mind back. Suddenly, she stopped and slapped her leg. "I know what it was. There was a warehouse fire that was blamed on Jewish dockworkers."

"I assume Mustafa accompanied you back so that he could report to Alessandro?" Rat asked. When Melody nodded, he turned to the boy and said, "Given what happened to Lalla Melody earlier, I don't want to give you a note. Can you remember what I tell you, Mustafa?"

"Yes, Sidi Matthew. Mustafa has an excellent memory."

"Excellent. Then I want you to tell him this: that the paper is the key and I have been able to decode the scrap of manifest. Then, I want you to tell him that I will be going to the docks tomorrow, posing as an itinerant worker to see what else I can learn."

At this, Melody's eyebrows shot up in surprise, but she held her tongue until the boy had left. Rat had Mustafa repeat the message back and then sent the boy on his way.

When they were alone, Melody asked, "Are you sure about this? How do you even know you will be taken on at the docks?"

"I know that they do take on foreigners quite regularly. This is an international port; it isn't necessary to speak Dutch, particularly for manual labour. The bigger question is what I should wear."

"Do you still have the clothes you wore that night we broke into the Giardini Della Biennale in Venice?" Melody asked.

"Yes. That's a good idea. They're certainly the roughest-looking clothes I have with me."

"And I think that, with Mary's help, we can make them look even worse. She could sew a few patches on and help us rough up the trousers a little. From what I remember, you wore a pair of old, scuffed soft-soled leather boots. Those should be perfect.

"And I still have the old flat cap I wore that night. That has to look like the kind of thing a man seeking work would own."

Rat went to dig out these clothes, and Melody went to her room to find Mary and ask her to return with her to assist with the costume.

An hour later, Rat stood before them in his lightweight black suit, which now had some patches and a worn spot on the knee that looked as though it might need a patch any day now. He wore his old boots and the flat cap.

"If I might mention it, Mr Sandworth, but your fingernails are far too clean and well-groomed," Mary observed. "To say nothing of your lack of calluses."

Rat looked at his hands. Mary was right, of course. "Well, there isn't much I can do to get calluses, but I can chew my fingernails down and ensure my hands are as dirty as possible tomorrow. Thank you, Mary. That was an astute observation. Is there anything else?"

Mary blushed. She wasn't accustomed to being the centre of attention. "I have a handkerchief that I think would make a good neckerchief for you. And those gloves are in far too good a condition."

Rat picked them up off the table. "They're all I have. What do you suggest?"

"Leave them with me, Mr Sandworth. I'll have them looking years old and more worn in no time."

"You're a marvel, Mary. Thank you."

And with that, a costume and at least the beginning of a plan were in place.

Melody would have insisted on accompanying her brother to the docks if there had been any point. However, even she couldn't think of an appropriate disguise for her to take on for Rat's outing the following day. Instead, she took comfort in ensuring his costume was believable.

CHAPTER 12

Early the following morning, Rat crossed Prins Hendrikkade, dodging a cart stacked with milk churns, and headed east along the Oude Schans canal. The city was awakening; shopkeepers opened their shutters, market vendors began laying out their wares, and the occasional sweep brushed horse dung into the gutter.

As Rat rounded Montelbaanstoren, he passed its crooked clock tower and cut south along Uilenburgerstraat, the old Jewish quarter. He kept his flat cap low as he crossed the Nieuwe Herengracht, which appeared to be a rather fancy part of town with its stone-faced townhouses and iron balconies, before turning east onto Sarphatistraat.

A steam tram hissed past him. It was tempting to hop on it, but Rat decided against it at the last moment. He aimed to enter the docks as inconspicuously as possible. If his narrative was desperation for work, Rat didn't want to do anything to reveal that as a ruse. Soon enough, he reached Kadijksplein, where the air was thick with coal smoke and tannin.

A flock of seagulls ahead was his first clue that he was almost at the water. The next indication was the noise. Even though it was barely past dawn, chains were already clanking, the gulls were screeching, and a constant sound of yelling filled the air. Then there was the smell: old salt, coal smoke, rope, and something sharp and spicy.

The old customs house loomed nearby. Beyond that, he could see the cranes and warehouses of the Entrepotdok, rising like a city of iron.

He reached the gate where a line of men stood, hoping for a day's work. Rat joined the queue and by the time the foreman shouted "Naam?" Rat had one made up: Ernie Thumbull.

Ernie Thumbull was someone Rat had known in his Whitechapel days. He always seemed to be down on his luck and had a sob story prepared about why he didn't have the coin to pay for his drinks in The Cock. Ernie's saving grace was his good humour; he always had an amusing tale to share and appeared to accept his lot in life with equanimity. Rat thought he would be the perfect person to pretend to be for the day.

Rat hadn't had to fall back on his cockney accent in a very long time. In fact, he had spent so much time and energy trying not to drop his aitches that he was a little worried he wouldn't be able to revert convincingly. But then he reminded himself that a Dutch foreman was unlikely to be an expert on how someone from Whitechapel should sound. He just hoped there wasn't anyone at the docks that day who might be more knowledgeable.

As he waited in line, Rat noted his surroundings. There was something quite impressive about the Entrepotdok. It seemed to stretch on indefinitely. Long lines of warehouses, brick and iron, jutted out over the water. Trams clattered by, flatbeds stacked high with crates marked in painted letters that resembled the markings Rat had seen on the scrap of the manifest.

Surrounding him, Dutchmen, also seeking a day's work, muttered and coughed into their scarves, stamping their boots against the cobbles of the quay. He didn't understand the words, but the tone was familiar – grumbling about work, weather, and wages, the universal language of the labouring poor.

A bell tolled from within the yard, and the heavy gate creaked open. The queue lurched forward. The foreman, a stout man in a wool coat and oil-stained cap, stood just beyond, flanked by two younger clerks with ledgers. The foreman had a face resembling a butcher's block: scarred, weathered, and indifferent. One by one, the men stepped forward, gave their names, and were waved in or turned away.

Rat shuffled forward with the others, keeping his gaze fixed on the ground. When his turn arrived, the foreman scrutinised him as if he were a butcher assessing a side of beef. Rat detected a flicker of suspicion in the man's eyes and compelled himself to cough, hacking as though he had spent the last month sleeping in alleys.

"Sprak je Nederlands?" the foreman asked.

Rat gave a vague shake of his head and mimed lifting something heavy with a grunt. The clerk chuckled. The foreman sighed, marked something on the ledger.

The foreman said something to one of the clerks, who asked, "Can you read?"

Rat nodded. "Yeah, I can read good, I can." The clerk said something back to the foreman, who jerked a thumb over his shoulder.

"Magazijn zeven. Kisten lossen," he muttered.

The man jotted something down on a piece of paper and handed it to Rat. "Give this to the clerk over in Warehouse Seven."

It didn't take long for the foreman to attend to all the men in the line. Rat followed the others through the gate and made his way towards Warehouse Seven.

At the warehouse, Rat and the other day labourers were greeted by another clerk. Rat approached and handed the man the piece of paper he'd been given. The clerk grunted and indicated that Rat should make his way to the right side of the warehouse.

An hour later, Rat was hard at work. The task he'd been assigned seemed simple enough, though hard on the back. He was to help unload a shipment from the *SS Prins Hendrik*, a freighter just in from the Dutch East Indies. The crates bore stamps from Batavia and Palembang and were stacked precariously on a splintered wooden pallet inside Warehouse Seven. His job, along with three other men, was to ease them down from the wagon, shift them onto a handcart, and wheel them to the far end of the shed where the clerks recorded the contents.

However, unlike the others, Rat had been assigned an additional task because he could read. When the foreman saw his slip and grunted something about "schoolmeester," he handed Rat a stub of pencil and a list, motioning for him to check the labels before the crates were shifted. While Rat couldn't read Dutch, all that was required was to match what was on the crate with what was on the list and confirm the city of origin and the supposed contents—coffee, rubber, tin, spices—against the manifest tags. It was meant to prevent errors in sorting, especially now with the increased volume coming in from the colonies.

It was dull, repetitive work, but it provided Rat with what he needed: time and proximity.

Each crate had a paper manifest nailed to the top, listing the goods scribbled in Dutch. Rat wasn't certain what he was searching for, but he assumed there was some sort of pattern indicating the manifests that were part of the German operation.

Rat recalled the marking that had appeared on the piece of manifest he had decoded: ZKL-3. The cypher key was poly-alphabetic, with "ZKL" serving as the key to the cypher, and "3" denoting a starting row, shift value, or column. While Rat was convinced this wasn't the only pertinent marking, it was the one he recognised, and so he kept a lookout for it.

The morning dragged on with nothing suspicious occurring. Rat realised he might be overlooking manifests because he didn't recognise the markings, but that couldn't be helped.

The men were given a brief break for lunch. Rat was glad he'd had the foresight to buy a bread roll filled with ham and cheese from one of the street vendors. He'd tucked it in his pocket, and now, as the other men sat in groups and chatted while they ate, Rat sat alone on a crate, hungrily munching on his food.

He'd barely had time to finish chewing his last bite when the men were hurried back to work. A new ship was being unloaded, and Rat returned to the monotonous labour. It was all he could do to pay enough attention not to miss anything.

Rat had left his fancy pocket watch back at the hotel, so he had no idea what the time was. However, it seemed as if he'd been working for many hours; his back and shoulders ached, which made Rat realise how soft he had become over the years since he'd left Whitechapel. While he had always been scrawny as a child, he'd been nimble and quite strong for his age and weight. Not anymore. He hoped he could uncover something that day, because he didn't relish the idea of returning day after day and doing this kind of work.

A new batch of crates was being unloaded from the ship, and the wagons were rolling into the warehouse. It took Rat a few moments of glancing at the manifest to realise that all these crates bore the marking ZKL, followed by a number. Was this what he was searching for?

Rat crouched by the stack of crates, pretending to retie his boot. The paper he'd glimpsed inside the foreman's open ledger had that same marking: ZKL, followed by a number. A fresh shipment. Four crates. All marked for Rotterdam. All listed at exactly 58,2 kilos.

It was all too neat and tidy. Rat had seen enough to know something was amiss. If he left without a record, the manifest could be gone by the following day, and he couldn't anticipate when the next relevant batch of shipments would arrive. Rat couldn't believe his fortunate timing in having even stumbled across one of them.

As Rat and the others unloaded the crates, the clerk entered the details into a ledger. Rat was uncertain about what had happened, either to the original manifest or the ledger. It wasn't until some hours later, as the day seemed to wind down, that he saw the clerk take the ledger into the foreman's shack, leaving without it a few moments later.

This was his chance.

Rat rose, moved behind a nearby crate for cover, and ducked into the foreman's shack under the pretence of needing a fresh pencil for time-tickets. The door creaked. No one called after him.

Inside, the stench of stale tobacco lingered in the air. The ledger lay open on the desk, next to a stub of pencil.

ZKL-4. Kist 2187. 58,2 kg. Huis Jansen. He continued to scan down the page of the manifest. There was a second entry, followed by a third. All starting with ZKL and all destined for Huis Jansen.

His heart raced. He ripped a blank receipt from the edge of a stack and copied the manifest as swiftly as possible.

2187 - Rubber - 58,2 kg - Huis Jansen - ZKL-4
2191 - Tin - 58,2 kg - Huis Jansen - ZKL-10
2192 - Dekens - 58,2 kg - Huis Jansen - ZKL-2

He heard a footstep outside, and Rat's chest tightened. He jotted down the remainder of the manifest as swiftly as he could. Someone cursed. The door handle twitched. Rat slipped the copy into his cap, flicked the ledger shut with one hand, and picked up a blank time slip as if he'd been searching for it all along.

The door opened. A large man stood there, his face unreadable beneath his cap. He looked quizzically at Rat, who held up the blank time slip and grinned. Whatever the large man thought, he seemed to decide he didn't care enough to question Rat. He went over to the desk, opened one of the drawers, took out a sheet of paper with something printed on it in Dutch, grunted again, and left.

Rat was tempted to take the paper and leave the docks immediately. However, he might want to return for work another time, so it made more sense to finish the day's tasks.

CHAPTER 13

Melody woke up early, aware that Rat must have already left for the docks. She felt far too anxious about his safety and curious about what he might discover to sit around the hotel all morning doing nothing. She recalled her conversation with Alessandro the previous day. They truly knew very little about the dead informant, Vermeer. Well, she amended that; they now knew he lived with a Dutch woman.

As Melody considered this, she snapped her fingers. "I need to talk to her. Who knows what light she might shed on Vermeer and his final days."

Of course, she didn't know who this woman was or where she lived; only, Alessandro might. The thought of returning to Alessandro's house and potentially encountering Fatima was more than Melody could bear. Rat had suggested that they use the hotel's telephone sparingly; they didn't know who might be eavesdropping on calls. However, Melody was sure she could make a seemingly innocuous call to Alessandro's house and ask him to meet her at the hotel.

Buoyed by the prospect of doing something productive with her day, Melody sprang out of bed. Even though it was early, Mary was already up and pottering about in the living room. She couldn't hide her surprise when Melody walked out of her bedroom fully dressed, despite it being only eight o'clock in the morning.

"You are up early, Miss Melody."

"Am I? Well, it looks to be a lovely day out and I think I need to get some fresh air."

Everything about this statement was patently absurd; actually, it appeared to be shaping up to be another uncomfortably hot day. Moreover, it was hardly as if Melody had been cooped up in the hotel for days.

However, it was not Mary's place to question her charge. Instead, she said, "Would you like me to accompany you?"

"As it happens," Melody said in an attempt at a casual tone, "I think I will ask Conte Foscari to walk with me."

Mary's pursed lips conveyed all the response she needed to give to this suggestion. Although she didn't know the details, she was aware that the conte had hurt her beloved Melody, and for that, Mary could never forgive him. It was not for a lowly servant like her to question why the man continued to travel with them, let alone why THAT woman did. While she would never be so bold as to voice such a statement about her supposed betters, as far as Mary was concerned, Fatima was no better than she ought to be.

Melody read Mary's expression accurately. However, she chose not to comment. Given the early hour, it was hardly reasonable to telephone Alessandro yet. However, perhaps if she went to have breakfast, it might be an acceptable time once she was done.

"I am going down to the restaurant to have some breakfast. Would you like to join me, Mary?"

A servant like Mary held an unusual status. If one considered her still to be Melody's maid, then it was inappropriate for them to dine together. However, if she were the young woman's companion, or even chaperone, then it was socially acceptable for her to do so. Melody typically inclined towards the latter view, whereas Mary herself could never shake off her lowly start in life and usually leaned towards the former.

Given this, she shook her head. "You go ahead without me, Miss Melody."

Melody was disinclined to argue with Mary about this for a change; she wished to make the telephone call to Alessandro without being in the shadow of the woman's disapproving glare.

Melody skipped out of the room before Mary could change her mind.

The dining room was quite empty at that time of the morning. Melody sat at her usual table and gratefully accepted a cup of coffee from the waiter. She wasn't particularly hungry and thought she might just have some toast and jam.

Just as she was about to call the waiter over, Melody saw Jemima Edwards enter the dining room, and her heart sank. The room was far too empty to hope that she wouldn't be seen. It was possible that Jemima would merely wave and then move to a table on her own, but Melody had a terrible feeling that the chirpy Miss Edwards would never be that unsociable.

Her worst fears were confirmed when Jemima caught sight of her, waved, but then proceeded to walk towards her. "Miss Chesterton! What a surprise. It seems you are an early bird as well."

"Not usually, but yes, this morning, I woke early and thought I would come down and miss the crowds."

If Melody had hoped this last statement might dissuade excessive friendliness, she was mistaken.

"Oh yes, I agree. It can get awfully busy in here later on, can it not? Might I join you?" Jemima asked, shattering Melody's last hope that she might escape.

Trying to make her smile as genuine as possible, Melody lied, "Of course you may. I would love some company."

Jemima took the seat opposite, and the waiter hurried over to take her beverage order.

"I wouldn't mind so much if all the other guests weren't so elderly. I do believe that we, and of course Mr Sandworth, are the only people under forty staying in this hotel."

Melody held no opinion on whether this was true. She had made no particular observation of this, but she also didn't really care. Her stay in Amsterdam was not for pleasure, and thus the presence of more age-appropriate guests with whom she might socialise hardly mattered to her.

Instead of saying anything like that, Melody simply smiled again.

Then, realising she would need to make some effort to uphold her end of the conversation, she asked, "Do you have travelling companions, Miss Edwards?" Melody assumed the young woman must have someone. It was not the done thing for an unmarried woman of Jemima's age to travel the continent unaccompanied.

"I am being chaperoned by my Aunt Beatrice. However, she has a rather nervous disposition and seldom leaves our room."

Like Rat, Melody pondered who could possibly believe that such a person would make a suitable chaperone or even companion for a young woman.

While good manners prevented Melody from voicing such a thought, she did remark, "That must be rather lonely, Miss Edwards. To be always alone, that is."

Jemima gave her a rather sad little smile. "It can be. It certainly can be. It is one reason I was so delighted to meet your brother. And of course, then you, Miss Chesterton. Usually, I am happy enough with my own company. I go to the museums, borrow books from the library, and take tea in the cafes. However, sometimes it can be a bit lonely."

As she listened, Melody berated herself for being so inconsiderate; Jemima Edwards merely craved some company, and here she was, resenting even the notion of sharing a cup of coffee with the woman.

"I am very grateful for my brother's company and that of my companion, Mary," Melody said with a genuine smile this time.

"Where else have you travelled to?"

The question was asked so casually that Melody didn't even consider it before she answered. "We began in Venice, then went to Morocco, before coming to Amsterdam." As soon as the words left her mouth, Melody realised how peculiar that itinerary was, if they were indeed nothing more than tourists exploring the continent. Why on earth would anyone leave Italy, travel all the way to North Africa, and then return to the Netherlands? It made no sense.

Melody searched for a reason that might render the travels more comprehensible, but came up with nothing.

If Miss Edwards was curious about their travel choices, she did not comment. However, she did observe, "Morocco must have been fascinating. And you must have been there when the Germans sent their gunboat to Agadir."

This observation was just a little too close for comfort, and Melody panicked. "Oh, did they? I didn't hear about that." This was an absurd statement to make. She would have had to ignore every single newspaper over the past month, not to have seen some mention of the German provocation.

Again, regardless of what Miss Edwards thought about this statement, she merely smiled and shifted to a far more mundane topic. "Did you ride a camel?"

"Luckily, I did not have to experience that. I rode horses and quite a few mules, but I was spared a camel."

"You would not have liked that?" Jemima asked. "I would love to ride a camel, given the chance. How romantic it must be to ride such a beast as you trek across the desert."

Given the hardships of her travels between Casablanca and Fes and then onto Tangier, Melody could imagine nothing romantic about an even more uncomfortable ride on a camel in the dunes. However, she kept her thoughts to herself.

Melody ordered toast, and Jemima hemmed and hawed for a few minutes before deciding on boiled eggs. The food arrived quickly, and the women chatted as they ate. The more they talked, the more comfortable Melody became with Jemima, and the more she regretted her initial assessment of the woman. Perhaps it wouldn't be such a bad thing if Rat were to end up with someone like Miss Edwards.

As this thought ran through her head, Melody realised that the subject of her brother had not come up at all. She wondered if this indicated a lack of interest on Jemima's part or merely a shyness in discussing a young man in whom she had a romantic interest.

Determined to investigate what this might be, Melody remarked, "My brother greatly enjoyed your outing yesterday."

"I am so glad to hear that. Mr Sandworth is delightful company, and so interesting."

Melody wasn't sure she'd ever heard her quiet, rather bookish brother described as in this way before. Her first sisterly instinct was to make a joke at his expense, but she caught herself just in time.

"I believe Matthew finds you equally charming," was what Melody said instead. Then, she asked coyly, "Will there be another such outing?"

"Absolutely! We are to visit the Rijksmuseum." This was the first Melody had heard about such an excursion. Should she be upset that Rat hadn't mentioned it? Melody wondered. Then, she considered that they had spent the previous evening consumed with assembling an appropriate disguise for Rat's trip to Entrepotdok and realised that a visit to a museum with Miss Edwards had not been top of mind for him.

"I am so happy to hear that there will be a second outing," Melody said with genuine pleasure.

When she had finished her eggs and had drunk a second cup of tea, Jemima wiped her mouth with her napkin and made her excuses. "This has been delightful, Miss Chesterton, and I hope we can repeat it again soon. However, I must get going. I have an appointment for which I will be late if I am not careful." With that, Jemima Edwards stood and left.

Melody watched Jemima leave and pondered how she might help further the budding romance. She had shifted from trepidation about the potential chaos Jemima, as Mrs Sandworth, could unleash, to contemplating the role she might assume as matchmaker for the young couple. Melody sat there considering the topic for several minutes before realising that she still needed to make a telephone call to Alessandro.

CHAPTER 14

M elody did not know how telephone calls were placed in Amsterdam. She approached Robert and told him she wished to make a call to someone, but all she knew was the name and the street. As she said this, it occurred to Melody that perhaps Alessandro was using an assumed name. However, she considered that he owned newspapers in the Netherlands. Surely, remaining incognito was pointless. Wasn't his entire persona as an operative about hiding in plain sight?

In the hope she was correct, Melody provided Alessandro's name and the street. Robert made a telephone call to the operator, and a few minutes later, he handed her the receiver. As she took it, Melody suddenly realised that Fatima might have answered. Steeling herself for an uncomfortable conversation, she nervously greeted whoever was on the other end of the line. Fortunately, it was Alessandro.

After overhearing Robert's earlier conversation with Alessandro, Melody was aware of how public the front desk was. She tried to keep her voice low as she said, "Conte Foscari. I was thinking about your deceased friend's widow and would like to pay a call of condolence. Would you be available to escort me?" Melody hoped this message was both vague enough not to attract the attention of anyone who might overhear it, yet clear enough that Alessandro would understand her point.

"I am sure the grieving widow would greatly appreciate a visit," Alessandro replied, seeming to understand Melody's drift. "I will meet you in the hotel lobby at ten o'clock, if that is convenient." Melody assured him it would be perfect and then handed the receiver back to Robert.

Glancing at the clock on the counter, Melody realised she had some time before Alessandro arrived. She looked down at the dress she had donned earlier and decided it was a touch too colourful for a condolence call. After all, the woman they were to visit had indeed lost someone close to her, even if she was only his common-law wife.

Melody returned to her room and, after explaining where she was going and with whom, asked Mary to assist her in finding something more suitable to wear. Mary continued to remain silent but conveyed her intense disapproval through her facial expressions and the occasional tut. Melody was surprised that the woman didn't insist on accompanying her on the outing with Alessandro.

Finally, they found an appropriately conservative navy dress and decided to pair it with her new bolero jacket that was pretty, but also quite simple and so would match the respectful tone of condolence for the visit. Melody changed her clothes and hurried back down to the lobby, realising she was now running late.

When she exited the lift, Melody saw Alessandro was already waiting for her. In that first moment, she forgot how he had treated her since Venice and every negative emotion she had towards him, simply taking in how strikingly handsome he was. His chiselled features, olive skin tone, and jet-black hair offset his green eyes, framed by thick, dark, curling lashes. Melody recalled the first moment she had laid eyes on him outside the train station in Venice. Tall and broad-shouldered, Conte Alessandro Foscari had thrown her off balance and continued to do so even many weeks later.

Then Melody remembered the kiss they had shared in the gondola and how, in that moment, she had been willing to throw caution and all sense of propriety to the wind. Memories of that moment made her blush and feel shame, both for her behaviour and for her naivety in believing that the suave, urbane man of the world could have any genuine interest in a young, innocent girl.

As much as Melody resented Alessandro for taking advantage of her innocence – and not even for genuinely romantic reasons – she realised she had played a part in enabling him to do so. She had been so eager to prove that she was sophisticated and worldly that she had ignored Rat and Mary's warnings, along with her own instincts. No one had forced her into that gondola. She had chosen a dress with a daringly low-cut neckline, despite Mary's protestations. She had wanted to be seduced. Well, to the extent that she had considered what that meant, she had wanted it.

Melody realised that she could either insist on being involved in this investigation or maintain a state of open hostility towards Alessandro, but she couldn't do both.

She took a deep breath, composed herself, and walked towards him. "I apologise for my tardiness, Alessandro," Melody said, making a point of using his given name for the first time in weeks.

A slight quirk of his lips indicated Alessandro had picked up on the subtle change in attitude, but he made no comment. Instead, he followed her lead. "It is no matter, Melody. I have only been here for a couple of minutes." Alessandro looked around to ensure they could not be overheard, then said in a low voice, "I assume you wish to visit Vermeer's widow."

Melody tried to be equally discreet as she replied, "Yes. She might know something, even if she doesn't realise its importance."

"It is certainly something worth pursuing," Alessandro acknowledged. "Then let us be on our way. I ensured I had the address before leaving home. I think that dress is appropriate."

Melody was tempted to give a sharp retort, but then considered what Alessandro was wearing. He was always dressed in the height of fashion, in clothes that spoke of the finest tailoring and the wealth to afford it. However, for this outing, while his clothes weren't tattered by any means, they were less well-made and less cared for. The trousers did not feature their usual knife-edged crease, and the cravat was not tied with the precision that only a highly paid valet could achieve. Overall, he resembled a middle-class bank or law clerk. Nothing could hide his good looks, but certainly, the appearance of a life of monied ease had vanished.

Instead of the biting comment that had sprung to her lips, Melody said, "Then let us be on our way."

"The house is in Plantagebuurt, which is only a fifteen-to-twenty-minute walk," Alessandro explained. "Or we can take a tram if you prefer."

Melody indicated her willingness to walk. It would give them time to converse.

They left the hotel and began winding their way south through the hustle and bustle of Damrak. Trams rattled past as they entered the narrower lanes near Nieuwmarkt, where patrons of the cafés spilled onto the cobbled streets and the aroma of roasting coffee made Melody yearn for another cup.

They walked in silence for several minutes until Melody asked, "What story will we give for our appearance?"

"I am going to say that I am a journalist and wish to write a piece about Meneer Brenner and wanted to know more about his history."

While it was a reasonable story, Melody wondered how she would fit into it. "Who am I then?" Alessandro reached into his pocket and pulled out a slim, lightweight pocket camera. Melody was astonished by the camera's small size and curious about how Alessandro obtained it. Maybe his work as a newspaper publisher gave him access to amazing new technologies.

"You are my photographer," he explained. It was a reasonable enough story. Although women weren't common in journalism, they had made some inroads.

There was another more pressing question. "What if she won't talk to us?"

"I can be very persuasive," Alessandro said in a teasing tone that was a little too close to the truth for Melody's comfort.

Choosing to ignore that provocation, she instead pointed out, "If she does know anything of what Karl Brenner was really doing, I doubt she will reveal that to a pair of journalists."

"I agree. However, I very much doubt she knows much. What she might know is why Brenner ended up in Amsterdam and what his feelings were towards his native Germany, and more to the point, why they were what they were."

The crowds began to thin as they passed the old city walls and moved eastward along Plantage Middenlaan, where majestic chestnut trees shaded the quiet boulevards. By the time they reached the leafy calm of Plantagebuurt, the noise of the city had muted. It was a quiet and pretty working-class neighbourhood, Melody noted. Brick row houses lined the street, ivy climbed over wrought-iron railings, and lace curtains fluttered in the tall windows that were so characteristic of Amsterdam's architecture.

They made their way to a house that was indistinguishable from its neighbours and knocked on the door. Given Vermeer's job on the docks, it was unlikely that he occupied the entire house, and indeed, the woman who answered the door had the look of a landlady that apparently transcended countries and cultures.

It seemed that Alessandro spoke Dutch or at least spoke it well enough to communicate with the woman. She heard the name Brenner, to which the woman nodded and then stood aside to let them in.

Inside, the house was clean, albeit somewhat shabby. The furniture was well-made yet scratched and battered. The woman led them into a front parlour and indicated that they should sit. She then left the room.

A few minutes later, the door opened again, and a woman, perhaps of around forty years old, with a kind, if worn face, entered. She had black hair and intelligent, warm, brown eyes. The woman was wearing widow's weeds, which made her already pale complexion look washed out. Melody thought the woman had probably been quite pretty before a hard life had worn her down.

Alessandro stood at the woman's entrance and introduced himself and Melody. He then spoke some more in Dutch, and the woman nodded her head.

"She is happy to talk with us and to have you take some photos," Alessandro explained.

The woman sat, and Alessandro began to ask her questions, which she seemed willing to answer. When he was done, Alessandro indicated Melody should take a photo or two. She hadn't expected him to translate everything he was saying and was content to wait to hear what Alessandro had learned.

CHAPTER 15

As soon as they left the house, Melody asked, "So, what did she say?"
Once more, Alessandro looked around before answering in a low voice, "Well, from what I can tell, she had no idea that he was a British informant. Of course, I could not ask her that directly, but the woman seemed entirely lacking in guile, and I don't believe she was attempting to hide anything."

"What did you learn?"

"She had no trouble telling me why Brenner hated Germany so much; in fact, she volunteered the information. I asked how long he had been living in Amsterdam, and she told me it has been three years. She was rather vague on the details, but I know what she was alluding to."

"So? What was it?"

"Mevrouw Brenner, which is how she referred to herself, as his wife, said that her husband was in the German Navy during the unrest in the Baltic provinces following the Russian Revolution in 1905."

Melody was embarrassed to admit that her knowledge of history did not stretch that far. She knew what the Russian Revolution was – who didn't – but regarding the rest of it, she didn't know what Alessandro was talking about.

Given that Melody had still been a child at the time, Alessandro must have realised that she needed more context. "After 1905, revolutionary unrest spread throughout the Russian Empire, including the Baltic provinces. All of these had large German-speaking landowning minorities who wielded significant power. Local peasants and workers, many Latvian nationalists and socialists, rose up against their German landlords."

Alessandro continued, "These Baltic German elites armed themselves with foreign support; it was suspected at the time that at least some of it was unofficially German backed. Or at least this is what the British Government believed. While Germany officially remained neutral, there was no doubt that individual agents, merchants, and military sympathisers acted, supposedly independently. But there were always questions regarding how independent they truly were or whether this provided the German Government just enough plausible deniability."

Where was this leading? Melody wondered. Perhaps realising he needed to get to the point, Alessandro explained, "Brenner worked on a German-flagged merchant vessel delivering supplies to Baltic German landowners, under the guise of trade goods. Mevrouw Brenner said he came to believe the ship's funding and direction came directly from the German Government."

By now, they were back at the edge of Nieuwmarkt, and the aroma of coffee and pastries reminded Melody that it had been quite some time since her breakfast. She suggested they stop to get something to eat. Alessandro agreed, but it was clear he was anxious about sitting somewhere they might be overheard.

Finally, they found a cafe that was less crowded than the others and had tables outside where they could sit in privacy. They settled themselves in and ordered. Once the waiter returned with a cup of steaming coffee for each of them, Alessandro finished his story.

"Brenner's ship was moored in the port of Riga when retaliatory violence broke out. He watched Baltic-German militias execute civilians, including women and children, using German-supplied arms offloaded earlier. The crew was ordered to keep quiet about what they saw. Apparently, he was so haunted by what he had witnessed that when the ship arrived in Amsterdam, he abandoned his post and changed his name. She doesn't know what his real name is; he thought it safer for her that way."

Melody was appalled by what she had heard. Of course, she wasn't so naive as to believe that terrible things weren't often done in the name of warfare, but there was something about this story that made it very plausible that a German citizen might have turned against his homeland.

"Did Mevrouw Brenner have any thoughts on why her husband had been killed?" Melody asked.

"No. Though, she did say that he had been jittery of late and she felt as if he was always looking over his shoulder. They had recently moved lodgings for no apparent reason as far as she could tell, and he had begun to talk of leaving Amsterdam soon."

This led to only one conclusion as far as Melody could see: Vermeer was worried that someone suspected he was acting as an informant against the Germans.

"She had nothing else of use to say?"

"Well, my Dutch is not up to a very in-depth conversation," Alessandro admitted. "However, I asked her to send a message to the newspaper if she thinks of anything else. I don't hold out much hope, though."

Melody sipped her coffee and contemplated what they'd learned. "I do wish we understood more about how Vermeer and Captain Somerset even came into contact with each other initially."

"Those of us in the espionage business have a sixth sense of when someone is itching to blow the whistle on colleagues or even friends and family."

This was the first time either Alessandro or Rat had admitted that William Somerset must have been a covert intelligence operative, and perhaps he still was.

Now, she asked, "Do you know what Captain Somerset's official and unofficial role was when he was in Amsterdam?" Melody was curious to see what Alessandro knew and what he was prepared to reveal. She observed his face, looking for signs that he was about to lie. Of course, Alessandro was a seasoned intelligence operative, and, as such, Melody assumed he was more than capable of masking his deceit. However, she knew him quite well by this time and thought she might perceive what a casual observer wouldn't.

"My understanding is that he was seconded to the Political Affairs Desk at the Foreign Office. His official title while he was in Amsterdam was Second Attaché, Commercial Affairs. From what I understand, he was not, nor is, an official part of the Secret Service Bureau. However, his analyses were used as strategic intelligence, especially regarding Dutch neutrality and potential German sabotage."

"Oh!" was all Melody thought to say.

Alessandro looked bemused. "You sound surprised. Is it at what Somerset's role was or that I gave up the information so easily?"

"Mostly the latter, I suppose," Melody admitted.

Alessandro's face took on an expression she couldn't interpret. "Melody, I know that you have decided that I am the enemy, but it just isn't true." To Melody's ear, Alessandro's tone as he said this was almost regretful. Or was he merely manipulating her? Again?

That was the trouble, wasn't it? Having fallen prey to his suave machinations once, Melody was loath to let her guard down. It felt as if the safest thing, indeed the smartest thing, was to view Alessandro's every action and every statement through a lens of suspicion. Perhaps suspicion wasn't the right word, but certainly a level of distrust. Even articulating this felt like a degree of candour that she was uncomfortable sharing.

Instead of saying any of this, Melody replied, "Not the enemy."

She felt tempted to say more, but refrained. Alessandro completed the thought for her. "But not a friend?" Melody didn't reply. "I would like us to be friends, Melody. I am sorry for any hurt I caused you. The work that Matthew and I do, which you wish to be part of, is vitally important, never more so than now. We do what we need to, even when perhaps our methods seem unreasonable, or even cruel."

Was that a warning? Melody wondered. Certainly, it was an attempt to justify, or at least explain, why he had feigned romantic interest in her while they were in Venice. Melody considered Alessandro's words; was she going to be expected to behave similarly if she continued working on investigations with him, even if in an unofficial capacity? Was she comfortable with that kind of subterfuge?

Her thoughts must have been evident on her face because Alessandro said, even more gently, "We will never ask you to do anything you are not comfortable with, Melody."

Even as she felt grateful for this reassurance, she wondered whether this meant she would never be a full investigative partner. Was that even what she wanted? Melody contemplated whether she needed to take a step back when this investigation concluded, and consider more fully what she did desire. Even before she'd left London, she'd known that she didn't want to follow the usual path laid out for a woman of her class: a socially acceptable marriage that quickly led to an heir, and another should misfortune strike.

Thanks to a fortune bequeathed to her by the dowager countess, Melody could shape her life as she desired. The money was not a dowry, nor was it dependent on any particular path – something that was astounding at the time to those who knew the dowager well. There was no doubt that the world was opening up to women. It was now far more common for them to attend university than it had been when Cousin Lily was Melody's age. Was that what she wanted to do? Continue her education?

As of a few years prior, women could even be elected to borough and county councils, though not to Parliament. Melody had never had any genuine interest in politics before. However, since getting a front-row seat to the ramifications of the government's foreign policies, she certainly had valuable insights now.

Pretending to be a journalist earlier made Melody wonder whether that might be a field she was interested in exploring. Alternatively, there was always the option of continuing to force her way into investigations with Alessandro and Rat, which brought her back full circle to Alessandro's comments. Was she prepared to do whatever was necessary to fulfil a mission?

While Melody didn't have an answer to that question, she knew what needed to be said in that moment: "I understand why you did what you did. That doesn't make it easier to feel I can be fully candid now."

Alessandro nodded in acknowledgement of her feelings. He extended his hand. "Perhaps we can agree to start anew."

"I can do that," she agreed taking his hand.

They walked back to the hotel in mostly companionable silence. It wasn't until they had just passed the train station that Melody asked, "Do you sense that we're being watched?"

Alessandro was far too seasoned an operative to turn his head and look around him. Instead, he continued staring straight ahead. "Yes, I've felt it as well. I wasn't sure at the cafe, but even since we've been walking, I've had the feeling that someone is following us. Is this the first time you've felt this?"

Melody pondered the question. Was it? "Well, of course, there was the supposed footpad the other day. Is that the person who is behind us now?" Given the earlier physical attack on her, the thought that the same individual was tracking her was more worrisome than she was willing to admit.

"Let us continue as if we haven't noticed, at least for now," Alessandro advised. "We are almost back at the hotel. We have no idea how long this person has been following us. If they saw us visit Brenner's house, that ship has already sailed. Since then, all we've done is sit in a cafe. I will be alert when I leave the hotel later, and you need to be as well."

What did that mean? Melody didn't want to appear weak and scared to Alessandro. She realised his willingness to involve her in the investigation was fragile, as was Rat's. Melody didn't want to give either of them a reason to change their minds. She considered the small Derringer pistol that Granny had given her for her birthday. The gun was compact enough to be carried even in an evening bag. She resolved she wouldn't leave the hotel without it in the future.

CHAPTER 16

By the time the foreman dismissed Rat and the other workers, it had been a long and tiring day. Rat had never felt more clearly that his day-to-day existence, while it had its challenges, was still much easier than the lives of most people. He often wondered what his life would have been like had he not turned up at the back door of Chesterton House with Melody all those years ago. Would he even still be alive? It was almost certain he would have become a criminal of some sort, either as a pickpocket or working for a gang leader like Mickey D. The lives of such individuals were often short and brutal, or they often ended up in a prison cell.

Whatever path he might have taken, long, physically arduous days would have certainly been far more routine than they were now. For the most part, Rat had no regrets and was thankful to Tabitha, Wolf, and Lord Langley for all they had done for him and Melody. Still, sometimes there was a faint voice in the back of his mind that whispered he had become soft and wouldn't survive a day back on the rough Whitechapel streets he had roamed as a child.

These thoughts swirled in Rat's mind as he walked back to the hotel. Although he had left so early that morning that he hadn't worried about walking through the lobby, he realised that returning in the early evening was a different matter. Dressed as he was, he couldn't risk attracting attention. He presumed the hotel had a back door. Once he found it, Rat ducked inside and ascended a staircase.

Fortunately, the corridor on his floor was empty, allowing him to slip quickly into his room, encountering no one. As much as he wanted to share all he had discovered with Melody, Rat needed to wash off the grime from the docks first. He took a bath and changed his clothes. By this time, it was nearly half-past seven, and he wondered if he would find his sister in her room or downstairs for dinner.

Rat knocked on Melody's door. Mary answered and informed him he would find his sister in the dining room.

Mary had been in service for too many years not to realise the impertinence of asking Rat how his mission had gone. Nevertheless, she had been so helpful in putting a costume together that Rat volunteered that his disguise had seemed more than adequate and thanked her for all her help.

A few minutes later, Rat entered the dining room and looked for Melody. To his surprise, he saw her sitting at their usual table, accompanied by Alessandro. Even more surprisingly, the two appeared relaxed and were laughing together. Rat wasn't sure what had changed, but he felt grateful for it. He hadn't enjoyed feeling caught between his beloved sister and his esteemed colleague. The tension that always arose when Alessandro and Melody were in the same room had been exhausting for the young man to endure for weeks on end. He could only hope that whatever had caused this rapprochement would last.

As Rat approached the table, Melody and Alessandro looked up and smiled. "We have just ordered, Matthew," Alessandro said. "Why don't you pull up a chair and join us?" Rat realised how hungry he was, and the chance to share his discovery with Alessandro and Melody at the same time as he ate something was too good to pass up.

The dining room was bustling, but the tables were spaced sufficiently far apart for Rat to tell both of them about the manifests without the worry of being overheard.

Once he had finished explaining everything he thought he had discovered, Alessandro leaned back with his hands behind his head. "And you have copies of these manifests?" he asked.

"I do. However, I have not tried to decrypt them yet. Why don't we retire to Melody's suite when we have finished eating? Now that I have deciphered the original scrap of manifest, I don't believe it will take me long to do the ones I copied today."

There seemed to be no reason to argue, and thirty minutes later, they had finished their food and made their way up to Melody's hotel room. Once again, Mary slipped out of the room silently. Rat had brought both the cypher key and the paper he had copied with him and he sat with a fresh sheet of notepaper, and a German dictionary, working to decipher what the manifests revealed. Alessandro and Melody sat quietly while he worked.

Thirty minutes later, Rat looked up from his work. "The manifests I copied are an incomplete set, but based on what I have managed to decipher and my rudimentary German, it seems that the Germans are planning to escalate their activities."

"What does escalate mean?" Melody asked.

"Again, I don't have all the information here, but there seem to be explicit references to a planned bombing at a theatre"

"Do you have information on when and how?" Melody demanded. "Or which theatre, in fact?"

Rat shook his head. "I need to go back to the Entrepotdok and see what is in those crates and where they go."

"Wouldn't they have left the warehouse by now?"

ALESSANDRO ANSWERED, "MAYBE OR MAYBE NOT. IT'S MY understanding that manifests are filed upon entry, but that, depending on the cargo, it might sit in the warehouse for two to three days. It is certainly worth going back tomorrow to see what more you can learn."

Melody contemplated the implications of a bomb being detonated at a theatre. "There are potentially hundreds of lives at stake. We need to stop this at all costs." Rat and Alessandro exchanged a glance. "What? What are you not telling me?" she demanded.

"Our job is not to stop such a bombing," Alessandro explained. "Our job is to prove definitively that the Germans are behind it. I assume that their intention is to blame this on anarchists, putting the Dutch people on edge and making them more willing to look to their neighbour for some security."

"Don't you care that a lot of people might die?" Melody couldn't believe what she was hearing.

"Of course we care. And of course, we hope to prevent the bombing from taking place. However, it is not sufficient merely to stop it; we need to do so in a way that provides us definitive proof that Germany is behind this and the other false flag operations. Otherwise, in the long run, far more people might die."

Melody understood what he meant; of course she did. However, the hypothetical large numbers of people who might die if the Netherlands were drawn into a war between Britain and Germany felt abstract; no one could predict what might happen. The very real number of people who would die in such a bombing, however, was not in question.

Turning to her brother, Melody asked, "Are you alright with this, Rat?"

Rat looked uncomfortable with the question, but didn't answer no.

"I cannot believe this!" Melody stood and looked at the two men. "You may have your mission. However, as you are both so quick to remind me, I am not an official member of the Secret Service Bureau and do not share the same obligations that you seem to feel you do. I plan to prevent this bombing and stop hundreds, perhaps thousands, of people from being killed."

"Melody, you cannot do anything that might jeopardise our work," Alessandro cautioned.

"Or what?"

"Or we will cut you out of the investigation entirely," he said in a firm voice. "Please do not doubt me when I say this. You are here, in this room, in Amsterdam, only because your brother and I have allowed it. That can change at any point."

Melody was furious. So furious that she was tempted to storm out of the room, slamming the door behind her. Only the realisation that it was her hotel room stopped her doing so.

Seeking to calm the heated tempers of his sister and friend, Rat said, "Melody, just do not go off on your own and do anything that puts our mission at risk. If you promise that, I promise in return to do all I can to ensure that no one is killed in a bombing."

Alessandro gave him a look that clearly questioned his confidence in making such a promise, but Rat ignored it. "Now sit back down, Melody, and let us discuss what else we need to do."

Melody realised they hadn't told Rat about their conversation with Karl Brenner's common-law wife. She and Alessandro filled him in on what they had learned.

When they had finished, Rat expressed much the same opinion she and Alessandro had shared earlier: "Well, it does make far more sense why Vermeer, or I should say Brenner, has betrayed his native country. Did you get any sense that this woman knew anything about that betrayal?"

"Nothing," Alessandro acknowledged. "All she knew was that he was nervous about something of late and had been planning for them to leave Amsterdam. She assumed that his murder was random or an attempted robbery."

"There was one more thing," Melody volunteered. She then told Rat that both she and Alessandro felt they were being followed. Initially, she wasn't sure whether she wanted to share this information with her brother. Melody was certain he would revert to overprotectiveness and insist she withdraw from the investigation. However, if she didn't tell him about it, Melody was equally certain Alessandro would at some point. At least this way, she maintained some control over the narrative.

As she predicted, Rat's first instinct was to be fearful for her safety. "I will be carrying my Derringer with me whenever I leave the hotel," Melody assured him.

"That wouldn't have helped you against that supposed footpad," Rat pointed out.

"If I learned anything from watching Tabby Cat and Wolfie over the years, it is that one can't hide in the shadows for fear of what might happen. After all, in Morocco, you were the one abducted, not me." Melody hated having to use this against Rat, but she felt she had no choice.

"Fine. But promise me you will be careful and let either of us know if anything else happens." Melody promised.

Alessandro wore a thoughtful expression. He then asked Rat, "You said that Huis Jansen was on the manifests you copied. Wasn't it also on the one Vermeer was holding when he died?"

Rat confirmed this and continued, "It doesn't seem to be part of the cypher, so I assume it indicates that delivery should be to a private trading concern or perhaps a family-run importer." "Huis Jansen?"

Alessandro mused. "I know I have heard that somewhere before. Melody, I think that tomorrow you and I may have somewhere to investigate."

Alessandro would not explain further and merely stated that he would send Mustafa with word in the morning. Melody was pleasantly surprised that Alessandro's default behaviour was not to exclude her, so she refrained from pressing him for more information that evening.

CHAPTER 17

The following morning, long before daybreak, Rat once again donned his disguise and made his way back to Entrepotdok. As he set off, it occurred to Rat that it was a matter of luck that he had been assigned to the warehouse where the coded manifests were arriving. He might not be as fortunate on a second day. If he wasn't, Rat realised his mission would involve more subterfuge than he had hoped for.

Rat stood in the same line that the same foreman was managing. The process was identical to the day before. If nothing else, this boded well for him being given work for the day.

After ten minutes, Rat found himself at the front of the line. The foreman recognised him and said, "Jij bent die Engelsman, toch?"

"English?" Rat answered. "Ja."

The foreman directed him back to Warehouse Seven. What a stroke of luck, Rat thought to himself as he made his way to his assigned spot for the day. Now that he was familiar with the process and the day's rhythm, Rat had a clearer idea of what he was searching for. First, he wanted to observe what happened to the crates designated ZKL-3. Even as this thought crossed his mind, Rat realised that perhaps such crates didn't arrive at the dock every day.

For the first two hours, Rat believed he was out of luck; there was nothing amiss. Then, just as he pondered whether the day would be a waste of time, the first such crate was unloaded. He had noted where all the other crates were sent, irrespective of their manifests.

As Rat paid more attention, he noticed some other unusual things: the crates marked ZKL-3 were handled differently from the others. It was subtle, which was why he hadn't seen it the previous day. He observed unspoken signals between some dockworkers when those crates came through. He also noticed there seemed to be a weight discrepancy. Large crates of nutmeg and other spices should have been heavy, but the ZKL-3 crates appeared to be handled as if they were light. What was inside them?

Then, Rat spotted the man. He wondered why he hadn't noticed him before, especially considering how much his clothes distinguished him from the other men. He wore a light grey suit and had a cigarette dangling from his lips. He held a sturdy wooden board with a brass clip to secure papers in place. Each time a crate marked ZKL-3 was unloaded, the man made a notation on his papers.

From what Rat could see, the crates were being moved to a separate part of the warehouse. He wondered whether they were being guarded or if there was an opportunity to investigate during the brief time allotted for the men's midday meal. Rat was curious about what the crates contained. If the manifests were the coded message, was anything of importance being sent through? He allowed for the possibility that there might be nothing interesting in the crates themselves, but he still wanted to check.

Most of the workers appeared to be Dutch, and they gathered together to enjoy their brief meal. The previous day, this had left Rat sitting alone, and he hoped the same situation would occur again.

When the bell rang across the docks, signalling that the men could take a break, the others huddled together, conversing in Dutch and laughing as they unpacked their meals. Everyone ignored Rat. He glanced around to see where the suited man was, but he appeared to have slipped away.

Rat positioned himself on a crate as far away from the other workers as possible. His chosen spot was particularly dimly lit and, after a few minutes, when he was certain no one was paying him any attention, Rat slipped further into the shadows and made his way toward the direction the crates had been taken, which turned out to be a separate storeroom.

He'd had the foresight that morning to put his lockpicks in his jacket pocket, but he needn't have worried; the door to the separate storeroom was unlocked. Was the storeroom empty already? Rat crept in stealthily, regardless.

He had also thought to bring his pocket torch with him, and once safely inside with the door closed again, Rat felt secure enough to turn it on. The crates occupied about a quarter of the storeroom. From what Rat could ascertain, the number there probably accounted for that day and the previous one. On his way into the storeroom, he had grabbed a crowbar that had been lying about. Now, he approached the nearest crate. It was meant to contain nutmeg, according to the manifest. He opened the top of the crate carefully, hoping he could reseal it afterwards.

Rat shone his torch into the crate and saw hundreds of shiny brown nutmegs. He was about to reseal the crate and try another when a thought struck him. Rat reached into the crate and felt around. As he dug down, he came upon stacks of what felt like paper.

Rat pulled some of the pile out and shone his torch on the top copy. It appeared to be a type of propaganda leaflet. It was printed on coarse, greyish paper, with the ink smudged in places as though it had been rushed off a basement press. A bold black header shouted, "Neutraliteit is een Leugen!" followed by additional text. Rat couldn't read it, but he had some idea of what the leaflet was promoting. Jagged red lines bordered the text, and a crude drawing of a torch over a shattered crown marked the bottom corner.

Rat took one leaflet and stuffed it in his pocket, burying the rest back under the nutmeg. He then resealed the crate. Could they all be full of propaganda material? he wondered. The crate he'd opened had been taken off a ship that day. He moved some crates around to reach one of the earlier ones from the previous day.

Once again, the seemingly innocuous top layer comprised nutmegs, but beneath it, he discovered pieces of equipment. There were fuses, fuse caps, timers, and wires; in fact, most of the components necessary to construct bombs.

Rat examined the pieces he had removed. The fuse cap bore a stamp on the metal. He inspected it closely, and it appeared to depict a crown with a broad arrow mark beneath it. Rat wasn't certain, but he believed that was the symbol found on British government materials, especially military equipment.

It made sense that if Germany wished to place the blame on Britain, or at least on the anarchists it was harbouring, having some form of physical evidence of British origin for parts that might survive a bomb's explosion would be sensible. Rat also slipped the fuse cap into his pocket, then quickly repacked the other materials and resealed the crate. He realised he was in danger of returning to his post late if he wasn't careful.

Rat returned to his spot in the warehouse just in time. He noted that the man in the suit hadn't reappeared, but he also saw no more crates marked ZKL-3 unloaded that day. As he continued to work, Rat pondered when the crates in the small storeroom would be collected.

Was it worth staying on after his shift to see what he could observe? Rat wasn't even sure how he would go about doing such a thing. When the end-of-day bell rang, the men would line up for payment. After that, they filed out through the gates. He couldn't imagine how one might remain behind. Even if he could, where was a suitable place to wait that was discreet enough, yet would provide a clear view of the warehouse?

Eventually, Rat decided to return to the hotel and inform Alessandro and Melody of what he had learned that day, and discuss the next steps.

Rat stood in line for his pay and then exited with the other men. As he made his way back to the hotel, he thought about what he had discovered. There seemed little doubt that a plot was afoot to set off a bomb and somehow lay the blame at Britain's feet. They knew that the theatre was at least one target, but which theatre, and was it the only one? And when was the planned bombing?

More to the point, what evidence did they need before approaching the Dutch authorities? On the surface, what he had discovered today appeared damning, but what did it truly prove? They had British-made parts that could be assembled into a bomb, but they hadn't yet been. There were the leaflets, but no definitive evidence that they hadn't been printed and shipped in by anarchists.

Rat was worried that the conversation the previous evening, which had so inflamed Melody, had hinted at what they needed to do: let a bomb be detonated and then prove the association with Germany. The thought sickened him, but he did understand that there were larger forces at work. He just wasn't sure that was a decision he felt he'd be able to live with.

CHAPTER 18

For the second day in a row, Melody woke early. It was closer to the truth to say she had slept poorly, tossing and turning all night as she replayed the conversation with Alessandro and Rat in her mind. Finally, she had given up any thought of peaceful slumber and had got out of bed. Now, she sat in the armchair in the living room of her suite, considering what she wanted to do next. Alessandro had said he would send word about the two of them making a trip to whatever or wherever Huis Jensen was. Should she just sit around the hotel until he made contact?

She had become involved in the investigation in Venice after discovering Signor Graziano's dead body. The elderly bookseller had been a friend of her new acquaintance, Marchesa Luisa Casati. These two facts combined to make Melody's involvement a natural, obvious next step, at least as far as Melody was concerned. It was only when she was already deeply engaged in the investigation that it became evident that Rat's interest in the murder was of a more official nature.

In Morocco, Melody's motivation for forcing her way into the investigation was equally clear: Alessandro had been accused of murder and arrested by the Sultan. Proving his innocence and ensuring his release from jail had been her primary aim. But what was driving her now?

Beyond her desire to find something meaningful to do with her life, what was truly at stake?

Even as she pondered this, Melody realised that peace in Europe was perhaps the highest stake of all. However, she was neither arrogant nor naïve enough to believe that whether Britain ended up at war with Germany and its allies would hinge on her involvement in an investigation.

Yes, a man had died. But he wasn't a man she knew in any way. People died all the time, yet she didn't feel compelled to involve herself in investigating their deaths. More than anything, Melody was weary; weary from having to defend her involvement in the investigations, and from having to force Rat and Alessandro to share everything they knew. Would it ever end? When would she have made a sufficient intellectual contribution that she wouldn't have to fight to be part of the inner circle?

"Why am I bothering?" Melody said out loud.

Mary was just entering the living room. "Bothering to what?"

Melody looked at her companion. Perhaps for the first time, she really looked at her. Mary was still a relatively young woman. What were her hopes and dreams?

"How old were you when you entered service, Mary?"

The older woman looked at her charge in surprise; in the fourteen years she had cared for Melody, the young girl had never shown much interest in Mary's life before arriving at Chesterton House, or indeed in Mary's life when she wasn't acting as a maid or companion.

This did not imply that Mary had any complaints; she had joined the staff at Chesterton House as a scullery maid. The opportunity to become four-year-old Melody's nurserymaid had immediately elevated her status within the household, and in the time since, she had become devoted to the girl.

While Mary had the occasional romantic dream over the years, which sometimes sparked hopes of having a family of her own, for the most part, she was content. She viewed her role taking care of Melody as the only mothering she needed to do in her life. As that role evolved over the years, she considered herself fortunate to be a respected and cherished confidante to the girl as she transitioned into womanhood.

Mary was the eldest of twelve siblings. Most of them were in service or hoped to enter it. Mary knew well enough how fortunate she was. Tabitha, Lady Pembroke, had hired a tutor for Melody, and had encouraged Mary and the other servants to study with him to learn to read and write. Mary was travelling across Europe in luxury, and her actual duties these days were minimal and not at all burdensome. Of all the outcomes that a girl from a large, poor, working-class family in the East End might expect, there was little doubt that where Mary found herself was far beyond any reasonable expectations.

She went and sat in an armchair, contemplating the beautiful young woman before her. Mary understood Melody was struggling, and not merely because of her failed romantic affairs.

"I entered service at fourteen years old," Mary answered. Then she added, "I counted myself very lucky to be working in as fine a place as Chesterton House, and I continue to count my blessings for all that His Lordship and Her Ladyship have done for me."

To the extent that Melody had ever considered Mary's life, she wasn't sure she would have described it as lucky. "But do you not have regrets?" she pressed.

"Regrets about what?" Mary asked, in genuine confusion. "What is the point in regretting that my father had to leave the family farm when he was a child? Should I regret that a search for work brought him to London where he met my mother? Certainly, if he hadn't made the move, I would not be here today. It is not for me to regret that my father came to care more for where his next drink was coming from than whether there was food on the table."

Melody wasn't sure she agreed with this statement, but she let Mary continue. "I am very content where my life has ended up today. I am staying in a beautiful suite in a luxury hotel, and my biggest concern today is whether I'm going to be able to darn that hole in your stockings. If I am content now, then I cannot regret the path and choices that brought me to this point."

It was a remarkably wise philosophy of life, and Melody had no rebuttal to make. It was all very well to be content with where life had taken one and then look back with no regrets, but Melody wasn't even close to being content. In fact, all she seemed to possess were regrets. Regrets that she had allowed herself to be taken in by Alessandro's charming words and handsome face; regrets that she's let William Somerset walk out of her life without fully exploring her true feelings for him; perhaps even regrets at leaving London altogether.

Mary was too astute not to realise that Melody had become entangled in whatever Rat was involved in. She didn't ask questions and made an effort not to eavesdrop, but she had gathered enough information to recognise that they were engaged in some sort of investigations on behalf of the government. It was not her place to question Mr Sandworth, who was, after all, Melody's brother. It had crossed her mind once or twice that perhaps it was her duty to report back to Lord and Lady Pembroke. However, Mary understood that once that trust was broken with Melody, she might never repair it. So, she simply stood by, watching and waiting.

Now, she rose and crossed the room to where Melody was seated. Stroking the young woman's hair as she used to when Melody was a child, Mary said, "Miss Melody, fate has smiled on you over and over again. Look where you are compared to where you might have been. What regrets can you possibly have?"

It was very unusual for Mary to allude to Melody's humble origins as the child of impoverished parents in Whitechapel. Most of the time, she maintained the pretence that the young woman was the child of the Earl and Countess of Pembroke rather than their ward, and had every right to her place in society.

Mary's explicit reference to Melody's East End roots, along with considerations of where she might be now if Tabby Cat hadn't taken her in and treated her like her own daughter, jolted Melody out of her self-pity.

"Thank you, Mary. What on earth would I do without you?" Melody said with a smile so sweet that Mary's heart swelled with love. Truly, she couldn't imagine a better way for her life to have turned out than to spend it looking after this young woman.

Melody stood, feeling reinvigorated by the conversation. She understood her purpose in life: to ensure that the fortunate hand she had been dealt was not wasted. Although she might not have complete clarity about what that might look like, she owed it to herself, Tabby Cat, Wolfie, Granny, and Uncle Maxi to make the most of the opportunities they had presented her with.

She possessed a good education, independent wealth, social status, and the support of a loving family. Although she might not know what a life that fully made the most of those assets might resemble, she understood that sitting around moping about minor slights and setbacks was not it.

"I am expecting word from Conte Foscari. In the meantime, I am going to get dressed now and would prefer breakfast up here rather than have people in the dining room wonder why I am suddenly dressed like a governess." Again, while Mary's expression suggested her thoughts on this, she said nothing.

CHAPTER 19

M ustafa arrived at Melody's hotel room door an hour later. She had dressed and finished the toast that had been sent up, and was just finishing her second cup of tea when she heard the gentle knock.

When she saw her caller was the young boy, Melody assumed he came with some kind of message from Alessandro.

"Lalla Melody," Mustafa began. "Sidi Alessandro has sent me with instructions. He did not want to return to this hotel and leave with you again. He feels that might look suspicious, particularly if someone is following you."

This made perfect sense to Melody, and she was curious to hear what the plan was.

"Sidi Alessandro has said that you and I should leave for the morning to run some errands. He suggested that you might want to visit a dress-maker or two and place some orders. Then, perhaps we might have some lunch at a café. At half past one, you should make your way to this shop," and with that, Mustafa handed her a card for what looked to be a millinery store. "They will know that you are coming. Tell them you are looking for a purple hat with a peacock feather."

Anticipating Melody's next question, Mustafa assured her, "They speak English. The woman who owns the shop knows what to do." Then, remembering something he was supposed to emphasise, Mustafa added, "He said to wear the green dress you had on the other day."

It was all very cloak and dagger, and reminded Melody of a play she had seen at the Drury Lane Theatre once. She was curious about what Alessandro had in mind. Of course, if someone really was following them and potentially still watching her, precautions of some sort had to be taken.

Melody realised she had little choice but to go along with Alessandro's directions. It was still early, so there seemed little point in starting their faux shopping expedition too soon. She did wonder about Alessandro's instruction regarding her outfit. Her green dress, while not the fanciest day dress she owned, certainly didn't lend itself to a believable middle-class disguise. She looked down at the very plain navy dress she had put on again and realised that if she went into expensive dressmakers wearing that, no one would believe she could afford their wares. She had to leave this hotel and go shopping in such a way that whoever was watching would not suspect subterfuge.

"I will go and change. There are some pastries left over from my breakfast if you are hungry, Mustafa." The boy eyed the plate eagerly and nodded in anticipation.

Thirty minutes later, Melody and Mustafa descended in the lift. As they made their way through the lobby, she heard, "Miss Chesterton, hello there."

Melody's heart sank. As much as her opinion of Jemima Edwards had softened, she didn't want to be delayed by her or have to explain where she was going.

What she couldn't do was ignore the voice calling out to her. Melody stopped and looked in the direction from which it had come. Jemima was leaving the dining room, presumably after a late breakfast.

"How lovely to see you, Miss Edwards," Melody lied. "I wish I could stop and talk, but I was just on my way out."

"So am I!" Jemima exclaimed. "We can walk together. I am going to the library again. Are you going in the same direction?"

Melody didn't know which direction she was heading in. Given Mustafa's ability to navigate Amsterdam, she was glad he was with her. Though, even as she considered this, it struck Melody that the young boy would have no clue about where the best dressmakers might be found.

Making a quick decision, Melody said, "Actually, Miss Edwards, perhaps you can help me. I would like to get some new dresses made. Do you happen to know where I might go?"

Jemima clapped her hands together in glee. "Oh, a shopping expedition. I love those. I am supposed to be meeting someone for lunch, but would you like company until then?"

As much as Melody's initial instinct was to decline, she then considered what Jemima's company might offer her. The woman seemed to know her way around Amsterdam and being in her company would add yet another layer of plausibility to her charade. And if Jemima needed to leave by lunchtime, then there was no cause for concern about how to part ways with her before heading to their ultimate location.

"That would be delightful, Miss Edwards. Do you know of a good modiste or two you can recommend?"

"Indeed I do. Can you wait for me while I go upstairs and get my hat and bag?"

No more than five minutes later, Jemima returned. "I know where we will go. P.C. Hooftstraat is one of the most prestigious shopping streets in Amsterdam. It is where all the bankers' and wealthy merchants' wives shop."

Melody wasn't certain she wanted to be dressed like the wife of a banker or a merchant. She then caught herself in that thought and realised it was the kind of thing Granny would have said imperiously as she looked down her nose at someone. As much as Melody adored the dowager countess, she also realised that the woman could be quite a snob, and that wasn't something to emulate.

"P.C. Hooftstraat sounds perfect. Do you have a place in mind?"

"I do! Madame Delacroix's Atelier. I have been meaning to visit it since I've been here. Perhaps I will order some new dresses as well. How much fun this will be."

Melody wasn't convinced of this, but she ensured her face conveyed nothing but delight at the prospect.

It appeared they would need to take a tram to P.C. Hooftstraat, and, like Rat during his outing with Jemima, Melody was grateful that the young woman seemed to know what she was doing and where she was going.

Alessandro's instructions suggested she was to bring Mustafa along. As they walked to the tram stop, Melody realised Jemima hadn't asked who he was, and that she had offered no information.

"I hope it is alright if Mustafa accompanies us," Melody said. "He joined our group in Morocco and while he is currently residing with one of our travel companions from that trip, he has come to help carry any packages."

"Of course. You are most welcome, Mustafa. I cannot wait to hear about Morocco. How exotic."

Melody hadn't wanted to reference Alessandro. She didn't know what Rat had mentioned regarding who they had travelled to Amsterdam with, and she was concerned about inadvertently revealing information that would contradict whatever story he'd told Miss Edwards.

Fortunately, whether because Rat had said nothing or because she was too busy chatting away to focus on what Melody had said, Jemima did not comment and asked nothing about these travel companions. Instead, she bombarded Mustafa with all sorts of questions about his homeland.

While there was no doubt Jemima Edwards was not the monster Melody had initially imagined her to be, her company could be rather wearing. The woman never stopped talking. The advantage of Jemima leading most of the conversation was that Melody could contemplate the morning ahead and Alessandro's apparent plan to shake off whoever was following her.

Of course, Melody reflected, Alessandro had assumed that she was the one being followed; what if he had been the target all along? She hoped Alessandro had taken similar precautions to ensure he lost whoever it was.

They had boarded the tram a few minutes earlier, and now Melody looked around, trying to ascertain whether her shadow had followed them onto it. The tram wasn't busy, and there were four other people on board along with the three of them. Two of those people had already been on it when they boarded, and the person who got on at the same stop as they did was an old woman. Unless she was wearing an astonishing disguise, Melody doubted that the petite septuagenarian was the person she was worried about.

Perhaps no one was tracking her movements today; perhaps they hadn't been the previous afternoon. Although Alessandro also sensed something, they might have both been on edge and imagining things. It crossed Melody's mind that Alessandro's elaborate precautions were likely pointless, but she had no way to contact him and might as well follow through with his instructions.

The tram ride wasn't long, and before she knew it, Jemima had rung the bell, and they were standing, ready to disembark. P.C. Hooftstraat was a broad, elegant avenue nestled between the greenery of a nearby park and what appeared to be a row of stately museums. Carriages clattered softly over cobbles, and the avenue was lined with elegant-looking shops featuring highly polished windows and gleaming brass nameplates.

The entire street exuded an air of discreet affluence. From what Melody could see, there were numerous dress shops that seemed to cater to the city's elite wives and daughters. Jemima appeared to have a definite idea of their destination. She strode past several rather fancy shops until she arrived at one that was announced on a tasteful brass plaque as Maison de Liseron.

A bell rang as they entered the modiste's shop, and almost immediately, an elegantly dressed woman appeared through a pair of curtains at the back of the store.

"Bonjour," she said with a French accent that sounded rather exaggerated to Melody's ear. She was well aware that in London, it was so desirable for anyone claiming to be a modiste, as opposed to a mere dressmaker, to be French, that women were known to style themselves as Madame and cover a broad cockney accent with a fake French one. It wouldn't be surprising if Amsterdam were no different.

CHAPTER 20

Later, Melody had ordered a new walking suit, an evening gown, and a lovely pale blue muslin day dress. Jemima had shown more restraint and only ordered a skirt and blouse set. Madame had taken their measurements, noted the name of their hotel, and promised she would be in touch.

Melody checked her pocket watch and realised it was nearly noon. If they were to have some lunch and then find the millinery shop, they would need to part ways with Jemima soon. Since the young woman had claimed to have lunch plans of her own, it didn't seem odd to ask what time she was planning to leave.

"Oh my, look at the time!" Jemima exclaimed. "Whatever was I thinking, letting the morning slip away like that? Do excuse me, dear Miss Chesterton, but I must leave you.

Since Jemima appeared to be late for her luncheon, Melody didn't see any harm in showing her the card for the millinery shop and asking if she knew its location.

Jemima took the card, looked at it for a few moments, then turned around, glanced up the street, and turned back. "I believe that if you go up here and turn right after two streets, you'll find it there, about halfway down. I've never been, but I've heard good things about it."

Jemima sighed. "Oh, but now I wish I didn't have to leave and could join you."

"No, no!" Melody said, in what she worried was too anxious a tone. "I cannot make you miss your appointment." In a calmer voice, she assured Jemima, "I will go and see how it is, and if I believe it worth our while, you and I can return on another day."

Jemima clapped her hands together in delight once more and seemed pacified. Melody let out a sigh of relief. Five minutes later, Jemima had left, and Melody found a nearby cafe for her and Mustafa to enjoy a light lunch together.

Mustafa was nearly as capable as Jemima in holding a conversation alone, so Melody didn't need to speak much during the meal. Instead, she muttered the occasional reply but mostly ate her food while watching the street ahead. She chose a table outside on the pavement so she could see if anyone had followed them.

Melody wasn't sure how to describe the feeling she'd had the day before of being watched. Saying that the hairs on the back of her neck stood up seemed too cliché. Still, the feeling had been very real. Had she noticed something without realising it? Melody wasn't sure how she might have done that, but it seemed the only logical explanation. She had heard Wolfie talk about the new, very radical ideas of Dr Sigmund Freud, who had many scandalous theories about how the mind works. Granny's response to hearing some of these ideas was to say, "I will not have an Austrian tell me how my mind works. I would barely let an Englishman do so."

Did she feel now anything of what she had experienced the day before? Melody couldn't be certain. Maybe she was trying too hard to tell. Finally, it was a few minutes before one o'clock. Melody paid the bill and collected her things.

As Jemima had promised, the walk to the millinery shop was a quick one. It was a charming little store and would have caught her eye even if Alessandro hadn't directed her there. Once again, a bell above the door announced their arrival. The shop was empty of customers, and there didn't appear to be any salesgirls about. Melody and Mustafa waited for someone to come and serve them. While they waited, Melody looked around at the hats on display. There were some very pretty pieces of headwear, and Melody wished she had the luxury of time and of choosing something she truly wanted.

After a few minutes, a handsome blonde woman entered from the back of the store and greeted them. While she spoke Dutch, it was clear that it was not her first language. Melody responded in English, and when the woman switched languages, it became more obvious that she was a native Italian.

"Good afternoon," Melody said. "I am looking for a very specific hat and was told you would be able to assist me."

"Of course, Miss. What are you seeking?"

"A purple hat with a peacock feather."

"Indeed, we can help. I have just what you are looking for," the woman replied. "But first, I have some other hats for you to try on. Might I suggest that you stand near the window so you can see how they look in daylight? There is a mirror right here."

For the next thirty minutes, Melody tried on hats. It was unclear how Signora Vecchi – for this was the woman's name – selected which hats, but Melody realised there was some kind of ruse underway, and so didn't comment.

Each time a hat was produced, Melody was encouraged to display herself in the hat very obviously. The last hat was enormous; far larger and more ostentatious than anything Melody would ever usually wear. As Melody donned the hat and looked at herself in the mirror, Signora Vecchi came towards her, holding a cup of something. She seemed to be offering it to Melody, but then appeared to trip slightly and managed to spill some of it on her dress.

"Mi scusi," the signora exclaimed while making very exaggerated hand motions. It seemed as if it was all part of a charade, but Melody couldn't imagine why. As it happened, very little of the liquid had spilt onto her, but the shopkeeper was acting as if her dress was soaked.

After a few ineffective attempts to mop Melody's arm with a lace handkerchief, she indicated the screen. "Perhaps you might go behind the screen and remove your dress so that I can have one of my girls dry it off," the signora explained.

Melody was about to protest that it wasn't necessary, but then wondered if this was the part she was meant to play. Instead of arguing, she went behind the screen only to find a curtain behind it, pulled aside. Standing just behind the drawn curtain was a young woman with hair much the same colour as Melody's. Or was it a wig? The other notable thing about the woman was that she was also wearing a green dress. While the two items of clothing were not identical, certainly the shade and style were quite similar.

The woman put her finger to her lips, then whispered, "Follow me," as she disappeared into the room, which was curtained off. Intrigued, Melody followed.

The woman led her through a workroom to a table at the back. "You will wait here for now, Miss."

Melody sat down and waited. She realised Mustafa was still in the shop. Would he be sent back to her? After waiting over ten minutes, she decided she would not see him again, at least for now. Melody was even more curious about what the plan was.

Fifteen minutes later, a young woman with chestnut hair, wearing an enormous hat that blocked her face from most angles, left the shop. She was accompanied by a young dark-skinned boy carrying a hatbox. The woman hurried down the street and back towards the tram. She took the tram all the way to the Hotel Victoria, and Mustafa accompanied her in the lift. Ten minutes after that, the boy came back down and left the hotel, and the young woman removed her hat and wig, stashing them in a dark corner of the stairwell, then slipped out the back door of the hotel.

At last, Signora Vecchi returned. She presented Melody with a burgundy bolero jacket to wear, along with a rather unattractive matching hat.

"Doesn't this make me look rather conspicuous?" Melody objected. She assumed the purpose of this exercise was to throw her potential shadow off her scent. If that were the case, then wearing such a hat seemed counterintuitive.

"Men do not look at the details of what a woman is wearing," the signora informed her. "Many years selling hats has taught me that. The number of times a woman has come in with her husband and asked him which he prefers of two or three hats and I have heard him say he cannot tell the difference." Melody thought about the last time she'd made the mistake of asking Rat's opinion about an outfit and had to agree.

"This hat is ugly and obvious by design. It's the kind of thing a man will notice, and given that you weren't wearing it before, he will then mark it as irrelevant. It will hide you even when you are seen."

Melody wasn't certain she agreed with this logic. Wasn't it better for someone not to notice anything? However, now wasn't the time to argue the point. She presumed that the woman who bore a passing resemblance to her had exited through the front door of the shop and had led away whoever was following, assuming that someone was.

"So, what now? Where am I to go?" was all Melody bothered to say in response.

"My man will escort you. It's on the other side of Amsterdam, and you won't find your way alone."

Melody could think of no good reason to refuse the assistance.

Signora Vecchi called out for a Johannes who turned out to be a very tall, very blonde young man of about Melody's age. The signora said something in Dutch and Johannes nodded his understanding.

"He speaks no English," the signora warned. "But he knows where to take you."

CHAPTER 21

Melody felt quite conspicuous in the ugly outfit and with the very tall young man at her side. She hoped that whoever had been following her had been fooled by the decoy who had left in her place, because she wasn't sure that the signora's logic about becoming invisible by being so obviously garish held water. Melody hurried along, trying to keep her head down and not do anything that would attract any more attention to them.

At some point, they got on a tram and sat on that for twenty minutes or so. When they disembarked, they were in a very different part of town. In fact, it looked as if they were close to the docks. Melody wondered if Rat was nearby, which caused her to wonder how his investigation was going. She hoped better than hers. So far, all she'd done was go shopping and have an overpriced meal.

Johannes led her to what looked like a small, rather rundown working men's tavern. Given that it was mid-afternoon, the place was empty. Johannes pointed for Melody to make her way in, alone. She hoped he had the right place because this didn't look to be the kind of establishment where a well-brought up young woman should be spending time alone. Actually, probably any young woman.

The tavern was dark and smelled of stale beer and smoke. She looked around to see where she was supposed to be going, and spotted Alessandro in a gloomy corner, drinking a mug of beer.

Melody made her way over to where he sat. As she got closer, Alessandro said, "Ah, Miss Smith, I'm so glad you could make it." For a moment, she was tempted to look over her shoulder to see who he was speaking to; then she realised she was Miss Smith.

In an equally exaggerated tone – at least to her ear – Melody said, "Yes, it took me a little while to follow your directions, but here I am."

Alessandro indicated she should take a seat and called over to the woman behind the bar to bring a cup of coffee. Melody was relieved; she had no liking for beer and didn't want to pretend to be drinking it.

After the coffee was delivered, the woman disappeared into the back of the tavern, and Melody and Alessandro appeared to be alone. Even so, he spoke quietly. "I assume Signora Vecchi helped you and you don't believe you were followed from there?"

"Honestly, I'm not sure I was followed there," Melody admitted. "But yes, we went through her charade and one of her men brought me here. Now, tell me, what is going on?"

"I found out what Huis Jansen is. As I suspected, it is a small family-run importer of spices. We need a legitimate reason to go in and ask to be shown around. We are going to pretend to be representatives of an Italian import firm looking to expand spice purchases from the Dutch East Indies. I am Signor Alessandro Marchetti of *Fratelli Marchetti.*, and you are my secretary, Miss Smith. We are hoping to find a new importer because we became suspicious of the business practices of our former one. Given this, we are hoping to verify shipping practices before making a decision."

Superficially, this sounded like a decent enough story, but Melody also saw some possible holes in it as she considered it more deeply.

"And we're just turning up without an appointment?" she asked.

"Not at all. I had Fatima call and make an appointment for us in twenty minutes," he explained.

Well, that was one question answered, but there was another, more significant one that had occurred to Melody. "Aren't they going to ask us who our former importers are?"

Alessandro smiled. "If they do, and I'm sure you're right about that,

I will feign professional discretion and withhold the name. I am sure there is enough malfeasance that takes places around these docks that whoever we talk to will draw his own conclusions." Melody hoped he was right.

It seemed she had time to drink her coffee and so she took a couple of sips while reviewing Alessandro's disguise. He was dressed quite smartly, but certainly not in his usual dapper tailoring. His outfit was of a much higher quality than the one he had worn when pretending to be a journalist, but still far lower than might be worn by the titan of industry he was in reality. Instead, he looked like a moderately prosperous merchant, who was still not so successful that he might have underlings make such visits on his behalf.

Alessandro noticed her review and asked, "Do I pass muster?"

"Indeed. Do I?"

He laughed. "Definitely. While the dress is well-made, it is quite ruined by that unflattering hat and jacket both of which have the look of a lower middle-class striver trying just a little too hard."

His assessment of the hat was just as Melody's own had been. One thing was evident: Signora Vecchi's observation about men not paying close attention to what women were wearing didn't apply to Alessandro.

"What about my accent?" Melody asked. Would she pass as a secretary, even to a Dutchman?

"Can you modulate it at all?" Alessandro asked. Could he? Of course, Melody couldn't imagine what a titled Italian, speaking Dutch, might sound like and how that might need to be modified.

Melody considered the question; could she? Unlike Rat, she had no memory of how she had spoken as a four-year-old in Whitechapel. However, she thought about how some of Granny's more unusual friends spoke. The Ladies of KB, an eclectic social gathering of London madams, were perhaps not typical role models, and Melody had only met them a few times over the years. Nevertheless, she had spent enough time around them to think of one of them now: Madame Zsa Zsa, whose real name was Laurie.

Whatever Madame Zsa Zsa's real roots, she now cultivated an accent that couldn't easily be placed, but which sounded as if she were trying just a little too hard not to talk like a cockney.

Melody tried to recall Laurie's voice, and said in her best attempt at an impersonation, "How's this instead?"

Laughing again, Alessandro said, "That's very good. It sounds like you're trying just a little too hard to cover up rather rough origins."

"That was precisely what I was going for."

Alessandro pulled out his pocket watch. "I think we might make our way over to Huis Jansen now." He pulled out some coins and left them on the table. He stood and Melody followed suit.

When they left the tavern, they turned down a quiet, narrow street. Halfway down, Alessandro stopped outside of a tall, narrow brick structure that sat between warehouses, its gabled roof capped with a small hoisting beam. The façade bore a fading sign painted in neat serif lettering: Huis Jansen – Specerijen & Koloniale Goederen. Two iron-shuttered loading doors were positioned over a small canal-side quay where barges once moored. Crates were still stacked beneath a rusted pulley arm.

Tall sash windows with small glass panes looked down over the street. Some had half-drawn curtains, suggesting living quarters above the trading floor. A brass nameplate near the front door read Jansen & Zonen, Est. 1843. As Alessandro lead the way to the door, Melody caught the faint smell of perhaps cloves and pepper. She started as a loud barge horn blared nearby.

The door was slightly ajar. Alessandro knocked and called out, but it seemed no one was around. He pushed the door fully open and walked in, followed by Melody. The moment Melody stepped through the heavy oak door of Huis Jansen, the scent enveloped her far more strongly than a moment earlier: warm cinnamon, cracked pepper, clove, and something sharper, like dried citrus peel and bay. The air was thick with spice and dust. The tiled entryway, worn smooth by decades of trade, led into a narrow corridor where crates were stacked in neat rows against the wall, each stamped with exotic ports: Batavia, Colombo, Surabaya.

Alessandro called out again, and still no one answered. Light filtered through tall, dust-dulled windows, illuminating floating specks in the air. A brass bell above the door had jingled on their entry, and from somewhere behind a sliding panel door, Melody could finally hear footsteps approach.

They walked into a large room. To their left, a dark walnut counter served as both ledger desk and display, with jars of turmeric, star anise, and cardamom arranged with careful pride. Behind it, shelves rose to the ceiling, lined with tin canisters and hand-labelled glass bottles.

The place had a quiet order to it; the sort of establishment that had earned its reputation not by flash, but by generations of meticulous, honest trade. Based on the feel of Huis Jansen, it would be entirely believable that Signor Alessandro Marchetti of Fratelli Marchetti. would have heard good things about their business practices.

The footsteps grew louder, and suddenly, a man entered the room and asked them something in Dutch. Alessandro responded.

"Goedemiddag," the man said, before quickly switching to English with a practiced ease. "You must be the buyers from Marchetti & Co., yes?"

CHAPTER 22

"Good afternoon," Alessandro replied, holding out a hand in greeting. "Yes, I am Alessandro Marchetti of *Fratelli Marchetti.*, and this is my secretary, Miss Smith."

The man took the proffered hand enthusiastically. "Ah, yes, yes. Cornelis Van Rhijn," he said. "As I mentioned to whoever called earlier, I handle most of the overseas accounts. Why don't you follow me? We can chat, and then I can give you a tour of our facilities."

Van Rhijn ushered them through a narrow passage flanked by burlap sacks and lacquered tea chests. The floorboards creaked as they entered a cramped office. A large map of the East Indies dominated one wall, marked with faded pins and curling edges.

Van Rhijn gestured for them to sit. "You mentioned an interest in our Ceylon stock. But... forgive me, did you say you were also looking into logistics?"

Melody nodded with the air of an efficient professional, "Our firm prefers to handle our own freight coordination. We've had... inconsistencies before. Crates mis-marked. Delivery discrepancies. In fact, this is the reason we are searching for a new, more reliable business to work with. We prefer to understand how our partners ship."

Van Rhijn studied them intently. "Can I take it you have been working with someone in Amsterdam already and have concerns?"

Alessandro modulated his tone to sound concerned but also wary. "Meneer Van Rhijn, I would prefer not to speak of other importers in Amsterdam. I do not think it my place to tarnish the reputation of others. Suffice it to say, I have been unhappy and am searching for a new company to partner with. Under my father, *Fratelli Marchetti*. was a minor concern in Milan. Since my dearly departed father left this earth six months ago, I have been working to streamline operations in order to expand throughout Italy."

"I am sorry for your loss, Signor Marchetti. Of course, I respect your discretion and can assure you that, whatever you may have experienced with other importers, Huis Jansen prides itself on both its efficiency and its scrupulous honesty."

Melody chimed in, "While we are not prepared to give names, we can say that some concerns Marchetti Brothers have related to underweight shipments, confused manifest numbers, and, sometimes, inconsistent invoice totals." Even as she said this, Melody worried she was being too assertive in the conversation. Was it believable that a Miss Smith, secretary, would speak up in this manner?

If he thought anything of this, Van Rhijn didn't express it in his manner. Instead, he spoke directly to Melody as he addressed her concerns. "I can assure you, Miss Smith, that Huis Jansen will never engage in such practices."

"Excellent, Meneer Van Rhijn. Huis Jansen seems to be just the kind of business that Marchetti Brothers can partner with for the kind of expansion I have in mind," Alessandro explained, rubbing his hands together as if genuinely delighted at the mercantile opportunity before him.

"Do you have a sense of how much you are hoping to expand the business in the coming year?"

"Indeed. I see a growing interest in more exotic flavours in Italy's major cities. The expansion of our railways will facilitate the domestic movement of goods, and I believe there has never been a better time to import the wares of the East Indies. What I am hoping to find is a business in Amsterdam to partner with in the truest sense of the word."

The look of avaricious pleasure on Van Rhijn's face made it evident that they had enticed the man sufficiently. Now, Melody felt comfortable making the request she and Alessandro had discussed. He had felt it would be better coming from a woman; it would seem less aggressive, or so he hoped.

"Meneer Van Rhijn, as Signor Marchetti says, we are looking not merely for an alternative company to work with now, but for a true partner for a future that we hope will greatly benefit both companies. To this end, we would like to request evidence that we are not stepping into a similar situation to the one we are hoping to leave."

A thoughtful look came over Van Rhijn's face. "What evidence is that, Miss Smith?"

"We would like time to review your books to assure ourselves of both the competency and integrity of Huis Jansen."

"That is quite an irregular request, Miss Smith. We don't typically open our books to outside parties. Indeed, we have never been asked to do so." Then, addressing Alessandro, Van Rhijn continued, "Signor Marchetti, would you share the ledgers of your business with total strangers?"

It was a fair enough question, and Alessandro acknowledged it as such.

"While I have no reason to question that you are who you say you are," Van Rhijn explained, "I cannot ignore the possibility that you are working for one of my competitors and have less than honest intentions."

Were they at an impasse? Melody couldn't blame the man for refusing their rather impertinent request; there wasn't even anything suspicious about his refusal to show them his accounts. If anything, it would have been odd if Van Rhijn had conceded immediately.

During their brief conversation on the walk from the tavern, Alessandro had explained that he didn't expect to find evidence of the suspect shipments in the Huis Jansen books; quite the opposite, he was hoping not to find the crates in the encrypted manifest referenced, as this would provide proof of questionable practices. It was this kind of proof that they might take to the Dutch officials.

Then, just as Melody was worried that this ruse had been for nothing, Van Rhijn continued, "However, you have given me no reason to suppose you are anything less than who you say you are. You both have a very honest air about you." Did they? Melody wondered. "While I cannot give you access to all our accounts, obviously, I feel comfortable sharing some examples which I hope will satisfy you as to the competency of our record keeping."

While this was good news, Melody hoped Alessandro had more of an idea of what records should look like than she did. Of course, he ran a significant international business, so she assumed he knew something about bookkeeping. However, how different might the records kept by an importer be from those of a newspaper? She assumed there wouldn't be much overlap.

Melody took comfort in the belief that Alessandro would never have suggested this plan if he didn't feel confident that he would have some idea of what he was looking at if they succeeded. Minutes later, they were ensconced in the small office with a pile of ledgers before them. While Van Rhijn had stated he wasn't comfortable making all the Huis Jansen accounts available, he certainly seemed willing to share a great deal. Perhaps the promise of significant business from Marchetti & Brothers was a sufficient temptation to override other concerns.

Initially, Van Rhijn stayed in the office with them, occasionally pointing to a record; eventually, he left them alone. As far as Melody could see, Alessandro seemed to know what he was doing as he scanned page after page in the ledgers.

Finally, he closed the books and sat back. "I think I have seen all I need to," he said. Melody had no expectations that he would elaborate further until they were well away from Huis Jansen, and so merely nodded.

They left the office and returned to where they had originally found Cornelis Van Rhijn. He stood at the back of the large room, counting inventory.

When he heard them enter, Van Rhijn turned. "I hope you found everything satisfactory."

"Indeed. Your bookkeeping is exemplary. I feel confident that Huis Jansen is everything that Marchetti & Brothers needs in a business partner. Miss Smith will be in touch over the next few days to formalise matters between us. I hope to have a letter of intent to you shortly, and then we can have our legal agents begin to work on the contract. Miss Smith will also provide greater details on the types of shipments, quantities, etc."

"We will expect standards credit and payment terms," Van Rhijn said in a tone that indicated the man was doing his best to suppress his excitement about the prospective business agreement.

"And I will be happy to provide them," Alessandro assured him. "Of course, I will expect regular access to inspect stock and facilities."

"Huis Jansen has nothing to hide and so that will not be a problem."

After a few more pleasantries and promises exchanged, they wished Van Rhijn a good day and departed from the premises.

Once they were far enough from the building, Melody asked in a low voice, "Did you find anything?"

Alessandro shook his head. "As I suspected, there were no references to crates marked ZKL-3. I would imagine there is a second set of ledgers used to track those. It depends on what they contain. If the manifest itself is all that matters, I might expect the contents of the crates to be recorded. However, given that they are not, I wonder if this import scheme allows for more than merely communicating in code."

"Perhaps, they don't track them at all," Melody suggested.

Alessandro laughed. "We are dealing with Germans and the Dutch; I am sure they account for and track everything. They are both very methodical and organised people."

He paused. "I need to go back at night and search that office."

Whether Alessandro realised he had said "I" rather than "we", Melody caught it. She would not allow him to use her as a prop when it was convenient and then cast her aside when there was actual espionage work to be done.

Instead of challenging Alessandro directly on his statement, Melody replied, "Why do we not see what Matthew has discovered and then assess what we should do next?" She placed heavy emphasis on the word "we." Because they were walking side by side, Melody couldn't see Alessandro's reaction, but she thought she caught a sigh.

CHAPTER 23

When the group reconvened later that evening and heard about Rat's discoveries, it became even clearer that they had no choice but to return to Huis Jansen under the cover of night.

"Bomb parts!" Melody exclaimed.

"Well, that is hardly surprising," Rat pointed out. "We already knew the Germans were planning a bombing."

He was right, of course. However, it was one thing to decipher a message and quite another to find physical evidence of an actual bomb; this made the possibility seem very real. Suddenly, this made the likely mass fatalities feel more than abstract, and reminded Melody of her earlier conversation with Rat and Alessandro regarding their main objective: to ensure that blame was appropriately assigned to Germany.

The fight to join the nighttime adventure was as Melody had antici-pated. "It's far too dangerous, Melody," was her brother's position.

"This is not about so-called fairness," was Alessandro's. "It is about a successful mission, nothing more."

Melody bristled at the idea that success necessarily precluded her involvement.

"We believe someone is watching and following us. What if they follow you to Huis Jansen tonight?" she posed to Alessandro.

"Then Matthew and I will deal with them. What possible help will you be if that's the case? All your presence will do is distract us if we need to protect you."

There was little that Alessandro could have said that would have set Melody off quite as much as that sentence did. "Protect me? Is that what you believe you will have to do? Need I remind you both that it was Captain Somerset and I who saved my brother in Morocco and in doing so facilitated your release from jail, Alessandro? Perhaps I will be called upon to protect you, again!"

Rat could see where this argument was leading, and it would not be helpful. He intervened. "Alessandro, Melody is correct; we do need her help. We need someone to be a lookout on the street. If we are followed there and caught inside, we will be like lambs to the slaughter." Rat realised this was hyperbole; he was sure that the two of them could manage whatever situation they found themselves in well enough. However, allowing Melody to accompany them but remain outside seemed the best compromise they were going to reach.

Whether Alessandro intuited the reasoning behind Rat's concession or was simply tired of arguing, he gruffly capitulated. "Fine, but you stay outside at all times. We will provide you with a mechanism to communicate with us if you believe we are in danger. Is that understood, Melody?"

She was tempted to continue the debate, but realised they needed someone to be a lookout, and it made the most sense for her to fulfil that role.

Alessandro looked her up and down. "You cannot go dressed like this."

"I have a black dress I can put on," Melody answered.

"A woman standing alone on a dark street at night is going to attract all the wrong kinds of attention," Alessandro pointed out. "Matthew, do you have clothes that would fit your sister and are dark enough?"

Fortunately, since Rat was slender and not very tall, he realised his clothes would likely fit his sister well enough. "I have a hat that is a little big for me that will accommodate her hair as well," he answered.

As eager as she was to accompany them, Melody wondered how believable a young man she would make. When she expressed this, Alessandro told her confidently, "During the day, not at all. At night, if we keep to the shadows, you will pass well enough. It will also throw off anyone who is following us."

They agreed to wait until nearly midnight to ensure the streets were as quiet as possible. They would need to walk to Huis Jansen, which would take at least thirty minutes, so they decided to leave the hotel shortly after eleven. Rat already knew how to enter and exit the hotel without going through the lobby and suggested that Alessandro return home to change, and that they meet him at the back of the hotel at the designated time.

It was fortunate that they had some time before the meeting, as Rat's clothes didn't fit Melody as well as he had hoped. It required some of Mary's needlework skills to assemble an outfit that was suitable for an evening of skulduggery.

While Mary usually asked no questions, even her typical reticence was overcome at the thought of her darling Melody leaving the hotel at night, dressed as a man. Although neither Melody nor Rat wished to provide her with a full explanation of their plans, Rat assured her that Melody would not be in any danger.

"I know it isn't my place to question your actions, Mr Sandworth, and I would never question your care of Miss Melody. Still, I am not sure how a situation that requires her to dress as a man and go out in the middle of the night can be considered 'no danger'."

"Mary, I promise you I will be safe," Melody assured her with just a hint of irritability in her voice. "Now, please, don't fuss." Mary pursed her lips and shook her head, but made no further comment on their evening plans.

By the time Melody had dressed in Rat's altered clothing and tucked her hair into a flat cap, it was easier to believe she would pass for a young man, at least in the night's darkness. Luckily, there was almost no moon that evening, making it simpler to stick to the shadows. Of course, the absence of moonlight meant it would be more difficult for her to see if anyone was watching when Rat and Alessandro broke into Huis Jansen.

At a quarter past eleven, Rat led Melody to the back staircase, and they made their way downstairs, hoping they wouldn't run into any hotel staff at that time of night. They slipped out of the back door and looked around for Alessandro.

"Over here," they heard whispered from the shadows. Alessandro revealed himself and looked Melody up and down. "You'll do," he conceded. "I hope you brought your gun," he added.

"I did. And we brought a torch and each of us has a knife."

"And of course, I have my picks," Rat added.

They walked in almost complete silence to Huis Jansen. No one wanted to risk anyone catching Melody's higher-pitched tones in the evening's stillness.

Then they arrived on the street where Huis Jansen was located, and Alessandro whispered, "I don't think we were followed."

"I didn't hear or sense anything," Rat agreed.

"Good. Then we are ready to go," Alessandro decided. Melody noted that neither man appeared to care what her assessment was.

Melody had observed that Alessandro was carrying something. Now, he held up what resembled a lantern. It was a compact, utilitarian item, made of blackened tin with four narrow panes of smoky glass and a hinged handle for carrying.

"The most important feature is this adjustable metal shutter," he explained, demonstrating how a sliding panel could be drawn across the front to block or reveal the light in controlled bursts. Alessandro pulled out a box of matches and lit a single wick inside the lantern, which burned low and cast a soft amber glow until he moved the shutter.

"The light can be dimmed to a sliver or extinguished entirely with a flick of the thumb, allowing you to signal discreetly or move unseen. I want you to stand across the street and keep an eye out. If you see anything suspicious, unshutter the lantern and hold it up so the light shines through the window."

Melody could immediately see the flaw in this plan. "When you are in the office where the ledgers are, you can't see into the main room that the windows look into."

"I know. I am going to have Matthew position himself so that he can see any light and can also keep watch for anyone coming in through the back. I will go into the office and look around."

It was a good thing that it was dark and Alessandro couldn't see Rat's face; he wasn't thrilled at being relegated to a role barely one step above Melody's as lookout.

Alessandro handed the lantern to Melody. Its body was warm to the touch, and when shuttered, it disappeared into the dark.

"Please keep your wits about you. It's late and dark, and this is a rough area at night. There is much danger lurking around these streets, besides whoever might be following us."

As tempted as she was to deliver a sharp retort, Melody knew he was right and merely nodded her head. With that, Alessandro tapped Rat on the shoulder, and the two men slipped into the darkness. Alessandro believed there was a narrow alleyway beside Huis Jansen, which he hoped would lead them to a back door. Melody hadn't wanted to ask how he could be certain the building had a back door, and instead prayed he knew what he was doing.

With the two men gone, Melody became acutely aware of how exposed she was, standing alone in the dark. While she was glad to be dressed as a young man, she wondered just how much protection that would afford her against drunkards, thieves, or worse. She did her utmost to shrink into the shadows, giving thanks for the cover of the night. It occurred to her it was so dark that if she heard or saw anything and shone the lantern into the window, Rat would not be the only one to notice it.

Then, Melody waited. Given how warm the days had been, she shivered. Melody pulled Rat's jacket close around her and used the lantern's heat to warm her hands. Had she done the right thing by insisting on accompanying them tonight?

CHAPTER 24

The more Melody thought about it, the more her behaviour appeared foolhardy and childish. She had the money, education, and social standing to choose to do almost anything a woman might do in 1911, yet somehow, she found herself standing alone on a dark and dangerous street in Amsterdam at night dressed as a boy while the others did the real work. How could that possibly be what Granny wished for her when she entrusted her fortune to Melody?

Alessandro's cutting phrase ran through her mind: "All your presence will do is distract us if we need to protect you." Was he right? Was she being stubborn and wilful, distracting the two men from their mission? After all, it was their mission, wasn't it? She was merely tagging along and forcing her way in.

Suddenly, Melody felt exhausted, and not just because she had been waking up so early. She was constantly fighting for her place in these investigations and wasn't even sure why. Alessandro clearly didn't want her involved, and Rat seemed to accept her assistance reluctantly. Once again, she thought of London and all that she missed.

Melody felt so despondent that she barely noticed her surroundings. All she wanted was for Rat and Alessandro to hurry up and find whatever evidence they were after so she could return to the hotel and put an end to the charade of her being a needed part of the investigation.

Just as she was feeling rather sorry for herself, there was a noise behind her. Before Melody could react, a hand covered her mouth, and an arm gripped her tightly, leaving her unable to move.

Melody felt a warm breath on her cheek and was gripped by fear as a voice whispered, "I'm not going to hurt you." She struggled in vain against her captor's vice-like hold. A range of possible scenarios flickered through her mind: was this a footpad who could be placated with whatever coins she hoped to find in Rat's jacket, or had they been followed despite their best efforts?

Another whisper, "Melody. It's me." It took her a moment to realise who was speaking and to cease struggling, but even then, she couldn't reply in amazement because of the hand over her mouth. "I'm going to remove my hand and let you go," the voice said. "Please don't scream."

The moment she was free, Melody whirled around. It was so dark she could barely see the face before her, but she could see enough to recognise it matched the voice.

"William!" she gasped in amazement. "What are you doing here?" By here, she meant Amsterdam, this street in the middle of the night, and with her. Ever since he had walked out of that door in Fes, Melody had wondered where he was. Had Captain Somerset stayed in Morocco? Had he been recalled to London in disgrace? The one thing that had never occurred to her was that he might be in the Netherlands.

"There isn't much time," William said hurriedly. "I wanted to talk to you without anyone around."

"And so you followed us here at midnight and scared me half to death? You couldn't have just sent a note?"

"I wanted to be sure," he answered cryptically.

"Sure of what?" As happy as Melody was to see William Somerset, she was more than a little irritated by what was starting to resemble a scene out of a penny dreadful.

"Melody, there is so much I want to tell you, but your brother and Foscari might return at any moment. Could you slip away tomorrow to meet me? Come to the Hortus Botanicus. I'll be waiting for you in the Palm House."

Somerset hadn't even waited to hear whether she was prepared to meet him before naming a spot. Was this arrogance or desperation?

Melody decided that the question could wait for now. "I'll come with my companion, Mary, and will meet you there at ten o'clock in the morning."

"I need you to come alone," William pleaded.

"Going out alone will look far too suspicious," Melody informed him pertly. She was about to tell him they had been followed and that she was worried she might be followed the next day, when something occurred to her. "Is this the first time that you've followed me?"

It was too dark to see William's reaction, but if a tone of voice could be sheepish, his was when he replied, "I've done it once or twice." Before Melody could berate him or ask anything more, William continued, "I wanted to find a time to speak to you alone but you always seemed to be with someone else: that Foscari fellow, your brother, or the Moroccan boy. Also, as I said, I needed to be sure of something."

"And now you are?"

"Can we talk about this all tomorrow, Melody?"

Melody couldn't imagine where this was all going, and was tempted to keep pressing. However, this was hardly the ideal time or place, and she was supposed to be keeping watch. Although, if it had been William following them all along, perhaps she didn't need to.

Finally, deciding that all her questions and admonishments could wait until the following day, which was probably later that same day, given the hour, Melody made it clear to William that she was willing to wait, but expected to hear the full story.

What was telling was that he asked nothing about why she was waiting out in the dark, dressed in men's clothing. It seemed he had some sense of what they were up to. There was a sound coming from across the street, and Melody turned her head for a moment. When she turned back, William was gone. From what she could see, the sound had come from some rats. Melody found this more of a consolation than she would under other circumstances.

Melody wasn't sure how long she'd been standing there when she saw movement in the alley. She hoped it was Rat and Alessandro and hesitated whether to shine the lantern. Just as she thought she should be better safe than sorry, she heard a bird's call. Not just any call, but the high-pitched trilling song of a canary.

Melody hadn't heard that sound in a long time. When she and Rat had lived on the streets of Whitechapel, it was the signal he used to tell her it was safe for her to emerge from wherever he had been hiding her for the night. A canary meant come out, the rasping caw of a crow meant she should stay where she was. He had used the bird calls occasionally since then, but not for many years. Indeed, not since they were children playing on the grounds of the Pembroke Estate. She understood what it signified; it was Rat and Alessandro coming down the alley. Melody breathed a sigh of relief.

In no time at all, they were in front of her. Melody hugged her brother, grateful their break-in had been so seemingly uneventful.

"Did you find what you were looking for?" she asked Alessandro.

"Why don't we have this conversation back at the hotel?" he replied. "I'd like to leave here and it's late. To answer your question simply: we found some interesting things, I believe."

Yet again, Melody would have to wait for information. Though Alessandro was right, it was late, and she was tired. She sighed but didn't argue. The walk back was in silence.

When they parted ways, Alessandro asked Rat, "You will let me know what you discover?"

"I will."

Well, that was cryptic, Melody thought. She wanted to insist that Rat meet her for breakfast and tell her what they found. However, considering how late it already was, and that she was supposed to meet William at ten o'clock, she decided it was best not to tempt fate by meeting her brother first and risking questions about where she was going.

Instead, Melody said nothing as she and Rat made their way back to their rooms. The back door of the hotel had been locked, but Rat had easily picked that.

When they had climbed the stairs and reached Melody's floor, Rat said, "I have some work to do tomorrow. Why don't you come to my room after lunch, and I'll explain everything?" That suited Melody's plans to meet William perfectly, so she agreed and then wished her brother good night.

Melody slipped into her hotel suite only to find Mary sitting in one of the armchairs, asleep, clearly waiting up for her.

At the sound of the door closing, Mary jolted awake. "Thank heavens. I was getting so worried. I won't ask where you went and what you did, but I am very glad to have you home safely." She gave the young woman a warm hug and then turned to go to her bed.

As late as it was, Melody didn't fall asleep as quickly as she hoped. Instead, she lay in the dark going over and over her conversation with William. How long had he been in Amsterdam? How many times had he followed her? What was he doing there, and what did he want to tell her?

It was some time before she finally fell asleep. She had set the alarm clock to wake her in a few hours; without it, she might sleep the morning away by the time she drifted off.

CHAPTER 25

R at was awake early the next morning. He had also set his alarm
clock, though it hadn't been necessary; after tossing and turning
before falling asleep and then, after experiencing a few restless hours of
sleep, he woke at dawn. He kept going over what they had discovered, first
when awake, and then even in his dreams. He and Alessandro had agreed
it was best to review everything properly in the morning with clear heads,
but Rat hadn't been able to consider sleep until he had decrypted the
manifests they had transcribed.

Before they crept out of Huis Jansen in the early hours of the morning, carefully relocking the doors, the men had agreed to meet again, but
without informing Melody. Alessandro had been the driving force behind
this decision, though Rat had agreed, albeit reluctantly and with a guilty
conscience. Alessandro's argument was that they needed to determine
precisely what was happening and what steps to take without the compli-
cations of Melody's naivety regarding the importance of saving lives.

Now, as he dressed in the morning's early light, Rat felt more guilty
than ever about their subterfuge. He understood Alessandro's point, but
he also recognised the validity of his sister's view that they couldn't even
consider allowing a bomb to detonate and kill or maim people.

Rat tried to push aside such thoughts and instead focus on the primary task at hand: gaining a complete picture of what Germany was plotting. Alessandro had suggested that they rendezvous at the townhouse rather than the hotel, to avoid running into Melody. While this made sense, it also made very clear that they were going behind her back in a way that he wouldn't be able to argue against if Melody ever discovered they'd met. And yet again, he was back to obsessing over their deception rather than focusing all his efforts on solving the riddle in front of them.

Finally, Rat decided he'd had too little sleep to focus his mind properly. Instead, he gathered his papers and sneaked out of the back door of the hotel, letting his thoughts drift wherever they would. If he felt guilty, well, he should. Perhaps dealing with that discomfort was the price he had to pay for deceiving his sister.

Rat pondered whether he should worry about being followed by someone who might or might not be shadowing them. In the end, he decided that, if they were under surveillance, it wasn't news that he was working with Alessandro. Therefore, a visit to the man's townhouse, even early in the morning, wasn't unusual in itself.

Alessandro's front door was opened by Mustafa, whose usual cheerfulness was a little much for Rat to deal with on so little sleep.

"Sidi Alessandro is waiting for you. Would you like me to bring you some tea or perhaps coffee?" the boy asked. Rat replied that very strong coffee would be welcome and then allowed himself to be guided into Alessandro's drawing room.

He wasn't sure whether he was happy or disappointed not to find Fatima waiting. Ever since they had arrived in Amsterdam and the beguiling woman's choice of living arrangements became clear, Rat had come to terms with the impossibility of pursuing his interest in her. Then he met Jemima Edwards and felt a flicker of romantic hope that began to dim his remaining foolish dreams of Fatima. Mostly. There was still enough of an ember left that Rat felt uncomfortable watching her play host in Alessandro's home.

Alessandro, still wearing a dressing gown, greeted Rat warmly. "Matthew! I wasn't sure how early to expect you, but I didn't imagine it would be before nine o'clock in the morning."

"Apologies if it's too early, but I wanted to share what I've uncovered and discuss what we saw."

"No apologies needed. It is more that I'm impressed by your resilience. Now, tell me, what have you learned?" Rat then explained that he had deciphered all the additional manifests they had discovered at Huis Jansen.

"I am not sure that we have all the manifests for the complete message, and there are some German words I need you to translate, but I do have a theatre name and a date." He paused, then said the words that would explain his inability to sleep. "August 6th."

"But that's tomorrow!" Alessandro exclaimed in horror. "Wait, you said you have a theatre name. What is it?"

"The Stadsschouwburg."

Alessandro leapt up and went to grab a newspaper from a nearby sideboard. He scanned the first couple of pages before saying in an even more horrified voice, "I knew I'd seen something." He returned to his seat and handed Rat the newspaper. It was in Dutch, so he couldn't understand all of the language, but what was clear was who was in the photograph accompanying the news story: Queen Wilhelmina of the Netherlands.

"There is a special opera performance tomorrow night that the Queen Wilhelmina and Prince Hendrik are attending," Alessandro explained.

Rat sank back in horror at Alessandro's words. Whatever they had imagined Germany was planning, an assassination attempt on the Dutch monarch was more terrible than anything they had expected. Rat thought about the flyers he had found along with the bomb parts.

"They are going to detonate a bomb at the theatre, then blame an actual or at least attempted assassination on anarchists." As he said this, Rat realised that in the excitement of planning their late-night visit to Huis Jansen, he had forgotten to show Alessandro the flyer he had taken from the crates at the port. While he was wearing a different jacket from the one he'd had the day before, he'd had the foresight to put the leaflet and the fuse cap into the pile of materials that he'd added to the night before when he'd deciphered the manifest. Now, he pulled them both out and showed them to Alessandro.

"I gather it says something about neutrality," Rat volunteered. "I have no idea what the rest says."

"It says that neutrality is a lie and that Germany cannot be trusted, essentially." Rat then handed over the fuse cap. "What am I looking at?"

Alessandro asked, turning the cap over and over in his hand, a bemused look on his face.

"It's a fuse cap. More importantly, it is stamped with a symbol indicating that it is British military equipment."

Neither man spoke for a few moments as the implications of their discovery sank in.

"Germany is planning not merely to suggest a weak link between the supposed anarchists and this bombing, they're going to make the connection explicit and perhaps even lead the Dutch to the conclusion that the British are behind it," Rat exclaimed. Then he had another thought. "Why would the Netherlands believe Britain would do such a thing?"

"Why would Germany? Both countries would like to sway the Netherlands out of its neutrality and towards themselves. If fear of anarchists might make this country more inclined to look towards its neighbour for security, one could argue that it could also make it lean towards one of its biggest trading partners across the Channel." Alessandro considered his claim: "Let's follow this narrative thread: Britain either arms these anarchists or perhaps commits the deed itself and plants evidence of anarchist group connections."

"As Germany is planning to do."

"Precisely. Perhaps the stamp on the fuse caps was something that was overlooked, or perhaps the expectation is that they won't survive the explosion."

Rat stood and began pacing the floor as he tried to follow Alessandro's logic. "So, if the caps won't survive the explosion, and I'm assuming they won't, how would Germany ensure this is traced back to Britain?"

It was a good question, and one Alessandro had to consider for a few moments. Then, he snapped his fingers. "Perhaps they will rig this in such a way that a fuse cap, even if it's not actually part of the bomb, will be found lying around. After all, they also have to ensure that the leaflets survive and are discovered. Who knows what they have planned? Whatever it is, this plan is devious and we need to stop it."

The men agreed that, regardless of their initial opinions on whether preventing the actual bombing was a priority, the situation had changed drastically now that it appeared to involve assassinating the Dutch royal family and planting evidence directly implicating Britain.

"I found those bomb parts yesterday morning, so they'll have to get them off the docks soon. But how are they planning to get them into the theatre and then assemble them?" Rat mused.

"Actually, there's a genius behind this plan. Consider all the equipment needed for a theatre production, from props to lighting. It wouldn't be difficult to sneak in bomb parts; in fact, it's much easier than trying to smuggle in an assembled bomb. We should go to the theatre and find out what we can about the upcoming performance."

Suddenly, Alessandro slapped his head and picked up the newspaper again from where Rat had rested it on the table in front of them, then translated, 'The royal gala performance will be of *Die Walküre*, presented by the Dresden Staatsoper, and promises a night of triumph for German music lovers in Amsterdam.' The theatre will be full of German cast and crew, and pulling this off won't even be a challenge."

He stood, and Rat followed his lead. They both knew they needed to act, but what should they do? They had no authority to search the theatre and limited evidence that might persuade anyone of an imminent bombing.

"We need to talk to Sir Alan," Alessandro decided.

"The British Envoy to the Netherlands? Do you think he can help?" Rat asked, his words heavy with scepticism.

"He may be the only person who can. We have no authority and little credibility; he has both. We can only hope he believes us."

With so much at stake, Rat hoped rather than believed that Alessandro was right. First, they had to persuade Sir Alan of their roles and then take him through all they had learned. While Rat did not doubt the truth of their information, he imagined it might seem less than convincing to an outsider. They had made many conjectures and drawn connections between those conjectures that might be seen as insufficient reason to cause a panic. Yet what if they were correct? Wasn't it better to appear foolish than to risk the alternative? Rat nodded in acceptance of Alessandro's plan.

CHAPTER 26

Melody had slept much more soundly than Rat. It was fortunate that she had set her alarm clock, or she might have slept right through her scheduled meeting with William. When the alarm went off, it took a moment before it penetrated her deep sleep enough to wake her. When it did, she shot upright, confused for a moment about where she was. She looked at the clock and realised she hadn't left herself much time to get ready. She could have done with a cup of coffee, but there wasn't enough time.

After hurriedly dressing, Melody went in search of Mary. While she dressed, she thought about what she was going to tell her. Was it plausible that they would visit the Hortus Botanicus together, and then somehow, she might slip away to meet William? Melody didn't want to explain anything more to Mary than necessary. Besides, the investigation was so convoluted at this point that she was unsure she could even make sense of it to someone else.

Finally, Melody decided not to mention her meeting for now. Of course, Mary was far too eagle-eyed not to notice the dark circles under Melody's eyes and, given her obvious exhaustion, question why she had to visit the botanical gardens that morning.

Melody was too exhausted to argue. "Mary, I want to go, is that not a sufficient answer? If you do not want to accompany me, I will venture out alone," she snapped. This was a cheap shot, and Melody knew it.

"I will fetch my hat and bag and be ready to leave whenever you are, Miss Melody," Mary said primly.

Sighing, Melody apologised. "I am sorry if I am being grumpy, Mary. I just need, I mean I want to go to the botanical gardens and I would like you to accompany me." She could see Mary's features soften at her words, and felt even guiltier at her manipulation of her companion. However, it couldn't be helped. There were weighty issues at play, and Melody was sure Mary would understand if she ever needed to be told the whole story.

Now, Melody faced a new dilemma: what if they ran into Jemima Edwards in the lobby? The very last thing she needed was Miss Edwards tagging along on the outing. She had seen enough of the woman to know Jemima was quite capable of doing just that. On the other hand, she couldn't imagine what excuse she might give Mary for sneaking them out the back of the hotel. Which was the lesser evil?

"Mary. I do have one more favour to ask of you," Melody said tentatively, trying to sound as casual as possible. "There is a young woman with whom Mr Sandworth has become quite friendly."

This was news to Mary, and she raised her eyebrows but said nothing. Melody pressed on, "There is nothing wrong with this woman, Miss Edwards. In fact, she is a charming young lady. I even went shopping with her yesterday." This also came as a surprise to Mary, her eyebrows rising even higher. Now, Melody reached the crux of her request. "However, I would prefer this morning's outing to be just the two of us."

Immediately, she could see Mary's eyes brighten with pleasure at the suggestion that Melody wanted some time alone with her.

Feeling terrible, Melody promised herself that once this investigation was over, she would do something lovely for Mary to make up for all the lies and deception. For now, though, she merely dug herself in deeper. "So, if we run into her in the lobby or on the street, you might hear me lie to her. I have found that she is very quick to invite herself along for outings and so a little white lie might be necessary. You do understand, don't you?"

Mary smiled. "I will follow your lead, Miss Melody."

Relieved to have one thing sorted out, Melody then realised she still needed to come up with a plausible excuse in case they bumped into Jemima. Perhaps they were going to lunch with an old friend of Granny's. Yes, that was it. No well-mannered young woman would dream of inviting herself to such a social occasion. And, just in case Jemima was not so well-mannered, it would be perfectly believable for Melody to decline.

The two women pinned on their hats, gathered their bags, and made their way to the lift and down to the hotel lobby. Despite having a fool-proof excuse in hand, Melody still stepped out of the lift nervously, glancing around to see if Jemima was nearby.

When she couldn't see the other woman anywhere, Melody whispered, "Let us make haste." Of course, it was still possible they might run into her on the street; Miss Edwards did seem to appear at the most inconvenient times.

Melody had looked on the map, so she had some sense of how to get to the gardens. The morning air was already warm, and sunlight flickered over the canals as they walked eastward. A milk cart clattered past, and ahead, a flower seller called out prices in sing-song Dutch. They crossed Muiderstraat, passing the theatre district, then turned on to Plantage Middenlaan. The street was quieter here, shaded by rows of horse chestnut trees and lined with stately buildings and quiet fences. Melody's heart beat faster as they drew closer to the botanical gardens. She wasn't sure what Somerset had in mind with this meeting, only that he'd been intentionally vague but also quite insistent.

At the gates of the Hortus Botanicus, Melody paid the entrance fee of just a few Dutch cents, and they stepped into the cool, green hush of the garden. The city noise faded behind them. Instantly, Melody felt as if they were in the peace of a rural estate. It was a tranquil and beautiful place, and she wished she had the luxury of appreciating it properly. As it was, she had an assignation to attend and a companion to shake off. She surveyed the grounds and then glanced at Mary. How was she to slip away?

As luck would have it, the solution presented itself with no effort from Melody. The walk to the gardens hadn't been long, but it seemed it was enough to tire Mary out. Looking at a lovely wrought-iron bench under a weeping willow tree, beside a charming pond, Mary admitted, "Would you be angry if I sat here for a while? It is surprisingly warm out, given that it is still morning, and you kept up quite a fast pace for the walk here."

Melody was elated at the opportunity to rid herself of Mary with no need for an excuse, but also felt terrible for exhausting her. "Are you sure you don't mind me leaving you, Mary?" she asked, though she couldn't imagine what she would do if Mary did mind.

Of course, the devoted companion was far too selfless and dutiful ever to begrudge her charge a morning's pleasure. "Of course I don't mind. The grounds seem perfectly safe and respectable. I am sure there is no harm in you wandering them alone while I rest. Far better that than I hold you back. You know where to find me when you're done."

Too eager to be off, Melody made no more half-hearted attempts to dissuade Mary and instead skipped away. A painted sign marked the path to the *Palmhuis*. Melody followed it, her skirts brushing fern fronds and plants that lined her way. The Palm House loomed ahead. It was a large, glass-and-iron building that glinted with condensation.

As Melody stepped through the entrance, a wave of humid warmth enveloped her. The air was thick with the scent of loam, damp wood, and citrus. Inside, towering palms cast long shadows and lent the place a somewhat menacing air, at least to her eye. Perhaps it was simply the nature of her visit that made her feel so nervous.

Melody knew she was being irrational; this was Captain William Somerset she was meeting, not some mysterious, dangerous stranger. She moved carefully, eyes searching each figure seated on benches or kneeling to admire exotic plants. Somewhere inside, Somerset was waiting. And although she told herself again that she had nothing to fear from him, the dampness of her palms was caused by more than the humidity of the building.

She felt as if she had walked the entire Palm House and was beginning to wonder whether Somerset was delayed or if she had misunderstood his instructions. Melody was exhausted and uncomfortably warm. While she was tempted to leave and go back to the quiet spot where Mary was sitting, Melody was drawn by the sight of a bench nearby, beneath a large palm tree.

She might have dozed off for a few minutes. How else to explain that she hadn't noticed she was no longer alone on the bench?

A gentle hand on her arm alerted her she wasn't alone, and a soft voice whispered, "It is wonderful to see you, Melody."

"William," she whispered back. "What is this all about? Why are you in Amsterdam, and why were you following us last night?"

Now that he was sitting beside her, any trepidation Melody had felt melted away. Instead, she looked at Captain Somerset's handsome face with his dark, close-cropped hair and soulful brown eyes, and realised how very much she had missed him. Their previous encounter in the early hours of the morning had been so sudden and fraught with the danger of the situation that she hadn't had time to consider her feelings at having him suddenly reappear in her life.

Without considering the wisdom of her words, Melody replied in a gentle voice, "I've missed you, William. Very much."

As she said it, Melody realised how true the statement was. She had missed everything about Captain Somerset, from his quiet, steady presence to his gentle smile. More than anything, she had missed how she felt when she was with him: capable and confident. William believed in her and made her believe in herself, and Melody hadn't appreciated until that moment all that this faith meant to her.

CHAPTER 27

"Why are you here, William? What's the reason for all the skulking about?" As pleased as Melody was to see him, she felt irritated by the secrecy. If he had something to tell her, why hadn't he contacted her days earlier, in broad daylight, and just said it?

Surely, this was more than just an over-the-top romantic gesture. William had always seemed so sensible and down-to-earth. Was she mistaken? Had he followed her to Amsterdam and found her on a dark, deserted street to declare his love? As soon as she thought of this, Melody realised how foolish it was. He was the one who had walked away from her, not the other way round. If he had wanted to fight for her, William could have done so in Morocco rather than saying goodbye.

"Melody, I had to warn you. I know what your brother and Foscari believe they've uncovered, but there's more to it than meets the eye. I voiced my concerns about the situation, but I was undercut, dismissed, and ultimately sent away to Morocco for my troubles. The unfortunate series of events there was considered my second black mark. I am meant to be back in London, but I had to follow you here and try to help."

He was still being so cryptic with these vague warnings that Melody was tempted to get up and leave immediately. Instead, she asked, "Can you speak more plainly? What concerns? What help do I need?"

"To be honest, I only have suspicions and haven't put it all together. Just before I was sent away, I grew worried that Vermeer had been compromised. I was uneasy about the authenticity of the false flag information; some of it seemed too perfect. I reported my concerns back to the Foreign Office and was told to stand down. The false flag narrative fits too neatly with what Sir Edward and his cronies want to believe about Germany and its intentions."

Melody was all too aware of the British Foreign Secretary, Sir Edward Grey's, sentiments towards Germany. He and his private secretary, William's brother, Adam, had been behind Alessandro's arrest for murder, or at least indirectly responsible for it. That had also been a tangled attempt to sway public opinion away from Germany. Was this happening again? Is that what William had uncovered? Melody asked the question.

In response, William looked thoughtful. "I'm not sure. I don't think so, but then it never would have occurred to me that they were behind all the mayhem in Morocco. What I do believe is that they are desperate to expose this so-called false flag operation and sway the Dutch away from neutrality."

Melody wasn't sure what to believe. Her experiences in Morocco had taught her that things are not always as they seem, even when it was her own government in action. Was there more to what was happening in Amsterdam than they realised?

"Why are you telling me?" she had to ask. "Why not tell Matthew or Conte Foscari? After all, they are the ones officially working this mission."

She heard William sigh. "Foscari is part of the problem. At least I believe he is. I don't have concrete proof, but I believe I was ordered back to London on his advice. Before leaving Morocco, I made another attempt to return to Amsterdam and pick up where I left off, aiming to get to the bottom of what I think might be going on. I heard rumours that the conte persuaded the powers that be to send him and Mr. Sandworth instead and keep me out of it."

Was this true? Melody couldn't believe what she was hearing. After all William had done to help save Rat and, in doing so, secure Alessandro's release, would he really betray William in such a way?

It wasn't much later when William said he had to leave. "I cannot risk being seen with you. I have no idea what danger that might put you in." Melody would have liked to ask more about this statement and about what he wanted her to do, but there wasn't enough time.

There was one question she did think to ask just as he was turning to leave: "William, did you slip the cypher key into my jacket pocket when I was leaving the library the other day?"

William looked at her sharply. "No. That wasn't me. I never had the cypher key. Vermeer had talked about finding it and bringing it to me, but I was ordered to Morocco before he had a chance."

He caressed her cheek with his palm. "Be very careful, Melody. Truly, I don't believe everything is as it appears. Why would someone give you the cypher key? How would they even know to approach you?"

And with that, he turned and disappeared down a narrow path between particularly lush foliage. It wasn't until he was gone that Melody realised William hadn't even left her a way to contact him. However, she rationalised, it was clear he knew where and how to find her. It comforted her knowing that William was in the shadows, watching out for her. However, he had left her with a big decision to make and no guidance as to what she should do: what, if anything, should she say to Rat?

It was unpleasant, but not unthinkable, to imagine Alessandro turning against William. It was preposterous to imagine Rat deliberately doing anything dishonourable in any way. Her brother was one of the most decent men Melody knew, and that said a lot, considering she was raised by Wolf and spent most of her life among men like Bear and Lord Langley. Melody understood what integrity and honour looked like, and Rat embodied both.

Though even knowing all that, should she tell him? If nothing else, Rat's sense of honour would almost certainly mean sharing this informa-tion with Alessandro, who, it seemed, already knew and had dismissed William's concerns. All that alerting him to Captain Somerset's presence in Amsterdam would probably do was get William into even more trouble than he was already in.

Melody decided to stroll through the grounds of the botanical gardens for a while. If nothing else, how would she explain to Mary why she had taken so little time otherwise? The walk also provided her with some time to think.

William's warning had been so vague. He had come to think that Vermeer might have been compromised. Might. Did the man's subsequent death support or detract from that possibility? Melody could see how one might argue it either way; if Vermeer was who he claimed to be and was stealing and leaking information about Germany, he might have been caught and killed. Or, perhaps he had been playing both sides and got found out.

She kept returning to one thing William had said about the authenticity of the information he'd received: it all seemed too perfect. Did it? It was fortunate that Vermeer had been clutching a piece of manifest when he did; was it more than fortunate? And she couldn't stop returning to the cypher key that mysteriously appeared in her pocket. At the time, they had been so grateful for it that none of them questioned too closely who might have given it to her. Now, this decision seemed shortsighted. Alessandro had seemed convinced that it had come from another informant. Had it? Was there a reason he had been so willing to adopt this theory?

Melody wandered the winding paths of the Hortus Botanicus, her hands brushing against the leaves of unfamiliar plants that lined the path. The air was thick with the scent of moss and turned earth, warmed by the morning sun; it was going to be another hot day. She paused near a trickling fountain at the edge of a large expanse of grass, admiring a fern while she reflected on her conversation with William. Children's laughter echoed faintly from across the lawn.

Vermeer might have confided in someone who, after his death, took on the cause themselves. The more Melody considered this, the more plausible the idea seemed. In fact, she wondered if Vermeer's wife knew more than they realised. After all, they had posed as journalists, so why would she reveal what she knew? Or what if someone he worked with at the docks was involved? It wasn't too far-fetched to imagine others wanting to steer the Netherlands away from aligning with Germany.

While this all seemed possible, she kept returning to the question of who had put the cypher key in her pocket. Whoever it was, it had to be someone aware that Rat and Alessandro had come to Amsterdam to take over the work William had been doing. More importantly, that person knew enough to put the paper in her pocket.

Melody saw a body of water ahead and decided to head there. As she walked, she reflected on the day her bag was stolen. She had been in the library, and her jacket was on the table beside her. Had she got up and left it at any point? She couldn't recall doing so, but perhaps she had. Then, Jemima Edwards had arrived, and they had spoken for a few minutes. After that, Melody left.

Wait! Jemima Edwards. No! It couldn't be. Overly chatty, Jemima Edwards couldn't possibly be anything other than the perky, too-friendly young woman she appeared to be. Or could she?

Now, Melody's mind was racing. Jemima had access to the jacket and could have slipped something in it, but why? Why would she have access to the cypher key? And why wouldn't she just give it to them if she did? Who was she really?

Melody remembered the words she had spoken to Rat during her initial irritation about Miss Edwards. She had said, "You bumped into her in the lobby, then carried her books up. That is all. She could be anyone." Had she sensed something at that moment, only to be later lulled into ignoring it by Jemima's friendliness? Melody knew they had discussed her travels over breakfast the other morning. At the time, she had the fleeting thought that the comment about the gunboat at Agadir was a little too close to the mark. Had it been more than just a passing remark?

If her conversation with William had disoriented her, she was even more flustered by these reflections. What did it all mean, and what should she do with this information? One thing was for certain: if she went to Rat with accusations about Miss Edwards but lacked proof, he would dismiss it as petty gossip on Melody's part. Of course, she had no proof. She wasn't even certain that Jemima had slipped her the paper.

Melody knew she needed more evidence before approaching her brother, let alone Alessandro. But how was she going to gather it?

CHAPTER 28

A lessandro's house was near the Golden Bend, where most foreign legations and consulates were housed in grand canal mansions. It was a short walk from Herengracht 76 down the canal to the Legation. In many ways, it was too brief a walk; there was little time for Rat and Alessandro to discuss what they planned to say. It seemed that Alessandro was somewhat acquainted with Sir Alan; they had often attended the same social functions. However, this would be the first time he revealed any involvement with the Secret Service Bureau.

They debated the pros and cons of Alessandro taking the lead in the conversation. "Well, he knows me, but only as a newspaper publisher. I am not even sure he knows my British heritage," Alessandro explained. "However, you are unknown, which might cause its own scepticism but also enables you to introduce yourself for the first time as an agent of the Bureau."

Rat's natural reticence and modesty, as well as his admiration and respect for Alessandro, made him disinclined to put himself forward. "I have no way of proving that I am who I say I am. If Sir Alan already has a relationship of sorts with you, surely you are better placed for credibility."

The conversation continued unresolved until they finally saw the black lacquered door of the British Legation appear. "Matthew, why do we not begin with you explaining your role? He will inevitably ask why I am present, and I can then explain that I too am involved with intelligence operations on behalf of the British Government." Rat wasn't convinced, but as he usually did, deferred to the older, more seasoned operative.

The building was a tall, narrow mansion with a polished brass knocker and windows that reflected the light like cut glass. The street was quiet aside from the gentle lap of canal water and the creak of a nearby barge. Rat brushed a faint trace of soot from his jacket before rapping on the door with the large brass doorknocker. Alessandro took the lead in requesting to see Sir Alan. His title was enough to gain them entry.

Inside, the British Legation was a study in hushed power. Polished wood floors gleamed beneath Turkish rugs; sparkling chandeliers hung from high plaster ceilings. They passed an oil portrait of King George V, and a framed map of the Netherlands annotated in spidery handwriting. A faint scent of tobacco lingered in the air.

The footman led them to a tall door at the end of the corridor. He rapped once, then opened it. "The Conte Foscari to see you, Your Excellency."

The room beyond was spacious, with bookshelves reaching the ceiling and tall windows looking out over the canal. Sir Alan sat behind a large mahogany desk but stood when they were introduced. His expression was unreadable.

Sir Alan was tall, slender, and impeccably dressed, with the faintly aquiline features characteristic of an aristocrat. His steel-grey hair was neatly parted, his moustache precisely trimmed, and his eyes a keen blue, sharp beneath heavy brows.

He was dressed not flamboyantly, but with the sharp tailoring and perfect necktie of a man who has put himself in the hands of an excellent valet: starched collar, navy morning coat, and a waistcoat of muted brocade.

When he spoke, Sir Alan had the clipped diction of a top-notch British education. "Conte Foscari, this is a surprise. I do not believe you had an appointment?" Sir Alan approached with his hand extended.

"We did not," Alessandro apologised. "Please excuse my intruding upon your Saturday morning, but there is a matter of some urgency." Alessandro then gestured toward Rat. "This is my friend and colleague,

Matthew Sandworth." Alessandro paused before saying, "A colleague in the British Intelligence services, most specifically, the Secret Service Bureau."

Rat offered his hand, and Sir Alan shook it. However, even his excellent manners and diplomatic experience couldn't hide his surprise at these words.

"Secret Service Bureau, you say? Can't say I've heard of it." Sir Alan indicated his guests should sit and then retreated to his seat behind the desk. "What is the Secret Service Bureau when it's around?"

Created only in 1909, the Bureau was so new and covert that many, including some involved in the government, often had little or no awareness of it.

Rat replied, "It was founded two years ago in order to investigate enemy espionage threats and foreign intelligence activity at home and abroad."

Sir Alan made a noise that could have meant a range of things: disapproval, perhaps confusion. Maybe it was even a clearing of his throat with no other intention. "Well, this is the first I am hearing about it. More to the point, I am assuming you are operating in Amsterdam without my awareness or approval."

Alessandro glanced at Rat; they both knew they had no need to gain the diplomat's permission or even give him notice of their activities. In fact, quite the opposite; they were to operate as discreetly as possible, alerting no one, if possible, not even other British Government officials. However, they needed Sir Alan's help at the moment and pointing out such a reality was hardly likely to recommend them to the man.

Instead, Alessandro said, "Sir Alan, the mission we have come to Amsterdam to work on is a delicate one." They hadn't yet provided any details of their assignment, and Rat wondered how much information Alessandro would offer. "I am sure you understand if we cannot give too many specifics. However, what we can say is that we have uncovered a very dangerous plot which we need your help to thwart." Well, that wasn't very detailed at all. Would it satisfy Sir Alan?

Thirty minutes later, they had their answer: no, it wouldn't. As they left the British Legation, Rat asked, "Now what?"

"Well, he didn't refuse to help. He merely said that he needs more evidence before he is comfortable alerting the Dutch authorities," Alessandro pointed out.

"We showed him the fuse cap and the copies of the manifests. He could see for himself what I had deciphered. How much evidence does the man need?"

Rat was frustrated and couldn't help expressing his frustration. Alessandro understood and shared his sentiments, but he had been in the field too long not to understand how such things worked.

He stopped walking and turned to Rat. "Sir Alan has no authority here. Diplomacy is all about influence and relationships. If he goes to the Dutch authorities with our concerns and it turns out there's nothing behind them, he will not only look foolish and bring disgrace to Britain, but that will be the last time anyone pays attention to him."

Rat was not normally headstrong, but he was young and impatient. "But there is something behind our concerns, and we just showed him the evidence! How much more does he need?" It was a valid question, and one to which Alessandro didn't have a good answer. Rat continued, "I found bomb parts, for goodness' sake!"

"Well, you found components of what might be a bomb. They could also be parts for something entirely different."

"Then why bury them in a crate labelled nutmeg?" Rat insisted.

Alessandro smiled indulgently. "You don't have to convince me. I agree with you. I am just pointing out that our so-called evidence isn't indisputable."

Rat wanted to argue the point, but knew that he would only be preaching to the converted. Still, he couldn't help but express his deepest concern. "What if the only thing that will be sufficient proof is to find the bomb in the theatre, by which time it might be too late?"

The men had resumed walking. Alessandro considered what they knew. "If the bomb is to detonate tomorrow evening, and the components were still at the dock yesterday afternoon, which was Friday, then the plan must be to move them today or tomorrow morning. I don't know much about theatrical performances, but if there is a different performance tonight, then presumably, the German company will be moving in to set up tomorrow. Our best bet is to monitor the theatre and once we are sure that the bomb parts have been moved in, alert Sir Alan."

This plan made sense, but something still worried Rat. "If the point of our operation is to expose that this is a German false-flag plot to discredit Britain, it's not enough to just find a bomb. After all, the fuse caps look to be British-made, and we know that the plan is to shift the blame onto anarchists."

Both men sighed; this wouldn't be easy, and getting the timing just right would be crucial.

Rat knew Alessandro spoke several languages. Now he asked, "How good is your German?"

"Probably as good as my Dutch, maybe a little better."

"Then, I have an idea. Tomorrow we are going to visit the Stadss-chouwburg Theatre and pretend to be part of the backstage crew. I won't say much, but if anyone questions us in Dutch, you will claim to be with the German company, and vice versa. We need to locate those crates and try to get a sense of where this bomb might be placed so Sir Alan can then send in the Dutch authorities."

"Of course, that still doesn't solve the problem of pointing the finger directly at Germany," Alessandro pointed out. However, they both agreed to tackle one issue at a time.

CHAPTER 29

Melody and Rat arrived back at the hotel within minutes of each other. Rat had decided to have a light lunch in the dining room before considering how he might productively spend his afternoon. He and Alessandro had parted ways with the agreement that they would meet the next morning, appropriately dressed as workers, to make their way to the theatre. Rat was pleased they had a plan of sorts, but felt uneasy wasting time until then; if only he knew what to do with himself.

Rat was just about to enter the dining room when Melody entered the lobby and caught sight of him. She hailed him, and Rat felt immediately guilty about having left the hotel to confer with Alessandro that morning behind her back. Usually, Melody could read her brother well, but he was spared from her suspicions by how distracted she was by what she had discovered herself that morning.

"I'll join you," Melody said, approaching him. Unbeknownst to Rat, her guilt matched his own. She was still unsure what to tell him about the information William had shared, and she was even more nervous about her epiphany regarding Jemima Edwards. Melody decided to sit with her thoughts during lunch, hoping the answer would reveal itself to her.

Given his subterfuge that morning, Rat would have welcomed an excuse not to dine with his sister. However, try as he might, he couldn't think of a convincing reason. So, they proceeded into the dining room together, where they were immediately greeted by Jemima waving cheerfully at them.

The sight of the young woman reminded Melody of her suspicions. She hadn't thought them through sufficiently to feel comfortable engaging in small talk with Miss Edwards, but it seemed as if she had no choice but to do so. And perhaps there was some benefit to her company.

Jemima gestured for them to join her, and Rat was evidently eager to do so. Both siblings had the same idea: perhaps Miss Edwards' chattiness would save them from the discomfort of concealing something from one another.

"Mr Sandworth, Miss Chesterton, how lovely to see you both. I have only just ordered. Let me call the waiter back over for you."

A few minutes later, they were settled at the table, and their food was ordered. Melody was too anxious about questions regarding where she had been that morning to notice Rat's similar nervousness. Fortunately, as they had hoped and expected, Jemima more than kept up her side of the conversation.

If she'd been asked, Melody wouldn't have been able to recall what they discussed, or, more to the point, what Jemima said. She found that all that was required from her was the occasional murmur of agreement and a nod of her head. Apart from that, she could concentrate on eating her lunch and planning her next steps.

Now that she was with Jemima, she reconsidered her earlier so-called insight; was this overly friendly and talkative young woman likely to be involved in international espionage and intrigue? Of course, she thought to herself, someone might look at Melody herself and wonder much the same thing. She was also aware of how she'd been taken in by the seemingly sweet, gentle, and devoted facade that Xander Ashby had presented. One could hardly expect someone involved in such activities to appear obvious.

Rat was lost in far more pleasant thoughts: Jemima Edwards truly was such a lovely and sweet young woman. As infatuated as he had been with Fatima, there was also a part of Rat that had realised, even at the time, that the woman was manipulative and cunning. Could he really imagine a life with such a woman, even if she had reciprocated his feelings? But a life with Jemima Edwards, well, that was quite a different matter.

As he ate his delicate sole, poached with herbs, his mind wandered, and he imagined a small townhouse somewhere in London. Not Mayfair, of course; he could never afford to live there once he was married. Perhaps Kensington or Chelsea. He would return home in the evening to find Jemima waiting for him in the parlour. She would be playing with the children, and everyone would gather around him as he sat in his favourite armchair by the fire, his pipe in his hand.

He was so absorbed in his daydreams that he wasn't paying attention when Miss Edwards said, "Do you have any plans this afternoon, Mr Sandworth?"

"No, nothing," Rat replied absentmindedly, without considering his words.

"Excellent! Then why don't we spend it at the Rijksmuseum as we'd discussed?"

What? Rat thought. Wait! He didn't have time to waste at a museum. However, it seemed it was too late for an excuse.

Jemima turned to Melody. "Would you like to join us?"

This was asked in a half-hearted tone that made clear that the hoped-for answer would be in the negative. Even if the invitation had sounded more sincere, Melody realised this was her opportunity to do some snooping in Miss Edwards' room. Perhaps the aunt wouldn't be there, and Melody could break in and go through Jemina's belongings. Even if she were there, it would be interesting to meet this relative and see what information she could pry out of her.

Politely, Melody declined the invitation, and just as politely but gratefully, her excuses were accepted. Miss Edwards decided they would leave immediately after lunch. Having accepted the invitation, however unwittingly, Rat could find no reason to object. Twenty minutes later, he found himself leaving the hotel with Jemima Edwards on his arm.

Melody wiped her mouth with her serviette and rose. She needed to make the most of Jemima's absence. She couldn't imagine they would be gone for less than two hours, but there was no point in delaying. She had heard Jemima give her room number when she ordered breakfast earlier that week, so she knew where she was heading. After a quick stop in her room to collect the lock picks Rat had given her and showed her how to use, Melody made her way to room twelve.

It was only when Melody was standing outside Jemina's hotel room that it occurred to her she needed a reason for coming, having just eaten lunch with the woman. Not so much an excuse to tell her aunt, but one that would be believable when, inevitably, she mentioned her visitor to Jemina.

Casting her mind back over the little of the lunchtime conversation she had paid any attention to, Melody wondered if anything had been said that would provide a plausible excuse. She couldn't think of anything. Then, she had an idea. Returning to her room, she rummaged through her jewellery box until she found what she was looking for: a pair of small pearl earrings she wouldn't miss.

Melody took one earring and returned to Jemina's room. She would tell the aunt that she had found the earring on the table after the pair had left and assumed it was one of Jemima's earrings.

With a reasonably good excuse in hand, Melody knocked on the door. There was no answer. She knocked again, this time a little louder. The one thing she didn't want was to break into the room only to find that the aunt was just waking up from a nap. Still, there was no answer.

Looking up and down the corridor, Melody determined there was no one in sight and made quick work of picking the lock. She slipped into the room and gently closed the door behind her.

The first thing Melody noticed was that this wasn't a suite, and there was only one bed in the room. Of course, Jemima and her aunt might share it.

There was no open book on the bedside table, nor any clothes left on a chair. Melody wasn't tidy by nature, and the only reason her room was neat was because Mary tidied up after her. This room was so tidy that there was no clear evidence whether one or two people were sleeping in it. Perhaps the aunt had her own room, Melody mused. Then she remembered Jemima saying "our room" over breakfast. She had definitely said that, Melody decided. So, either they were sharing a bed, or there was no aunt.

Feeling somewhat guilty about going through another woman's belongings, Melody examined the drawers and the cupboard and concluded there was no sign of a second, older woman living there. What did that imply? By itself, it didn't necessarily suggest guilt. However, it was unusual, almost unheard of, for a young, unmarried, well-bred woman to travel alone.

Melody approached the writing desk. It had an inkwell and a neat pile of blank notepaper. The desk featured drawers, the first of which contained nothing of interest. However, the second held a folder. Melody pulled it out and looked inside. She found newspaper clippings there.

The clippings were in Dutch, so she couldn't understand their content, but one detail caught her eye. In the top one, there was a date and time that even her Dutch was good enough to recognise: 29 July, 2 pm. Wasn't that when Rat was supposed to meet Vermeer at the cafe? Of course, this might be a complete coincidence. However, the classified ad explicitly mentioned Café Suisse. She couldn't remember if Rat had told her which cafe he'd been waiting in.

She decided to copy the classified ads onto a piece of notepaper. Then, she copied a few others. They all had dates and times, though the others were at least six weeks earlier. Melody's breath caught. Six weeks ago was roughly when William had left Amsterdam. If she was correct, these were the newspaper classified ads that the captain and then Rat had used to communicate with Vermeer. How did Jemima know what they were?

Outside, a door slammed. Footsteps passed. Melody froze. If someone were to come into this room now, what excuse could she possibly make? Unless something unexpected had happened, there was no way Rat and Jemima would have returned from their museum excursion yet. Even so, the noise was a reminder that she should be as quick as possible. Melody folded up the notepaper she'd written on and put it in the pocket of her dress.

Before she left the room, Melody took a final look around. Was there anywhere else she should check? She was nervous about rummaging through too many things and alerting Jemima. Someone as tidy as the young woman seemed to be might notice if the slightest item had been moved. As it was, Melody just hoped she had returned the folder exactly as it had been.

Finally, Melody decided she had enough information for now and slipped out of the room.

CHAPTER 30

W hen Rat returned to the hotel several hours later, he felt he had
never been happier in his life. As much as he had worried about
spending precious hours he could ill afford at the museum, once he had
left the hotel with Jemima, he completely forgot all his concerns. Instead,
he walked beside the captivating woman, shyly answering questions but
mostly happily listening to her lyrical voice as she flitted from one topic to
another.

Rat couldn't have described what he saw in the museum; he had been
too absorbed in Jemima Edwards. She truly was the most charming girl.
Although she was petite in stature, Jemima's presence seemed to fill any
room she entered. If Rat was charmed by her at lunchtime, by later that
afternoon, he was completely infatuated. In fact, if he had been challenged, he might have even gone so far as to say he was in love.

After escorting Jemima to her door, Rat gently took her hand. "Miss
Edwards, Jemima, thank you for a lovely afternoon. I know we've only
known each other a few days, but I feel I must tell you how much I admire
you."

Another young woman might have blushed or batted her eyelashes.
Jemima smiled coquettishly. "Well, perhaps you ought to kiss me then,"
she challenged.

Rat had felt daring merely taking her hand. The thought of a kiss had never crossed his mind. Well, perhaps that wasn't true; it had crossed his mind a few times during their outing, but each time he had dismissed the idea. To steal a kiss would be the behaviour of the worst sort of rake and scoundrel. Still, this didn't stop him from sneaking furtive glances at her perfect bow lips. Now that Jemima spoke of kisses, Rat wondered in horror if he'd been less discreet than he believed.

"I would not want to take advantage of you," Rat stammered in reply.

Jemima laughed. "You are hardly taking advantage of me if I invite you to kiss me. Are you?"

Her logic was unassailable, yet Rat felt rooted to the spot, unable to close the few inches needed to hold Jemima Edwards in his arms and press his lips to hers. He stood there, her hand still in his, trapped and motionless.

Finally, with a giggle, Jemima took a step toward Rat, raised her head, and kissed him. It was a fleeting, gossamer brush of her lips, but it sent a shock through Rat, and it took all his willpower not to recoil from the sensation.

Then, as quickly as it had begun, the kiss was over. Jemima stepped back, reclaimed her hand, and said, "Thank you for a lovely afternoon, Mr Sandworth. I hope we can repeat it soon."

Rat mumbled something, though he later couldn't recall what he had said. Then, Jemima opened her door and slipped inside, leaving Rat standing in the hallway, uncertain of what had just transpired. He lingered for a few moments before turning around and heading back to the lift. Rat was so dazed that he forgot where he was going and nearly returned to the lobby. At the last moment, he snapped out of his daze and took the lift back to his floor.

As he opened the door to his hotel room, Rat felt he had never been happier. That thought lasted only a brief moment until he saw his sister sitting in the armchair, a look of fury on her face, tapping her fingers impatiently.

"Finally!" Melody exclaimed. "I was starting to wonder if you'd eloped with the lovely Miss Edwards." This was said in a tone of such nastiness that it took Rat aback.

"I'm sorry, Melly, but did we have an appointment that I've forgotten?" Rat wasn't being sarcastic; he genuinely couldn't imagine any other reason for his sister's attitude.

Even as she was biting Rat's head off, Melody knew she was being unreasonable; he had done nothing wrong. Far from it, in fact. If Rat hadn't accepted Jemima's suggestion of an afternoon excursion, Melody would never have been able to break into the woman's hotel room. Even though she knew this intellectually, the lovestruck look on her brother's face told Melody all she needed to know. Mostly, her irritation was masking concern at how Rat's heart was going to be broken at what she had to tell him about Jemima Edwards.

Melody couldn't imagine any scenario in which she and Fatima would have become true friends. Even so, at the very heart of Melody's dislike of the other woman was how she flirted mercilessly with Rat with no regard for how seriously he might take her coquettishness. The thought that her brother might have finally moved on from that infatuation, only to have his heart stamped on yet again, saddened and infuriated Melody. The easiest person to take that out on was standing in front of her, looking confused.

"An appointment? What about an investigation that we seem to be getting nowhere with?" Melody spat. She'd had some time to consider whether what she'd discovered in Jemima's room altered her calculation on what to reveal to Rat about her conversation with William.

She had concluded that she couldn't act alone. In a calmer voice, Melody continued, "I've discovered some things today and we need to decide what to do about them."

For his part, Rat had been too absorbed with his delightful companion to further consider what he should tell Melody. Now that it seemed she was about to make a revelation of her own, Rat realised he had to confide in his sister what he and Alessandro had discovered. He knew this meant admitting to leaving her out intentionally that morning and braced himself for her inevitable accusations.

"Actually, I need to tell you something as well, Melly," Rat admitted. He considered whether there was a way to tell Melody what he and Alessandro had surmised without confessing that they had met without her. He quickly realised Melody was far too perceptive, and more importantly, too attuned to the risk of being excluded to miss what had happened.

Instead of dissembling, Rat sat in the other armchair, ready to admit everything and be properly berated for it. "Alessandro and I met this morning and discovered that Germany plans to bomb the Stadsschouwburg theatre tomorrow evening when Queen Wilhelmina and Prince Hendrik will be present." He didn't pause long enough for Melody to jump in and berate him. "I am sorry we didn't include you, but we had our reasons, and I need you to accept that if you can."

This was the moment he expected her to explode, so when Melody simply sat looking at him in silence, Rat wasn't sure whether to feel grateful or worried.

For her part, Melody was unsure what attitude to take. She was genuinely furious that Rat and Alessandro had met without her. However, she hadn't told them about her late-night encounter with William, let alone her morning meeting with him. Also, she realised that her brother's guilt at excluding her might go a long way to offsetting his anger at her own behaviour.

As Melody contemplated how she wanted to handle this conversation, she sat in silence, which only threw Rat further off-balance. The only way he could interpret her silence was that Melody was too furious to trust herself to speak.

"Melly. I really am sorry. You're right; I said that you should be included in the investigation and then agreed to leave you out of a key discussion as soon as things became complicated. You have every right to be angry."

Still, Melody said nothing. Just as Rat was beginning to despair of his apology being accepted, she finally said, "I was contacted by Captain Somerset." Melody chose to be vague about when and how that contact occurred, confident that Rat was far too contrite at that moment to question her.

"Somerset is in Amsterdam? I thought he was supposed to have gone back to London with his tail between his legs," Rat blurted out.

Now, that was an interesting way to phrase things, Melody thought. After William said farewell to her in Fes that day, his name was never mentioned again. Indeed, Rat had shown no sign of knowing what had happened to the captain or where he was. Yet, it seemed he did know something, or thought he did. Melody filed this fact away for another time. They had far too many matters to discuss to waste time and frustration pulling that thread for now.

"Apparently, he didn't return to London but instead followed us here. Do you know why he was sent to Morocco and removed from what he was investigating in Amsterdam?"

Rat hesitated just a moment too long and was unable to control his facial expression sufficiently. Without waiting for him to lie to her, Melody continued, "So, you do know that he expressed concerns about the reliability of Vermeer's information."

"I heard something," Rat admitted with a shrug. "It is one of the reasons the operation moved from the Foreign Office to the Secret Service Bureau. It was felt that Somerset was insufficiently skilled to make such an assessment and that he would be better utilised in Morocco. Of course, when that went sideways as well, the second strike against him was seen as evidence that the man should be taken out of field operations altogether."

"And you and Alessandro said nothing to defend him?" Melody asked, appalled. "You knew what happened, and that William was nothing but the hero of the hour, saving your life and helping to liberate Alessandro. Yet you let him receive a black mark for his involvement." Even though William had implied as much about Alessandro, the thought that Rat had also been in the know, even if he hadn't explicitly spoken out against William, was appalling.

Rat spread his hands in a gesture of helplessness. "It is hardly as if we weren't also reprimanded, even though all we did was to fulfil the mission to which we were assigned. The politics of the situation were fraught, and neither Foscari nor I would have been the best apologists for Somerset." Even though Rat knew this was true, Melody's accusation touched a raw nerve for Rat; he did feel guilty about what had happened to Captain Somerset.

Again, this was a thread better left unpulled for the moment, Melody decided. Instead, she focused on what was most important at that time. "Have you not considered how relatively easy it has been to find out about these false-flag plots?"

"Vermeer is dead. I would hardly call this operation 'relatively easy'," Rat pointed out.

Melody couldn't dispute that point. Instead, she pivoted and showed him the notepaper she had written on in Jemima's room. "Do you recognise this wording?"

Rat took the papers and looked over what Melody had transcribed. "These look like copies of the classified advertisements Vermeer placed to communicate with Somerset and then with me. How did you get these?"

Taking a deep breath, Melody prepared herself for the hardest part of this conversation. "I found the newspaper clippings in Miss Edwards' room."

"You broke into her room and snooped around?" Rat exclaimed, outraged at his sister's impertinence.

"I think you're missing the point. Why did she have these cut out and stored in a folder? Who is she, Rat? Because the one thing I am quite sure of is that she is not who she claims to be, that there is no aunt staying in that room with her, and that bumping into you the other day was not an accident."

Rat's first instinct was to argue with Melody and defend Jemima. He could still feel her kiss on his lips, and just the thought of it made him want to smile. However, if Melody had truly found the newspaper clippings in Jemima's room – and why on earth would she lie about such a thing? – then, he had to question everything he believed about the young woman.

CHAPTER 31

Perhaps it was Rat's natural modesty that made him so easy to convince about Jemima's ulterior motives. After all, hadn't he been wondering what such a beautiful, vivacious young woman wanted with him? It made sense that the answer was: she wanted nothing more than to get close to him to manipulate the situation in some way.

As happy as Melody was that her hypothesis about Jemima Edwards hadn't led to a huge argument with Rat, it was so terribly sad for her to see how quickly her brother was willing to accept that Jemima had never had any genuine romantic interest in him. When had her brother become so lacking in self-esteem? she wondered. Of course, Melody had some sense of when and why: all those years of being treated as if he wasn't good enough by the young society women he encountered, simply because he wasn't titled and had to work for a living.

While it was heartbreaking to see her brother like this, it was expedient, at least for the sake of the investigation, that he be so accepting of this fact; they simply didn't have time to bicker. It was already late Saturday afternoon, and if they were correct, a bomb was set to go off at the Stadsschouwburg in just over twenty-four hours.

Rat told Melody about their failed attempt to persuade Sir Alan to intervene and alert the Dutch authorities. He then updated her on their plan for him and Alessandro to pose as backstage crew members the next day.

"What role am I going to play?" Melody demanded.

Rat sighed; he should have anticipated this question. "Melody, you can hardly dress as a man again and join us. In daylight, no one will be fooled."

"Let me be very clear about this. I am not going to be left behind. You need all the help you can get, and I know that I can be of use. I will pretend to be an assistant wardrobe mistress. While I am hardly fluent in German, I can certainly speak enough to get by." Given that Melody had never given her language lessons the attention she should have, this might have been an exaggeration. Nonetheless, her German was probably her best foreign language, and she felt it was important to make her point. She continued, "Honestly, I am sure that if I carry some costume pieces around with me, no one will think to ask. The German crew will assume I am Dutch and work for the theatre, and vice versa."

It actually made sense. As with his plan with Alessandro, the assumption was that everyone would be too busy preparing for the evening's performance to question random people closely.

Just then, there was a knock at the door. Rat answered it to find Alessandro there. If the conte was surprised to see Melody with Rat, Alessandro didn't show it.

Before Alessandro could begin any sort of charade for Melody's benefit, Rat said, "I have told my sister everything, and she will be joining us tomorrow." Before Alessandro could do more than show surprise at this statement, Rat continued, "And, she also has news of her own."

Alessandro raised his eyebrows at this statement. "What is your news?"

Melody then told him what she had discovered in Jemima's room. Rat noticed she said nothing about her liaison with Captain Somerset. He caught his sister's eye, but if she understood why, Melody chose to ignore it. When she was finished, Alessandro leaned back in the chair Rat had brought for him from in front of the writing desk. He clasped his hands behind his head and mulled over Melody's words.

"Tell me again how you met this Jemima Edwards," he asked. With only a slight blush, Rat recounted how they had accidentally bumped into each other in the hotel lobby and subsequently gone out to a cafe one afternoon.

"Then, she turned up while I was at the Anglo-Continental Lending Library," Melody interjected. "I first became suspicious of her when I realised she could have slipped that cypher key into my jacket pocket. So, when I knew she and Matthew were out this afternoon, I sneaked into her room and looked around."

"And found the newspaper clippings?"

"Exactly. Oh, and I had a long chat with her at breakfast the day before yesterday. She was curious about our travels, but not excessively so. Or at least, that's what I thought then." Melody considered the conversation. "However, she was remarkably knowledgeable about the situation in Morocco and mentioned the gunboat in Agadir, but perhaps that simply means she keeps up with current events. Though, I did notice it at the time."

They all sat in silence, reflecting on this information. Finally, Rat spoke up. "Let us assume for a moment that Jemima Edwards isn't who she seems to be..."

"I don't believe that's an assumption any longer," Melody interrupted.

"Alright. Jemima Edwards isn't the innocent tourist travelling Europe that she claims to be. Then who is she? If Melody is right and Jemima put the cypher key in her jacket, then she cannot be a German agent, can she?"

Melody reflected on everything that had occurred over the past week. More specifically, she considered William's warnings about the reliability of Vermeer's intelligence. She was tempted to mention this to Alessandro, but then remembered how William claimed to have been sidelined from the investigation for raising the issue.

Deciding not to mention William yet, she agreed, "The cypher key helped us. Why would a German agent do such a thing?" Then, she thought of something. It seemed an outrageous thing to suggest, yet it had to be said. "Is it possible she works for British Intelligence and that neither of you has been informed?"

It was clear that Alessandro's initial reaction would be to deny such a possibility. Rat's expression showed he regarded the idea more favourably.

"Absolutely not!" Alessandro exclaimed, confirming Melody's instincts yet again.

"Well, I didn't know about you when we were in Venice," Rat pointed out. "And we didn't know about Somerset's role in Morocco, and I'm quite sure he didn't know about ours when we first met. It's possible, isn't it?"

Melody could tell that Rat wanted this to be a possibility, perhaps more than believing it could be. If Jemima Edwards, or whatever her name turned out to be, was a British operative, then, while he might still feel like a fool for falling for her machinations, he at least would feel like a fool for the right reasons.

"Surely it could be the case," Rat insisted. "She might work for the war office, for example."

"I suppose," Alessandro conceded. "Though, why would she slip us the information secretly?" No one had an answer for that, and so Alessandro pressed home his point. "Until we know who she is, we need to assume the worst. While I don't know why an enemy would give us the cypher key, that doesn't mean that isn't what happened. Our identities have been compromised, and you are being watched. We need to move you both out of this hotel immediately."

"Into your townhouse?" Melody asked in alarm. She would prefer not to have to cohabitate with Fatima if it could be avoided.

"No. If Jemima Edwards and whoever she is working for know about you and Matthew, it's likely they are aware of me as well and that I'm being watched. After all, Melody's bag was snatched on the way to my townhouse. While I wasn't certain the robbery was connected at the time, now I'm not so sure."

Alessandro explained that they all needed to move to a new location discreetly. He suggested they should not only keep their hotel rooms, but that Mary would stay in Melody's and make herself more conspicuous than usual.

"Let Miss Edwards believe you are still here. Meanwhile, I have some-where we can go. Pack a small bag with the essentials, including an outfit for tomorrow if you are determined to join us. I will return home and send Mustafa to meet you at the back of the hotel in an hour. It goes without saying, I am sure, but be careful and discreet."

Five minutes later, Melody had returned to her room and was consulting with Mary. She explained she would be leaving the hotel but needed the other woman to stay on and pretend that both she and Mr Sandworth were still there. It was likely that Mary had many thoughts about this plan, but she kept them to herself.

Then, Melody explained the costume she needed. Mary, an excellent seamstress, quickly described how Melody could appear authentic.

"So, you think my black dress will suffice?"

"Yes. It is conservative, but more importantly, plain and practical. Your hair needs to be pulled back simply so that it is completely out of your face. Oh, and I will give you pins, needles, and some thread. Put some of the pins in your cuff and perhaps thread a needle and place it somewhere obvious on the dress. A good seamstress is always ready to take up a hem, and I'm sure a costume mistress is no different. Oh, and I have a hat and apron you can borrow."

Melody deferred to Mary's expertise in this area, and they soon assembled a costume. Mary then packed a few more items of clothing, and Melody added her lockpicks and revolver to the bag.

"Miss Melody, please be careful," was all Mary said upon seeing these.

"I promise. Now, Mary, I need you to be a bit more conspicuous in the hotel lobby than you have been. Perhaps go to the front desk and make some rather loud requests on my behalf. We have no idea if Miss Edwards is working alone. Regardless, you need to be evidence that I am still in residence." Mary nodded.

Not long after, there was a soft knock on her door. It was Rat, ready with a bag of his own.

"Let's slip out now while it's quiet. We'll go down the back staircase again and let's hope we don't run into anyone."

"And if we do?" Melody asked.

"Let us just hope that we don't."

Fortunately, no members of the hotel staff were in sight, and the siblings managed to slip out through the back door of the hotel. Mustafa was waiting for them in the alley behind.

"Sidi Matthew and Lalla Melody, I am to take you to Sidi Alessandro," the boy said, clearly proud of his role.

They followed Mustafa, who stayed away from main roads and intersections, anywhere they might run into Jemima Edwards. Soon enough, they were in a much poorer, working-class neighbourhood. They walked for a few minutes more before stopping at a rather dilapidated house.

Mustafa hurried up to the front door and knocked on it in a very particular pattern. After a few moments, Alessandro opened the door and quickly waved them in.

CHAPTER 32

After a restless night on a rather uncomfortable mattress, Sunday morning finally arrived. Melody rose and dressed, wearing the clothes she was using for her disguise. Bearing in mind Mary's warning about her hair, she scraped it back into a tight and rather unflattering bun. She tied the apron around her waist and took some pins, placing them in a neat line on her cuff. Mary had already given her a few threaded needles, and she took two and put them through the material of her bodice, then neatly wound the thread around them.

Melody peered into the small, cracked, and rather dirty mirror and decided she looked the part. Mary had suggested that she carry a bag and put some clothes in it so she wouldn't have to find costumes to carry around as she pretended to be busy. Now, Melody emptied her carpetbag, took a chemise and a petticoat, folded them, and put them back in. Then she made her way down to the kitchen to see what was for breakfast.

The previous evening, Alessandro had been rather vague about whose house it was and how he gained access. Whoever owned it seemed to keep it stocked with enough and suitable food for very last-minute stays. There was tea, sugar, some hard biscuits, and flour. Mustafa was sent out to see if he could find any shops still open to buy at least some eggs, bread, and milk. He returned with enough of all three, plus some cheese.

They had assembled a modest yet sufficient evening meal of bread and cheese. This meal included some mediocre wine that Rat had discovered in the pantry. Melody didn't know how to cook and was unsure if Rat did. She was certain Alessandro had never prepared a meal for himself. Perhaps Mustafa would know how to use the remaining supplies to make something for them to eat.

As Melody descended and made her way to the rather dark and dreary kitchen, delightful aromas wafted down the corridor. When she stepped into the kitchen, she was surprised to see Alessandro standing at the stove, tending to something frying in a pan. He looked up as she entered and must have noticed the shock on her face. "I've learned a few things over the years. It seemed practical to know how to cook at least a few basic dishes for myself."

As he said this, Alessandro slid whatever was in the pan onto a plate.

"Eggy bread," Melody said as her stomach gurgled hungrily.

"There's tea in the pot." As Alessandro said this, Rat entered the kitchen with Mustafa at his side.

"I think Mustafa should go to the theatre as soon as possible and monitor the situation. We have no idea if the crates are already there or are being moved this morning." Rat remembered from his own childhood helping Bear and Rat in their thief-taking work that young children were usually overlooked.

Alessandro agreed and suggested that Mustafa eat quickly, then make his way to the theatre. The boy grinned; he was happy to be of service and proud to be entrusted with such an important task. They sat and ate breakfast, which was surprisingly tasty. No one spoke much as they ate, each absorbed in thoughts of the day ahead. Mustafa finished his breakfast and then headed out to the Stadsschouwburg.

"I don't want you to do anything other than observe," Alessandro reminded the boy. "We'll find you when we arrive and you can report on what you've seen." With that, Mustafa was gone.

The group would have preferred to start investigating at the Stadsschouwburg Theatre early in the morning. However, Alessandro advised that he'd made some discreet enquiries, and the crew wouldn't begin to arrive to set up until just after lunch.

"I think the earliest we can plan to get there is perhaps one o'clock," he suggested.

"One? That doesn't leave us much time," Melody complained.

"If we arrive too early, it will seem suspicious," Rat pointed out. Melody knew he was right, but even so, sitting around doing nothing all morning felt wrong.

As painful as the wait was, eventually it was time to leave. Everyone ensured they had their guns, lockpicks, and, in Rat's case, his pocket torch. He also carried a knife.

Just before they left the house, Alessandro reminded them, "Our primary goal is to locate the bomb or its parts, then alert Sir Alan so he can inform the Dutch authorities. Let us not worry too much about politics in this matter and indeed hope that a British attempt to prevent this assassination will speak for itself in the end."

Rat wasn't convinced that this couldn't also be viewed differently: that the British had organised an elaborate hoax to come in at the last minute and save the day. However, he didn't voice this concern; such matters weren't in his remit.

They took the tram to the Stadsschouwburg theatre. They decided they shouldn't be seen together, so Rat and Alessandro stood at the back of the tram, while Melody sat up front.

After exiting the tram, Rat and Alessandro walked ahead while Melody dawdled a little to put some space between them. She clutched her carpetbag tightly against her chest, nervous about what lay before them. The plan was dangerous but necessary: infiltrate the theatre pretending to be backstage staff, locate the planted explosive, and prevent an international incident. She knew that Rat and Alessandro believed there was another crucial element to this plan: to prove once and for all that Germany was responsible for the bomb. No one had any idea how they were going to achieve this.

There was already enough commotion in and around the theatre that it was trivial for Melody to slip in through the stage door. She found a secluded spot in one of the many corridors in which to stash her carpetbag, put her gun and lockpicks in her dress pocket, and then pick up the folded clothes.

Meanwhile. Rat and Alessandro approached from the alley side of the theatre. Dressed in dark, soot-smeared trousers and jackets, they blended in effortlessly among the crew as they filtered in to prepare for the evening's opera.

They stopped outside the theatre and looked around for Mustafa. As they looked, Alessandro said casually, "I have one of my journalists coming later. He'll have a pocket camera with him and I'm hoping he can capture whatever happens here today. Whatever we can and can't persuade the Dutch authorities of, we have the power of the press behind us."

"What is this man going to do? Trail behind us all afternoon?" Rat asked sceptically. Alessandro shrugged.

At that moment, Mustafa appeared beside them. The boy had approached so quietly that neither man realised he was there until he cleared his throat to draw their attention.

"Good lad," Alessandro said softly. "Anything to report?"

"I saw crates taken in twenty minutes ago. I cannot be sure they were the ones Sidi Matthew described, but they came separately from everything else and were taken in by three men who then left immediately after."

"Excellent work." Alessandro wondered whether there was any point in asking the boy to stay or if he had already done everything they needed him to. Finally, he handed him some coins, told him to find something to eat, and then to come back and keep watch for anything suspicious. "Come and find us inside if necessary." Mustafa nodded and then slipped away as silently as he had come.

"You're making the assumption that he'll be able to get into the theatre to find us," Rat pointed out.

"He's a resourceful lad. He'll manage." Again, Rat thought about himself at that age and had to admit Alessandro was right.

Alessandro led the way through the stage door, where they encountered a rather flustered man holding a list clipped to a piece of wood, who asked them a question in Dutch. Alessandro replied in very broken Dutch that was much worse than his usual command of the language, then said something in German.

It didn't seem as if the man with the list spoke German or cared to question them further. Instead, he waved them through. Alessandro said something in his broken Dutch, and Rat grunted and nodded as they slipped into the shadows.

Backstage, people were coming and going in all directions. Rat could hear shouting in Dutch and German as the visiting and local crews hurried about with props and tools. It was hard to believe that a polished performance would emerge from this chaos in less than eight hours. However, Rat assumed this wasn't much different from what it took to stage any theatrical performance, and that both crews must be used to working under these conditions.

Backstage at the Stadsschouwburg was filled with dust and shadow in the early afternoon, hours before the house would open its doors to the evening's audience. The gas lamps had not yet been lit, and the air was cool with the scent of sawdust, varnish, and old clothes. The stage stood empty, the curtain drawn, while a handful of workers moved with the quiet efficiency of those accustomed to the lull before the storm.

Rat and Alessandro entered through the rear entrance into the backstage labyrinth. No one paid them more than a passing glance. There were set builders, lighting riggers, and a harried man pushing a cart filled with props who shouted at them as they crossed his path. Rat noticed a pile of rope with some tools sitting nearby and signalled to Alessandro. They moved towards the pile. Then, Rat grabbed the rope, and Alessandro took a couple of the tools.

"Where should we start?" Rat whispered.

"Well, if the crates the lad saw were the ones you opened, then they were brought in recently. That's good news. I cannot imagine they've been unpacked and a bomb already assembled in such a short time."

Rat nodded; this made sense. However, it didn't answer the question of how they were to locate the crates. "Why don't we make a tour of the theatre and do some reconnaissance to begin with," he suggested. "It occurred to me that the aim might be to have this explosion be quite localised. After all, there will be German citizens in the cast and crew. Surely their government will want to ensure their safety."

"Perhaps," Alessandro responded in an unconvinced tone. "Or perhaps not. I recognise this is a rather cynical view of what countries might do to serve their national interests. However, as we experienced in Morocco, elements within the British are willing to kill and imprison their own to push forward a foreign policy. Is there any reason to think that Germany would behave differently?"

Despite his scepticism, Rat's words did make Alessandro consider where it might be most sensible to place a bomb. "I think a tour is a good idea; I want to see where the Royal Family would be seated. I assume there's a royal box."

CHAPTER 33

I t seemed Melody's disguise was convincing enough; no one challenged
her as she walked through the theatre, carrying the pile of clothes. At
one point, she glimpsed herself in a mirror propped up in a corridor,
waiting to be taken on stage. In her plain dress and apron, with her hair
pulled back and the clothes in her arms, she genuinely looked like she
worked in the costume department.

As much as Alessandro had initially opposed her joining them that
afternoon, he was eventually persuaded, though reluctantly, that a
wardrobe mistress could access different parts of a theatre than propmen
could. However, now that she was actually in the theatre, Melody wasn't
sure where to begin.

They suspected they weren't the only ones pretending to be part of
the crew, and that at least one German in the theatre was assembling the
bomb and executing the rest of the plan. If Rat and Alessandro were
searching for the bomb parts, perhaps she should try to identify this individual. But how?

Melody considered their plan to blend in while doing something other
than working on the sets and costumes. Perhaps she should look for
someone similarly pretending to work. This was easier said than done.

There was also only so long she could wander around holding the same pile of clothes before someone questioned what she was doing!

Finally, she spotted a chair to the side of the stage and decided to sit and watch while pretending to sew. Neither Granny nor Tabby Cat had ever suggested that Melody gain proficiency in any of the usual skills that refined young ladies were expected to know. She couldn't play an instrument, hadn't painted anything since she was in the nursery, and had no idea how to do needlepoint. Instead, she had played chess with Uncle Maxi, learned to fence, and was an excellent shot. In fact, the dowager had insisted that Melody take self-defence lessons.

Until that moment, Melody had questioned no aspect of her education. However, sitting on a chair with a needle and thread in her hand, she hoped no one could actually see what she was doing with it, because her disguise would be utterly unbelievable as soon as they saw the mess she'd made of the chemise.

As she sewed - or rather jabbed her needle into the fabric in a poor imitation of sewing - Melody watched the comings and goings backstage. She wondered if anyone would ask why she was sitting where she was, sewing instead of occupying the usual spot of a wardrobe mistress, but no one did. Perhaps she was benefiting from the convergence of two theatre companies from different countries, each assuming she belonged to the other, who did things a little differently.

After thirty minutes, Melody wondered whether this plan was a waste of time; she had no clue what she was looking for. She hoped Rat and Alessandro were having more luck than she was. Just as she thought this, she saw a woman cross the stage with a pile of clothes; that must be the actual wardrobe mistress.

Suddenly, Melody worried that if anyone was going to question who she was or what she was doing, it would be this woman. The wardrobe mistress stopped to talk to someone, and Melody was just about to stand and move away to a place where she wouldn't be seen, when something about the woman caught her eye. The wardrobe mistress looked very familiar, but why on earth would that be?

Melody stood and moved into the shadows, gaining a better view of the other woman's face. The woman had red hair, which, for some reason, didn't seem right to Melody. She tried to imagine the woman with a different hair colour. As soon as she pictured that face with much darker hair, she realised who the woman was: she was Mevrouw Brenner, Karl Brenner's wife. Of course, the woman might have a job as a wardrobe mistress, but why was her hair a different colour?

She stepped forward slightly to try to hear the conversation and realised that the so-called Widow Brenner was speaking German. Again, there was nothing inherently suspicious about that. Melody assumed many Dutch could speak the language of the neighbouring country.

Melody's German wasn't perfect, but even she could understand what the woman had said: "The materials are here. Get ready for assembly." Get ready for assembly? What did that mean?

The wardrobe mistress began walking away, and Melody decided to follow her. It wasn't easy keeping sight of the woman as she navigated the maze of dark backstage corridors while maintaining a careful distance to avoid being noticed, and more importantly, recognised.

Finally, the woman turned a corner, and by the time Melody had followed at a safe distance, she saw her enter a room. What should she do next? Every instinct told her something was unusual about this situation, but she wasn't sure how to act. That was her last clear thought before she felt a sharp pain in her head and blacked out.

When she woke, she was lying on the floor with her hands and feet bound. Melody could hear voices speaking German. German! Perhaps the woman wasn't Dutch after all. She lay still, keeping her eyes closed, pretending to still be unconscious. The voices were low, and she strained to listen and understand what they were saying.

One word she didn't need to translate was "bomb." Melody was sure the female voice, speaking as she heard that word, was Widow Brenner, and the other was a man. Her mind raced, trying to make sense of what this meant. Was Vermeer not just an informant but working for Germany all along? Is that what was implied? But if that was true, why was he killed?

Melody thought back to what Alessandro had said about Karl Brenner's wife. He'd said that when Brenner didn't return home for two nights, she'd gone to her local police station to report him missing. At that point, they'd had her identify the body. Melody assumed that was how Alessandro's journalist had discovered her address. Would the police have questioned whether the woman was who she claimed to be? Why would they bother? They'd pulled a body out of a canal, and she had conveniently come along and identified it. Melody couldn't imagine the police in London caring much beyond that if the man wasn't someone of significance.

Yet, if she wasn't Brenner's common-law wife, why provide a real address? And when they visited, she was dressed in widow's weeds and appeared quite genuine. Melody even recalled Alessandro remarking on how guileless and honest the woman seemed. Even amidst her fear and confusion, Melody was amused by how ironic it would be if Alessandro, the seasoned operative, turned out to have been so completely mistaken in that judgement.

One thing was certain: Melody had to escape and take this information to Alessandro and Rat. First, these people needed to leave. Trying to make as little noise as possible, Melody tested how well her hands and feet were bound. The rope didn't seem overly tight, and she believed she had a chance of freeing herself. For now, though, she had to lie there and pretend she hadn't woken up.

Soon, the woman left, but the man remained. Melody had nothing to do but review everything they knew, or thought they knew. She kept returning to what William had told her: "I became worried that Vermeer had been compromised. I was concerned about the authenticity of the false flag information; some of it seemed too perfect."

Melody vividly remembered his words. He'd suspected Vermeer had been compromised and had warned the Foreign Office, who not only ignored the warning but also dismissed him. Was this how the informant had been compromised, through his wife? Or was the woman even that? Melody considered again that there was no reason to believe that was who she was, except that she'd told the police that story. A story she'd repeated to Melody and Alessandro.

If the woman wasn't his wife, why had she stayed in that house as his widow? Melody's eyes opened with a start. If she could have sat upright with surprise, she would have. What if she'd stayed in that house waiting for them? What if she'd known they would come? Even if Brenner, the man they'd known as Vermeer, was who he claimed to be, William worried he'd been compromised. Perhaps that was why he'd been killed. Maybe this woman had killed him and then gone to the police pretending to be his wife. She'd given an address and then waited, somehow knowing that Alessandro would discover it and visit.

Then, Melody thought about the story the woman had told about Vermeer. It had been so convincing. Perhaps it was even true. Certainly, it made the informant credible and kept them all following the trail he had left. Then, she reconsidered William's words that the information seemed too perfect. She thought about how easily Rat had found the crates at the docks. Not too easily to be immediately suspicious, but easily enough. He'd assumed it was luck, but what if it wasn't?

Melody realised she needed to escape and find Rat and Alessandro. As if answering her prayer, at that moment, the man rose and left the room. Finally, she had the opportunity she needed.

As soon as Melody began wriggling her hands, she realised how badly they were bound. She pushed herself towards a wall and managed to get upright. Then, she leaned down to her hands and started using her teeth to unravel the knot. It was lucky they hadn't bound them behind her back. It took some time, but eventually, she was able to undo the knot and free her hands. From there, it didn't take long to free her equally badly bound feet. Standing up, she checked her pocket, hoping her lockpicks hadn't been taken. Relieved, she found they were still in one pocket and her revolver was still in the other.

The door was locked, as expected, but easy to pick. It only took a few minutes for Melody to free herself. Now, she had to find Alessandro and Rat without running into the man and woman who had tied her up. She knew what the woman looked like but hadn't been able to see much of the man from where she'd been lying, pretending not to be conscious. The only thing she had seen was that his boots looked new and not at all the kind of footwear she'd expect stagehands to own or certainly not to wear to work. It wasn't much to go on, but it was something.

CHAPTER 34

R at and Alessandro discovered they could move around the theatre freely, with no challenge. Carrying the rope and tools, it was credible that they'd been sent by someone to fix something. Certainly, it was believable enough that other busy workers had no interest in looking up from their labours and asking questions.

They made their way through the backstage area, weaving past crates of set pieces and stacks of painted props. Their plan was straightforward: search the theatre from top to bottom for evidence of bomb materials, false compartments, or anything that looked out of place. The German plan might depend on hiding something in plain sight.

"Should we split up?" Rat asked.

Although doubling the area they might otherwise search if they stayed together seemed logical, there was the language barrier if Rat was challenged, and also the concern about what one of them would do alone if he encountered something suspicious. While time was critical, they risked wasting a lot of time searching for each other if they separated, so they decided to search together.

"I know that we have a working hypothesis that the Germans won't be prepared to blow up the entire theatre because of the German theatre company, but I don't think we should let that stop us from searching the stage thoroughly," Alessandro said carefully.

"What do you suggest?" Rat asked.

Alessandro looked upwards at the rafters above the stage. Rat followed his gaze upwards. From the stage floor of the Stadsschouwburg, looking up into the fly loft of the theatre, it appeared like a chaotic jumble of rafters, ropes, and pulleys. Thick hemp lines hung in ordered rows, stretching from the beams overhead down to the stage floor, each connected to backdrops, curtains, or pieces of suspended scenery. Some quivered with tension, others hung slack, swaying ever so slightly with the draft.

If Rat squinted, he could see the narrow wooden catwalks that stretched across the fly loft like rickety bridges. Standing on those catwalks, stagehands moved silently along narrow planks, checking rigging or preparing the next cue. A few thin beams of daylight filtered through rigging windows up high near the roof, catching the dust and creating a haze that made the space feel dreamlike and vast.

"Do you really think that's where they're planning to put the bomb?" Rat asked sceptically. "Apart from anything else, there are quite a few people up there working. I can't imagine it would be simple for someone to get up there and set something up without being noticed and challenged." While Rat genuinely felt this, he also had little desire to climb up to and then balance on those rafters. He wouldn't have said he had a fear of great heights so much as a sensible awareness of his balance and coordination skills.

Of course, Rat thought, Alessandro might have been offering to be the one to climb up to the fly loft. However, it seemed that was not the case. Instead, Alessandro said, "Perhaps you're right. Let us start with the areas around the royal box. You can always go up if we don't find something."

Both men looked out towards where the audience would be seated later that day. As was usually the case, it looked as if the royal box was centred in the first balcony tier, directly opposite the stage, offering the best view in the house. Like most of the theatres in London's West End, this box was easily distinguishable by its decorative elements, grander design, and gilt trim.

Rat looked around them. Everywhere, workers were busy. The entire stage and what they could see of backstage were a hive of activity. Men were hammering, moving props, and yelling from the rafters. It was as good a time as any to move.

They walked down from the stage, skirted the edge of the stalls, and exited through the door. Once out in the hall, they glanced around to ensure no one was nearby, then slipped into the grand stairwell that led to the tiers above. Gas wall lamps hissed faintly, unlit but ready, their mantles waiting for the theatre's gas master to pass with his taper before that evening's performance.

The theatre was very ornate; polished marble, grand and wide, swept upward in elegant curves. At the first landing, a massive mirror reflected the two of them in their disguises, with their caps pulled low on their heads. They didn't look any different from the many other men working.

"How are we going to manage this?" Rat asked as they passed gilt-framed portraits of long-dead impresarios. "Won't the royal box be locked? And guarded, tonight of all nights?"

"Exactly," Alessandro said. "If I were hiding something explosive meant to cause a scandal, I'd put it somewhere symbolic. Somewhere guaranteed to draw attention. And what's better than blowing up the queen's box? But the bomb doesn't have to be in the box itself to cause damage. So we need to look out for anywhere nearby."

Rat didn't argue. They reached the first balcony tier, its wide hallway carpeted in deep blue with gold trim. Here, the theatre's grandeur was most evident: double doors lined the inner wall, each leading to private boxes. Floral plasterwork curled across the ceiling like vines. A pair of golden sconces flanked the central royal box, its door larger, with a subtle crown motif carved above.

Rat slowed down. The corridor was empty, but a faint humming echoed from somewhere nearby. Someone was humming a tune, however badly.

Alessandro held up a hand. "Someone's here."

They pressed against the wall, creeping forward. The humming grew louder, until they finally saw their singer: a porter in a waistcoat too tight for his belly, holding a feather duster in one hand and a tin of polish in the other. He was swaying on his feet as he wiped down the balustrade outside the royal box, unaware of the intruders. They faced a choice: wait for him to move on, or stroll in as if they had been given a task to do.

Making a decision, Alessandro stepped out. He began speaking in German to indicate that he wasn't one of the Dutch workers. Then, quickly apologised in Dutch and switched his language. He hoped that anything that didn't sound like a typical worker's accent when he spoke German would be explained in this way.

The porter was startled by his words, nearly dropping his tin. "What...? Who...?" he said in Dutch.

"Stage crew," Alessandro replied. "Special inspection. They're worried the structure beneath the royal box might be..." For a moment, he couldn't think what the right word was in Dutch. Then it came to him, "that it might be compromised."

The man frowned. "No one told me anything about that."

"Course not," Alessandro said smoothly. "They're trying to be discreet because no one wants to take the blame that this hasn't been dealt with until tonight. They're concerned about vibrations from the new drop curtain system. Apparently, the foundation underneath this side isn't quite level."

This seemed to persuade him.

"I always said it didn't feel right," the porter muttered, nodding. "Feels like it sways when people laugh too hard. Can't have that when the royals are here tonight, can we?"

He turned and waddled away towards the stairwell, humming again. They waited until he was out of sight before moving to the royal box door.

Unsurprisingly, it was locked. "Of course it is," Rat muttered, pulling a thin roll from his coat pocket. He selected two narrow tools and crouched. "Keep an ear out."

"That it's locked makes it even less likely they are planning to assemble a bomb in the box itself," Alessandro pointed out. "But we need to be thorough, just in case."

The lock was old, well-made, but finicky. Rat's fingers carefully worked the tumblers, persuading rather than forcing. The stakes were higher than usual: if they were caught breaking into the royal box, they'd find it difficult to explain themselves convincingly. And Alessandro wasn't certain Sir Alan would vouch for them.

Finally, Rat heard a soft click, followed by another. He turned the handle, and the door creaked open slightly. Rat slipped in first, and Alessandro followed, gently shutting the door behind them. Fortunately, the entire audience section was in darkness; there was no need to light it until closer to the time when the doors opened.

It was a luxurious private chamber decorated in cream and gold, with a thick carpet and velvet banquette seating. A single chaise longue stood at the back, beneath an oil painting of Queen Wilhelmina as a girl. Gilded railings overlooked the stage directly. The view was perfectly centred on the stage. Although it was quite dark, the men worried about being seen and tried to stay as low to the ground as possible.

Rat pulled out his torch, but hesitated to use it. They moved swiftly, checking by feel where possible beneath seats, behind wall panels, and along the skirting boards. Then Alessandro frowned. He crouched beside the side wall and ran his fingers along a small air vent just above the floor. He pulled, and the vent came loose.

"Give me your torch," he said to Rat. Then, he crouched as far as he could and shone it into the air vent that had made him suspicious.

"Anything there?" Rat asked eagerly.

"Nothing," Alessandro sighed.

They searched every inch of the royal box, but found nothing except some mouse droppings. Even though they hadn't expected to find the bomb so easily or in the royal box, it was still frustrating. Rat took out his pocket watch, which he had tucked into his jacket pocket, as it was far too valuable to be owned by a theatre worker. It was now nearly half-past two. If they hoped to find evidence of a bombing and then convince Sir Alan of it, they'd better hope they discovered something soon.

Rat cracked the door to the box to check if anyone was in the corridor. It was empty, so he and Alessandro silently slipped out, and Rat locked the door again. They looked along the hallway in both directions. Where would it make sense to leave a bomb to ensure maximum damage to the royal box?

They began examining the doorways leading off the corridor. Most opened into other boxes. However, one, on the opposite side of the corridor, was locked. Rat quickly picked the lock. The door opened onto what appeared to be a small, opulent drawing room. There were silk-covered couches and chairs, as well as paintings all around the walls.

As Alessandro examined the paintings, he said, "I believe there is a painting of every Dutch king or queen going back years. I think this is the royal reception area."

Rat had no idea what such a thing was, so Alessandro explained. "The Queen and her guests will be shown in here when they arrive at the theatre. There will also be refreshments laid out during the intermissions." As Rat looked around, this made sense. He could see that some champagne flutes were already on a table in the corner.

As Rat looked at the cloth-covered table, he realised he could see something beneath it, barely visible under the cloth. He approached and pulled back the cloth, revealing a crate. Then the men pulled out the crate, which clearly showed the ZKL-3 markings.

"This is it!" Rat exclaimed. Just as he was about to open the crate to inspect it, they heard a noise. Both men froze; was it the porter returning? It appeared to be, but he wasn't alone this time. He had two burly looking men with him.

Rat couldn't understand what was said, but from the expressions on the men's faces and the tone of voice they used, this wasn't good. They spoke to Alessandro in Dutch, and he replied. He shrugged his shoulders, spread his hands, and seemed to be doing his best impersonation of a workman, just doing what he was told to do.

The three burly men conferred briefly, and then one of them grabbed Rat by his jacket while the other seized Alessandro. Rat's first instinct was to try to shake the man's hand off and run, or fight. However, a quick shake of Alessandro's head told him not to attempt this.

Rat and Alessandro hadn't been able to get much information from the men who had taken them. Now, they were led into an office that looked as if it probably belonged to the company director. There was a desk with two chairs in front of it. Sitting behind the desk was a harried-looking man who had one pair of spectacles on top of his head, and another perched on the bridge of his nose. He had little hair on his head, but what little there was seemed to be standing up in every direction.

The man looked up as they were brought into the room. He said something in Dutch, and one man addressed him as Directeur. Then, the man turned to Alessandro and Rat and said something in Dutch.

Would Alessandro continue pretending that they were workers? Rat wondered. Of course, the director of the company would know they didn't work for him. Was it worth trying to convince him they were part of the German company? It seemed not, as Alessandro appeared to be claiming they were British.

"So, what are two Englishmen doing sneaking around my theatre, pretending to be workers?" the director asked in flawless English.

Alessandro glanced briefly at Rat before saying, "We have reason to believe that a bomb is going to be detonated tonight in this theatre."

While Rat was surprised that Alessandro had been so blunt, he understood that they had little choice but to hope the shock of this news would grab the director's attention. It seemed to have worked. The director sat back in his chair and pushed the second pair of glasses up onto his head to join the pair already there.

In an incredulous tone, he said, "A bomb you say? And who is going to be detonating this bomb?"

"Germany," Rat replied, before considering what he was saying.

The director laughed sardonically. "So, you expect me to believe that Germany is planning to blow up its own theatre company tonight? Why would they do that?"

What was a credible reason? While the false flag plot made sense if you knew the entire backstory, it was hardly suitable for them to reveal that to some random Dutchman.

"It doesn't matter if you believe us. We found the crate containing the bomb parts upstairs in the room these men found us in. Go and see for yourself," Rat explained. He then briefly described where they had found it in the room.

The director said something to one of the men who'd escorted them down. He left the room, presumably to find the crate, closing the door behind him.

"While we wait for Johan to return, why don't you tell me how you came to know about this so-called bomb?"

Rat returned Alessandro's glance; he didn't want to be the one to decide what should be revealed. He suspected Alessandro had far more experience dealing with this sort of situation than he did.

Instead of answering that question, Alessandro said, "Please contact the British Envoy, Sir Alan Vanden-Bempde-Johnstone, who heads up the British legation. I can give you the address."

In a voice that dripped with sarcasm, the director asked, "And will this Sir Alan fellow tell me why two Englishmen are looking for a bomb in my theatre?" When neither man answered, he continued, "Well, let us take things one step at a time and see what Johan finds."

Five minutes later, Johan returned. While Rat couldn't understand what he said, the anxious look on Alessandro's face spoke volumes.

"There is no crate and certainly no bomb," the director said caustically, confirming Rat's worst fears: someone had taken the bomb parts and might be constructing it already. How had they managed to get the crate out in the short time since he and Alessandro had been discovered in the room?

He voiced his fears to the director, who laughed. "So, someone was watching out and as soon as they saw Johan and Pieter march you out of the royal reception room, they ran in and moved this crate? How convenient."

"Why would we lie about this?" Rat pleaded.

Alessandro appeared as stunned by this turn of events as Rat. "Please, contact Sir Alan." As almost an afterthought, he added, "Directeur, please consider the worst-case scenario if we are correct: we believe the aim is to harm the Dutch Royal Family. If we are mistaken, then you may face a little embarrassment, but if we are right, you are the person who was warned about an assassination attempt on your queen and ignored it."

This seemed to be persuasive. "Write a note and the address. You seem to believe this Sir Alan will vouch for you, so let us see if he comes when you summon him."

All Rat and Alessandro could hope was that Sir Alan would, in fact, answer the note.

CHAPTER 35

It would not be easy navigating backstage while searching for Rat and Alessandro, and staying clear of the false Widow Brenner and her associate. Melody didn't know how far into the backstage area she had been taken after being knocked unconscious. She took several wrong turns before finally finding a corridor she thought she recognised. Except it turned out she didn't.

Eventually, she reached a staircase. She couldn't imagine where it could lead, unless she had been taken down to a basement, yet this one led up to the main stage area. She climbed quietly and carefully. At the top, there was a black door. To her relief, it was unlocked. Melody pushed it open and realised she had been right; she had been taken downstairs. Now, she had a clearer sense of her location.

Carefully and keeping to the shadows as much as possible, Melody crept along the corridor. She was about to turn a corner when she heard voices. Was the man speaking Dutch Alessandro? Melody peered around the corner and saw Rat and Alessandro being marched into an office. She heard more voices. While she couldn't understand what was being said, she caught the phrase, 'Mijnheer de Directeur', and assumed they'd been taken to the office of the theatre director.

Now what? she wondered. Had they discovered the bomb? Were they about to be arrested? How would they prevent the assassination now?

Of immediate concern was what she should do next. Was there any point in continuing to sneak around the theatre? Suddenly, she wished William was there with her. Confusion and worry threatened to over-whelm her. Unsure of what to do next, Melody decided to make her way out of the theatre and speak to Mustafa. Of course, she couldn't imagine the boy would have any more idea what to do than she did, but she felt the need to speak to someone, at least.

It turned out to be simple enough to make her way back to the stage door. Stepping outside, she was momentarily blinded by the bright sunlight after the gloom of the backstage corridors. As her eyes adjusted to the glare, she looked around for Mustafa. Though she didn't see him immediately, Melody finally spotted him leaning against the neighbouring building.

As Melody approached Mustafa, he looked up anxiously. "Lalla Melody, I am so pleased to see you. I wasn't sure whether to come in and try to find you."

"Why? What has happened, Mustafa?"

In a quiet voice, the boy explained, "I believe I just saw the crate brought out that was taken in this morning."

Melody considered his words. What did they mean? It was possible the bomb parts had been taken out and were being assembled, and now they were simply disposing of the crate. Though why bother?

"Did you see what happened to it?" she asked.

"It was loaded onto a transport wagon and driven away," Mustafa explained. Melody closed her eyes, hoping inspiration would find her. The crate had vanished; Rat and Alessandro appeared to be under some kind of arrest, and after seeing the woman they had believed was Vermeer's wife, she wasn't even sure what of the investigation was real.

It was a sign of her desperation when Melody asked Mustafa, "What should I do? I feel as if I have most of the pieces of a puzzle, but I am running out of time to put them together. Mr Sandworth and Conte Foscari have been captured, and I am unsure of what our next move should be."

"I do not know, Lalla Melody," the young boy said seriously, his eyes wide with alarm at the panic in her voice.

"Let me help," a calm, steady voice said from behind them.

Melody started. How had she not noticed that they had been watched?

A figure stepped out from the shadows. Like Rat and Alessandro, the man was dressed as the other theatre workers and wore a flat cap pulled low over his forehead. Nevertheless, Melody recognised him instantly and sighed in relief.

"William! You have no idea how glad I am to see you." Melody had to stop herself from rushing into his arms. "How did you know to be here?"

"I've been watching you all closely," was all Somerset said.

"And we thought we were being so careful, and even changed accommodation," Melody said as much to herself as anyone. She quickly and quietly outlined everything they thought they'd discovered, what they believed was planned, and then what had happened since they'd arrived at the theatre.

Melody explained how a woman claiming to be Karl Brenner's wife had identified his body at the police station, and that Alessandro had discovered this and obtained an address for the woman through one of his journalists.

She continued, "But now I wonder if she was his wife at all or merely set up as such to lure us down a particular path."

"So, you were taken captive by a woman who had previously been posing as Vermeer's wife?" Somerset asked thoughtfully. "Was this woman the wardrobe mistress?"

"Yes! How did you know that?"

"Because I crept into the theatre and saw her. The woman is a German operative, who goes by the name Helga Meier. The Germans have been very clever and Foscari just walked into their trap," Somerset said with a trace of bitterness.

"My brother uncovered shipments containing bomb parts at the docks, which Mustafa saw unloaded here and taken into the theatre this morning. However, he just saw what looked like those same crates loaded back onto a transport wagon and taken away." Realising she hadn't yet told him one of the more critical parts of the story, Melody then described what she'd seen in the corridor a few minutes ago when it seemed Rat and Alessandro had been apprehended.

"I don't believe that anyone in the Foreign Office or British Intelligence realised that Helga Meier was in Amsterdam," Somerset explained. "The woman is a brilliant and ruthless operative. Knowing that she is involved helps explain what has been going on. I think the entire thing from beginning to end has been a trap."

"Everything? Every false-flag operation?" Melody asked in amazement.

"We may never know for sure. Perhaps Vermeer was a genuine informant, or perhaps he was meant to feed me compromised information from the start."

"Surely that he was murdered implies that he was who he said he was," she suggested. Somerset's only response was a shrug of his shoulders. As Melody considered the timeline William had provided her in the botanical gardens, she pointed out, "So, at some point, Germany knew that Matthew and Alessandro had been given this mission. How would they find out?"

Somerset shrugged again, but then said ruefully, "Perhaps we are far less subtle than we believe. More likely, Germany has a mole somewhere in the Foreign Office or British Intelligence. If not, they must have a way of intercepting our communications because you're right, they seemed to have known that your brother and Conte Foscari were the specific operatives who would be sent in my stead. They even knew, or anticipated, which hotel you were to stay in. In either case, I need to get word back to Whitehall as soon as possible."

The entire situation was so convoluted, and Melody felt a headache coming on just from trying to wrap her mind around its twists and turns. However, this wasn't the time to give in to a fit of the vapours; they had to stop a bomb going off and free Alessandro and Rat.

Melody shared her thoughts with William, who shook his head. "I do not believe there is a bomb." He said this with great certainty, yet could they be so sure? "The entire bomb plot has been theatre. There was never meant to be an explosion, only a crisis the British would rush to solve in front of the Dutch. I think that Vermeer figured at least some of this out, and that is why he was killed."

While she wished to believe in William, Melody couldn't help herself.

"And what if you're wrong?" Then, she recalled Alessandro's words before they left the house. "The plan was to contact the British Legation, a Sir Alan, and have him summon the Dutch authorities."

Everything they knew, or thought they knew, was swirling around in Melody's head. Had anything been what it seemed? What could they prove?

"The manifests, the cypher key, was any of it real? If we're right, then this Helga Meier went to the police and claimed to be Karl Brenner's Dutch common-law wife, yet now is here, working as a wardrobe mistress as part of the German theatre company. She is tangible evidence that Germany has been involved in this from the beginning. We need to have her restrained and get her in front of the Dutch authorities, who will surely recognise her from when she identified the body."

William looked sceptical. "It isn't that it's not a decent idea, Melody. However, these people are professionals. They'll vanish as quietly as they arrived, before anyone can ask the right questions. They may already be gone. They've been two steps ahead of us throughout all this. There's no reason to believe they haven't anticipated this move as well."

Melody considered William's words. "I don't think Helga is going anywhere until this operation is complete. At least not if she's the mastermind behind it that she seems to be. After all, it's still possible that Alessandro and Matthew will be kicked out of the theatre and totally ignored. Then, what have the Germans achieved except to irritate Britain and waste the time of some of its operatives?"

"You're right, Melody. However, we can't just confront her directly; she is far too wily to allow that to happen. And anyway, she knows who you are and that you're here. We need to trap her somehow. I just have no idea how. I wish we knew who was working with her. Given that the visiting company is German, it could be anyone within it. Certainly, the idea of installing their operative as the wardrobe mistress was both brilliant and easy to execute."

Melody reflected on what they knew and how they had been manipulated so far. Suddenly, her mental fog cleared, and she believed she understood what was happening. "As you said, the Germans have been two steps ahead of us throughout. Is there any reason to believe they still aren't?"

Wiliam conceded that. Melody pressed her point. "They led us here.

They know our beliefs because they supplied us with the information that underpins them. They want us to involve the Dutch authorities and cause a fuss."

"But perhaps you are right and we can prove that Helga Meier pretended to be Karl Brenner's wife," William insisted.

"Can we? Do you truly believe that our word will hold much weight? And as for whichever policeman she spoke to, I am certain she was clever enough to disguise herself. She knew this was all going to happen. Why would she leave such an obvious flaw in her plan?"

William sighed in frustration, but he could see Melody's point. "Then what do we do?"

"Nothing."

"Nothing?"

Melody smiled. "I have a plan. We need to go to the British Legation and ensure that Sir Alan doesn't contact the Dutch authorities no matter what he is told. And then, we do nothing." She addressed Mustafa. "I need you to go into the theatre and keep watch. Sidi Matthew and Sidi Alessandro have been taken into an office. If they are taken from there before we return, I need you to follow them. But be careful. Do not put yourself in harm's way."

She did her best to describe the way she had come from the corridor where she had seen Alessandro and Rat being taken. After she gave the boy yet another direction to be careful, Melody let him go, and he slipped inside.

It was clear from the look on his face that William wasn't entirely convinced by Melody's plan, but he didn't argue, and as soon as Mustafa had disappeared inside of the theatre, they left.

CHAPTER 36

Melody and William were fortunate and hailed a cab easily, and ten minutes later, they pulled up outside the British Legation. In their disguises, they found it harder to gain entry than they might otherwise have done. It took a lot of persuasion and threats of dire consequences before the butler hesitantly opened the door and allowed them to wait in the drawing room.

"I will let Sir Alan know you are here," the man said in a tone of great condescension that left no doubt of what he thought of them sitting on the expensive silk chairs.

Five minutes later, Sir Alan entered the room. He looked them both up and down rather dismissively. "Who are you and what is this about? I hope it's no more hokum about German plots and bombs."

Melody and William exchanged glances; this didn't bode well.

"I am Captain William Somerset, and I work for the Foreign Office."

Sir Alan's expression softened slightly. "Somerset, you say? Any relation to Sir Edward's private secretary?"

"Adam is my brother."

"What ho!" Sir Alan said, his face breaking into a grin. "So, you're George's son, are you? Which one are you now? Five of you boys, if I remember."

"Six, actually. I'm the youngest."

"Are you now? Your father and I were at Eton together. Fine cricket player."

Melody felt relief at this unexpected turn of events, but was also eager for the pleasantries to end so they could focus on the matter at hand. She looked at William and raised her eyebrows slightly, hoping to prompt him to keep things moving.

William understood her point. "Sir Alan, we need your help."

"Anything for Georgie Somerset's boy."

They explained what they needed. Sir Alan listened, shaking his head occasionally but saying nothing.

"So, the other day, I had two chappies from something called the Secret Service Office... wait, no, Bureau here. They were begging me to contact the Dutch authorities, and now you're asking me not to. Do I have that right?"

"Yes. That's correct. We had reason to believe a bomb was being planted in the Stadsschouwburg Theatre to explode when the Royal Family is there tonight," William explained.

"Indeed. This is what those other two told me. Yet they had no evidence to support that, and I told them I wouldn't do anything without something more concrete to go on. Britain is walking on eggshells in the Netherlands. The concern is that the slightest thing could tip them in Germany's direction. Certainly, making a big fuss and pointing fingers with no proof is hardly something anyone will thank me for doing."

"I understand, sir," William said respectfully. "And if we had time, I would explain in more detail what we believe is happening. However, we don't. So, please take my word for it that you may be asked to intervene, and I am asking you not to."

"So, you are asking me not to do something I wasn't planning to do anyway?" Sir Alan asked with a shake of his head. "I think I can agree to that." His smile made clear that Sir Alan was nonplussed by the entire conversation.

Perhaps they needn't have come, Melody thought. It didn't seem as if the man was inclined to do anything, anyway. However, they had no idea how persuasive Rat and Alessandro had been during their conversation with the theatre director. Perhaps they had found the bomb and explained the situation. Perhaps the director suspected them of planting it, and they had pleaded with him to contact Sir Alan and ask him to ensure the Dutch authorities were alerted, as well as vouching for them. Certainly, she could see they would be eager to have the British Legation firmly established as the ones who had saved the day.

"Is there anything else?" Sir Alan asked. "Perhaps a glass of sherry? You can catch me up on how old Georgie is doing these days."

No sooner had Sir Alan asked this than there was a tap at the door. The butler entered and handed Sir Alan a note, which he unfolded, read, then refolded.

"Damndest thing, I have just been called to the Stadsschouwburg by the company director. Apparently, there is the threat of a bomb and two men who claim to be British and want me to vouch for them. If I can do that, then I should bring the Dutch authorities with me."

Melody and William sighed with relief at having arrived before the note.

"Indeed, sir," William said in a respectful but firm voice. "And I am asking that you don't contact the Dutch authorities."

Sir Alan shook his head. "I really do not know what to make of all this. If you weren't George Somerset's lad, I'd be inclined to wash my hands of all of you."

"I appreciate that, sir. I believe it will be enough to reply to the note, vouch for Mr Sandworth and Conte Foscari, and request their release."

"I suppose I can do that," Sir Alan said with another shake of his head. It might be time for retirement, he thought, as he sat at the writing desk in the corner of the room to reply to the note. He gave the note to the butler, who presented it to the man waiting in the vestibule.

It seemed Sir Alan would have been happy to pour that sherry or order tea and sit and reminisce with them about his school days with William's father. However, eventually, they managed to make their excuses and rush back to the theatre.

Melody and William returned to outside of the stage door. What should they do now? Should they go back into the theatre? As they considered their options, a large, out-of-breath man appeared. He wasn't dressed like one of the backstage workers, so they hoped he was the person who had brought the note and had now returned to the theatre.

The man entered the building, and William and Melody looked at each other. Should they just wait? They stood there for a few minutes. Finally, just as they worried that something had gone wrong, the stage door opened, and Rat and Alessandro were led out by the man who had delivered the note. He said something forcefully in Dutch before slamming the door shut behind him, leaving the two men blinking in the sunlight.

When Alessandro realised that not only was Melody waiting for them but also that they were in the company of William, he snarled, "What is he doing here?"

"He is helping to save you both and, more to the point, trying to salvage something out of this situation for Britain," Melody said indignantly.

"And how exactly is he doing that? With more of his nonsense? Is that what he's been telling you, Melody? That this entire situation was contrived by Germany? The Foreign Office didn't believe it when he first said it, and I doubt anyone will believe it now." Then, turning to address William, Alessandro said in the nastiest tone, "You should have slunk back to London with your tail between your legs while you had the chance, Somerset."

"Enough!" Melody commanded. "And this is not the place to discuss this. Let us return to your townhouse, and Captain Somerset and I can explain everything to you."

It seemed as if Alessandro was about to continue arguing, but Rat placed a hand on his arm. "She is right. We should not be discussing any of this here."

"We just need to wait for Mustafa," Melody explained. "He went inside to keep an eye out for what was happening to you. He is probably making his way out."

Twenty minutes later, the boy still hadn't emerged from the theatre.

Mustafa had survived enough time alone on the streets of Casablanca to know how to stay hidden when needed. He had no trouble sneaking through the theatre's corridors, which were sufficiently dark to make the task much easier than it had been in the sunlit streets of the Medina.

Melody's instructions had been clear enough, and soon enough, the boy found himself in the corridor she had described. He made his way to the door. Over the past few months, the boy had been learning to read in English and knew enough letters to recognise the word Directeur.

As he listened at the door, Mustafa heard Alessandro's voice and then Rat's. The boy felt too exposed to stay there, so he moved to the corner where Melody had hidden earlier and waited in a dark shadow, crouching low enough that someone passing by might not notice him. He sat there for some time, listening, watching, and waiting.

Suddenly, Mustafa heard someone walking down the corridor towards him and tried to make himself even smaller and less conspicuous. As the footsteps drew nearer, Mustafa glanced up. Not only could the boy remember any writing or drawing he was shown, but he could also recall any face he had seen, however briefly, and he realised he had seen this face before. He immediately recognised it, but in a very different setting: the hotel. This man had been at the front desk of the hotel when he visited Lalla Melody the other day.

Mustafa was a quick child and realised that something was wrong; a man working in a hotel didn't suddenly appear backstage at a theatre. While Mustafa didn't know exactly what the adults were working on, he understood enough to know they were trying to prevent something terrible from happening. The brief conversation he'd overheard between Melody and Somerset outside the theatre made that clear enough.

Now, Mustafa made a decision: he needed to follow this man. Although it wasn't what Lalla Melody had instructed him to do, his instincts told him this was important. He waited until the man had passed him and turned the corner, then stepped out of the shadows and silently followed him. The man navigated the maze of corridors until he reached a collection of props. Keeping his distance, he watched a red-haired woman join the man. While he couldn't understand what the two were saying, Mustafa could hear enough to know they were speaking German. Of course, the visiting theatre company was from Germany, so this wasn't suspicious in and of itself.

If their tone of voice was any indication, the man and woman were arguing. She appeared to be in charge and was berating him. Mustafa remembered what Lalla Melody and Captain Somerset had just been discussing; was this woman the Helga Meier they were talking about?

Then, the woman handed the man a note. After speaking sharply to him once more, she turned and walked away. The man slid the note into his jacket pocket.

The second time Mustafa had encountered Alessandro in Casablanca, the latter had accused him of trying to pick his pocket. Mustafa had adamantly denied it. While it was true that he was not attempting to pickpocket on that occasion, it was also true that Mustafa had become quite skilled at it since he was orphaned and had to fend for himself. Now, he considered how he might put that skill to use.

He needed to see that note.

Mustafa looked around. A bundle of wooden prop poles, wrapped in old muslin, was leaning nearby. He grabbed it and stumbled forward just as the man stepped into the light. The boy collided with the man's chest, poles clattering between them.

The man shouted something in German as he struggled to regain his balance. "Pardon, meneer," Mustafa muttered, reaching out one hand to steady the man's arm, while his other hand smoothly slipped into his jacket pocket. His fingers closed around the folded note and skilfully slipped it free.

Mustafa's light touch hadn't been enough to stop the man from falling. As he hit the ground, he shouted again. Mustafa turned away briefly to look at the note. Then, he bent down as if to help the man up. As he did so, he slipped the note back into his jacket pocket. The man pushed him away and stood up on his own. Then, spitting one final German curse in Mustafa's direction, he stormed off.

By the time Mustafa returned to the office where Alessandro and Rat were being held, the door was open, and no one was inside. What did this signify? Where had Sidi Sandworth and Sidi Alessandro been taken? Mustafa's heart sank. While he didn't regret following the man, he had failed to keep watch as he was instructed.

He was unsure of his next move. Eventually, Mustafa decided to leave the theatre to check if Lalla Melody had returned. He would admit his mistake and accept any reprimand he received. With a heavy heart, Mustafa made his way out of the theatre. Did this mean he would be banished from Sidi Alessandro's household? He reached the stage door and paused for a moment before leaving. Mustafa was deeply grateful for the new life he had been unexpectedly given. He wasn't ready for that life to be taken away from him. However, his mother had taught him the importance of honour. The honourable thing was to tell the truth and admit he had not followed the instructions he'd been given.

As Mustafa exited the theatre, it took him a moment for his eyes to adjust. Before he even realised who was standing in front of him, he found himself pulled into an embrace.

"Thank heavens you are safe," Melody exclaimed. "We were so worried when you didn't follow them out."

Pulling away slightly from the embrace, Mustafa looked up and confessed everything. Then, he hung his head, waiting for his scolding.

"So, the man you followed was someone you recognised from the front desk of the hotel?" Mustafa nodded before describing what the man looked like. "Robert!" she exclaimed in surprise.

Whatever his punishment was destined to be, it appeared it would be decided later. Instead of berating him, the group left the theatre with the boy's hand held tightly in Melody's.

Back at Alessandro's townhouse, Fatima opened the door. Melody noticed that Rat coloured slightly upon seeing her and was surprised by how sad she felt about Jemima Edward's duplicity. She would have liked her brother to have a romance to distract him from this woman, even if it was with someone as irritating as Jemima had appeared to be.

If Fatima was curious about where Alessandro had been all night or what they had been doing, she said nothing. However, her eyes lit up as William entered the house.

"Captain Somerset," Fatima purred. "What an unexpected surprise." When Melody first met William, she was at a party in Morocco with Fatima beside her. Contrary to all expectations, he had barely glanced at the beautiful Moroccan woman and had focused all his attention on Melody. It seemed Fatima had either forgotten that rebuff or taken it as a challenge.

Despite William's earlier disinterest in Fatima, Melody's heart sank; she was all too aware of the effect Fatima's focused flirtation had on most men. It seemed that even her seemingly domestic cosiness with Alessandro didn't stop her from directing the heat of her sultry gaze on a new victim.

William's eyes flicked up to Fatima's face at her greeting. "Ah, Miss Amrani," he said stiffly. Melody knew it was petty of her, but she couldn't help smiling at Fatima's clear displeasure at further proof of how immune William was to her charms.

Fatima sniffed, said, "I will send in some refreshments," then turned and left.

The group proceeded to the drawing room. They had spoken little on the tram journey there. Now, as they all took their seats, Alessandro asked Mustafa to repeat what he had muttered to Melody outside the theatre.

The boy explained once more how he recognised the man and followed him to where he met a red-haired woman, who then passed him a note.

"And you got a look at this note?" Alessandro asked.

Mustafa nodded. "I picked up some poles and then bumped into this Robert. He fell, and I managed to get the note out of his pocket and look at it." If this reminded Alessandro of how he first met Mustafa and the boy's adamant claim that he hadn't been trying to pick his pocket, the man was kind enough to say nothing.

Instead, Alessandro asked hopefully, "Did you keep the note, Mustafa?"

"No, Sidi Alessandro. I thought it might be better if the man didn't realise it had been read." While this made sense, the group let out a collective sigh of frustration. "But I remember what it said," Mustafa continued. "Mustafa has an excellent memory!"

Cautiously optimistic, Alessandro rose and found a piece of paper and a pen, then brought them over to Mustafa, who wrote out a perfect copy of what he had seen so briefly. When he was finished, Alessandro examined the writing and then passed it around the group. Everyone shook their heads.

"It is in code," Rat said. "But not in the same code they were feeding us."

"Well, that makes sense. We weren't meant to see this one," Melody pointed out. She then explained to Alessandro and Rat everything she and William had deduced about the so-called false-flag operations, the manifests they were led to find and imagine they were deciphering.

"I don't believe it," Alessandro insisted, with barely restrained anger colouring his voice. He didn't say more, but his clenched fists and the tense line of his mouth made clear enough his dawning fear that they might be right.

Despite Alessandro's refusal to accept what had happened, Rat sighed; he suspected that everything Melody and Somerset said was true. It explained so much. It certainly explained how they had conveniently obtained the cypher key.

"Wasn't it all just a little too easy?" he suggested gently. Alessandro's scowl was all the response he received. Instead of pursuing that thought, Rat said, "While I can't decipher this note, I will send it securely to Whitehall and see if there are any new German cyphers we've uncovered recently that might."

"Well, do make sure it's truly a secure telegram," Somerset pointed out ruefully. "It seems our communications may be leakier than we realised."

Still, Mustafa waited for his punishment. At last, it seemed the group had remembered what he had done.

"Mustafa," Somerset began. The boy lowered his head. "Excellent work, lad. This note might turn out to be pivotal in understanding what has been happening here," Captain Somerset said as everyone smiled.

The boy beamed with pride.

Rat didn't hesitate to add, "And excellent work, Melody. As bad as this situation is, it would have been much worse if we had pulled the Dutch authorities into it."

Melody waited for Alessandro to agree, but instead, he scowled even more. As she looked at him sitting there, pouting and utterly unable to admit how he had failed in this mission, Melody realised he wasn't nearly as handsome as she'd initially thought. In fact, while his features undoubtedly had an almost perfect symmetry, the sharpness of his jawline and cheekbones failed to affect her as they once did. Instead, the childish petulance suffusing his face at that moment made him look almost ugly.

Epilogue

What was next? Melody sat in the armchair in her suite and pondered her immediate future. It appeared that William had redeemed himself somewhat at the Foreign Office. He had sent a note that morning to ask if he could call on her and had hinted at such an outcome.

She hadn't seen or spoken to Rat or Alessandro since the previous day. She suspected that, unlike William, they were licking their wounds, or at least Alessandro was. While Rat could probably claim he was merely doing as he'd been directed, if William was right, then Alessandro had been involved in dismissing his concerns and ensuring that Captain Somerset didn't return to Amsterdam, at least officially. As much as Alessandro had wanted to argue against the obvious the previous day, Melody was sure that even he secretly realised they had been made to look like fools.

While Melody didn't know precisely what had been said and done in Morocco, it was hard to believe that this Dutch mission reflected well on the conte. After all, without her and William's help, he would have walked into Germany's trap and caused the British to seem paranoid and heavy-handed. More importantly, the Dutch might have started to doubt Britain's competence or honesty and to question their neutrality. As it was, who knows what Germany had gleaned about their operations?

Melody couldn't decide whether this Amsterdam puzzle had put her off international espionage and intrigue or confirmed how well-suited to it she was.

Just then, there was a soft tap at the door. Melody rose and went to open it. After the note, she wasn't surprised to find Captain William Somerset standing there, in uniform and holding his hat.

"It is good to see you, William," she said softly and sincerely. "It is especially good to see you back in uniform. Please come in."

William smiled so sweetly that it was all Melody could do not to rush into his arms then and there. Instead, she stepped back to let him in. The day they'd met in the botanical gardens, she had told him she missed him, but he had not reciprocated. Perhaps he had reconsidered his feelings towards her, especially given what he believed she felt towards Alessandro.

"I felt we left things awkwardly yesterday. It was such a chaotic scene, and I wanted to come and say goodbye properly."

"Goodbye?" Melody asked in alarm. "You are leaving already?"

"I have been summoned back to London, at least to debrief on this operation. Not only did we walk straight into the trap set for us, but in doing so, we provided Germany with a great deal of valuable information about our operatives and methods. In fact, we do not even know everything they managed to learn as they moved us about like marionettes. Although we haven't deciphered the note that Mustafa memorised, there is reason to believe we might crack it soon enough, and who knows what that could reveal. There is strong reason to suspect a breach of confidential information somewhere within the Foreign Office or British Intelligence that allowed Helga Meier to anticipate our actions so thoroughly. I must return and report to Sir Edward."

Because Melody hadn't heard from Alessandro or Rat that morning, she was unsure if they had also been recalled. She asked now, and William smiled ruefully. "Conte Foscari definitely has some explaining to do. It appears he not only walked into a German trap, but it was one with clear warning signs he chose to ignore. He was so eager to prove his acumen over mine that he made some quite basic errors in judgment."

Melody reflected on her earlier concerns about how conveniently the cypher key had been handed to them and how arrogantly Alessandro had dismissed those worries, and she had to agree. It appeared William didn't have any details on how this mission might impact Alessandro's work for the Secret Service Bureau, but from the look on his face, he wouldn't mind if the man was brought down a peg or two. Melody only hoped this wouldn't harm Rat's career.

As she thought about her brother, Melody recalled a question she'd wanted to ask before they parted the day before, but hadn't felt comfortable mentioning in front of Rat. Now, she told William about finding the clippings of the classified ads in Jemima's room.

"Of course, this led us to believe she was involved with Germany, but there was nothing we uncovered yesterday to support this. Given Robert's involvement, or the man we thought was Robert the desk clerk, I now wonder if those clippings were just another piece of misdirection left for us to make us suspicious of Miss Edwards. It is clear Robert was watching our every move and reporting back to Helga Meier. He must have noticed our interactions with her."

William smiled. "Actually, your brother mentioned this Miss Edwards to me yesterday. Having observed this hotel and your comings and goings for days, I can tell you that I believe she is exactly what she appears to be."

"Then why lie about travelling with her aunt?" This was the question Melody kept returning to.

"Perhaps because the social mores against a young woman travelling alone make it easier to conjure up a fictional chaperone who keeps to her room," William suggested.

Melody considered his words and nodded her agreement. As annoying as Jemima Edwards was, she knew her brother would be thrilled to receive this news. The more she thought about it, the happier she was for Rat.

William sat, and they chatted for some time about nothing in particular. Melody admitted she didn't know what she wanted to do next, and William encouraged her not to doubt her abilities, boosting her spirits.

"You are clever, insightful, and brave, Melody. Whether or not intelligence work is where you choose to spend your time, don't ever doubt what an excellent operative you make." With this, he stood. "I should be going. I have some reports to write and telegrams to send."

Melody also stood. This was it; William Somerset was about to walk out of her life again. In Morocco, she let him go. Now, she had a second chance if only she were brave enough to take it. William had praised her courage, but somehow, expressing her feelings to the man before her seemed far more terrifying than confronting a villain or escaping from ropes and a gag.

"William, I..." she said hesitantly.

"You don't have to say anything, Melody," he replied as he moved closer and took her hands in his. "Things between us don't need explanation."

He was about to release her hands and turn towards the door. "No! I do. I have to say something. No, that's not right either. I want to say something. You left me in Morocco before I could explain." Was that true? The expression in William's eyes told her that her actions at the time had been enough explanation.

Trying again, Melody said, "I know what you thought you saw. Perhaps what you did see when Alessandro first appeared. And it's true, I had a girlish infatuation in Venice and it was not entirely extinguished in Morocco. But now..."

William had turned fully towards her at these words, and now he stepped closer, so close that Melody could feel his breath, warm on her face.

"But now?" he asked eagerly.

"Now, I see what I believed I felt for Alessandro for what it truly was. He is handsome and charming, and he swept me off my feet. He also used me, overlooked me, and belittled my contributions at every turn. He doesn't respect my intellect or value my involvement in these investigations." Even to her own ears, these words sounded inadequate. They were marks against Alessandro, but not reasons to love William.

Melody tried once more. "I was heartbroken when I thought I had lost you forever and giddy with joy when you revealed yourself the other night."

She reconsidered her words. "Well, I was scared at first, of course. After all, I had been grabbed from behind on a dark street in the middle of the night." She smiled. "But after I realised it was you, those feelings turned to joy. I have come to realise how much you mean to me. You have trusted me, confided in me, and treated me as an equal. You have respected me, not only as a woman, but as a person of intellect and worth, and have not been threatened by my contributions. Even when I have doubted myself, you have cheered me on and pushed me to believe in myself. I cannot tell you what that has all meant to me."

Even as she said all this, Melody realised that as true as those words were, they could just as easily be the underpinnings for a good friendship and that she still hadn't said the words that mattered. "I love you, William. And I'm sorry it took me this long to realise it."

Captain William Somerset said nothing in reply. He didn't have to. Instead, he took Melody into his arms and pressed his lips to hers.

~

FOR SHORT STORIES, BONUS CHAPTERS, INSIDER INFO, AND more, find the link at sarahfnoel.com.

~

MELODY'S STORY BEGAN WITH TABITHA & WOLF. IF YOU would like to start at the very beginning, enjoy an excerpt from A Proud Woman, the first book in the prequel series...

TABITHA HAD BEEN STANDING IN FRONT OF THE MIRROR FOR A full five minutes, transfixed by her own image. To the undiscerning eye, not much had changed, only that she had moved from full to half-mourning. Her rich chestnut hair coiffured as conservatively but stylishly as usual. Her maid Ginny would allow nothing less. Her jewellery was minimal, tasteful, and clearly extremely expensive. Her now-deceased husband had deeply cared that she was always a visual representation of his power and influence. But what did seem different were her eyes. Over the two years of her hellish marriage, she had become used to seeing dead, emotionless eyes staring back at her, eyes that spoke to a crushed soul. But today, for the first time since the night of her marriage to Jonathan Chesterton, the Earl of Pembroke, those eyes had some life in them.

Jonathan's death should have ended her suffering, but it didn't. The police investigation and the attendant sensationalist publicity consumed the six months following the death. And, of course, there was the faux horror by the upper echelons of society who were secretly lapping up every bit of gossip and enjoying the spectacle of the disgrace of one of the formerly untouchable families. In the end, Tabitha was still untouchable enough, and the death had been ruled death by misadventure. After all, when the police inspector had examined Jonathan's body lying at the bottom of the marble staircase, the unnatural angle of his neck making clear that his neck was broken, the smell of whiskey emanating off him was undeniable.

Since the ruling, she had barely left the house. Of course, society had generally shunned her, and that was more than fine with Tabitha. She had always found high society's etiquette and unspoken rules suffocating. Long before her coming out at eighteen, her mother had bemoaned how Tabitha could possibly be a product of her womb and upbringing.

But even though Tabitha had strained against her mother's and society's expectations for her, she ultimately complied. Because what else could a young girl do? But now, she didn't need to shun society; it had shunned her. Even her mother could barely bring herself to visit when she was still in London before leaving for the family country seat a month before. And so Tabitha had been left alone in the palatial Mayfair home that Jonathan's great-grandfather had built to impress society with his wealth and might. Alone except for the large staff. Tabitha sensed that despite most of the staff having worked for Jonathan and his family long before Tabitha had married him, they didn't miss their master and had a fondness and profound sympathy for their new mistress.

And so today, for the first time, her eyes reflected a woman returning to life. Tabitha had known for a while that she was a wealthy woman. With the dowry she had brought to the marriage and the not-inconsiderable monies she'd inherited from Jonathan's many business ventures, minus the entailed property, she would never have to worry about money. As a widow, her rights were somewhat more expansive than those of single women, even if they were still limited compared to men. With her father recently deceased, Jonathan's solicitor had explained that, assuming she wanted to, he could help establish Tabitha as the head of her household, leaving her total control over her wealth. She had always thought that Jonathan's man of business was honest, straightforward, and loyal. His willingness to manage her business and lack of condescension during their conversation had quickly confirmed her instincts.

Today, as she shrugged off her full mourning, almost certainly much earlier than most in society would consider appropriate, she looked at the face of a woman who was finally as free and independent as a woman in 1897 could be. She wasn't sure what she was going to do with this freedom. She was neither welcome back into high society nor desired a return. She certainly didn't want it enough to endure the obsequiousness and self-flagellation her mother had suggested would be necessary to ensure her entry back into the best drawing rooms in London. So she took one last look at this new woman in the mirror and took a deep breath before preparing to make her way downstairs. Because she would need every ounce of her new feelings of fortitude to deal with her caller that morning, the Dowager Countess of Pembroke, her mother-in-law.

Tabitha had seen very little of Jonathan's mother since his death. The few times she had seen her, including the funeral, the older Lady Pembroke had made it very clear that, despite the final ruling, she believed that Tabitha was responsible for her son's death, either directly or indirectly.

Afterword

Thank you for reading The Amsterdam Enigma. I hope you enjoyed it. Want more historical mysteries, bold heroines, and secret plots? Follow me on social media or join the newsletter to see what's next, including *Tabitha & Wolf*, the prequel series set in 1898.

SarahFNoel.com
Facebook
@sarahfNoelAuthor on Bluesky
sfnoel on Instagram
@sfnoel on Threads

If you enjoyed this book, I'd very much appreciate a review (but, please no spoilers).

About Sarah F. Noel

Originally from London, Sarah F. Noel now spends most of her time in Grenada in the Caribbean. Sarah loves reading historical mysteries with strong female characters. The Tabitha & Wolf Mystery Series and its spin-off, The Continental Capers of Melody Chesterton, are exactly the kind of books she loves to curl up with on a lazy Sunday.

Visit Sarah's website (sarahfnoel.com/) to join her mailing list, connect with her on social media, and see what's coming next!

www.ingramcontent.com/pod-product-compliance
Lightning Source LLC
Chambersburg PA
CBHW060212180626
46813CB00007B/2807